A Vow of Shadows

Elle Backenstoe

Paperback ISBN: 979-8-9878042-3-0

Hardcover ISBN: 979-8-9878042-4-7

E-Book ASIN: B0CLSYHK38

Cover Design: Artscandare

Editing: The Crafted Draft Author Services

Interior Designs: Art Muse Graphic Designs

A VOW OF SHADOWS

Note from the Author

This novel is intended for adults and may not be suitable for young readers. The following book contains instances of mature language, violence, and other topics which may be sensitive to certain readers. While the romantic aspects of this book remain light, the topic of death is a heavy one. If you would like a more detailed description of the sensitive themes and materials contained within, please visit my website:

www.ellebackenstoe.com/content-warnings

A Vow of Shadows is the first book in a planned trilogy. I promise there will be a happily-ever-after... eventually.

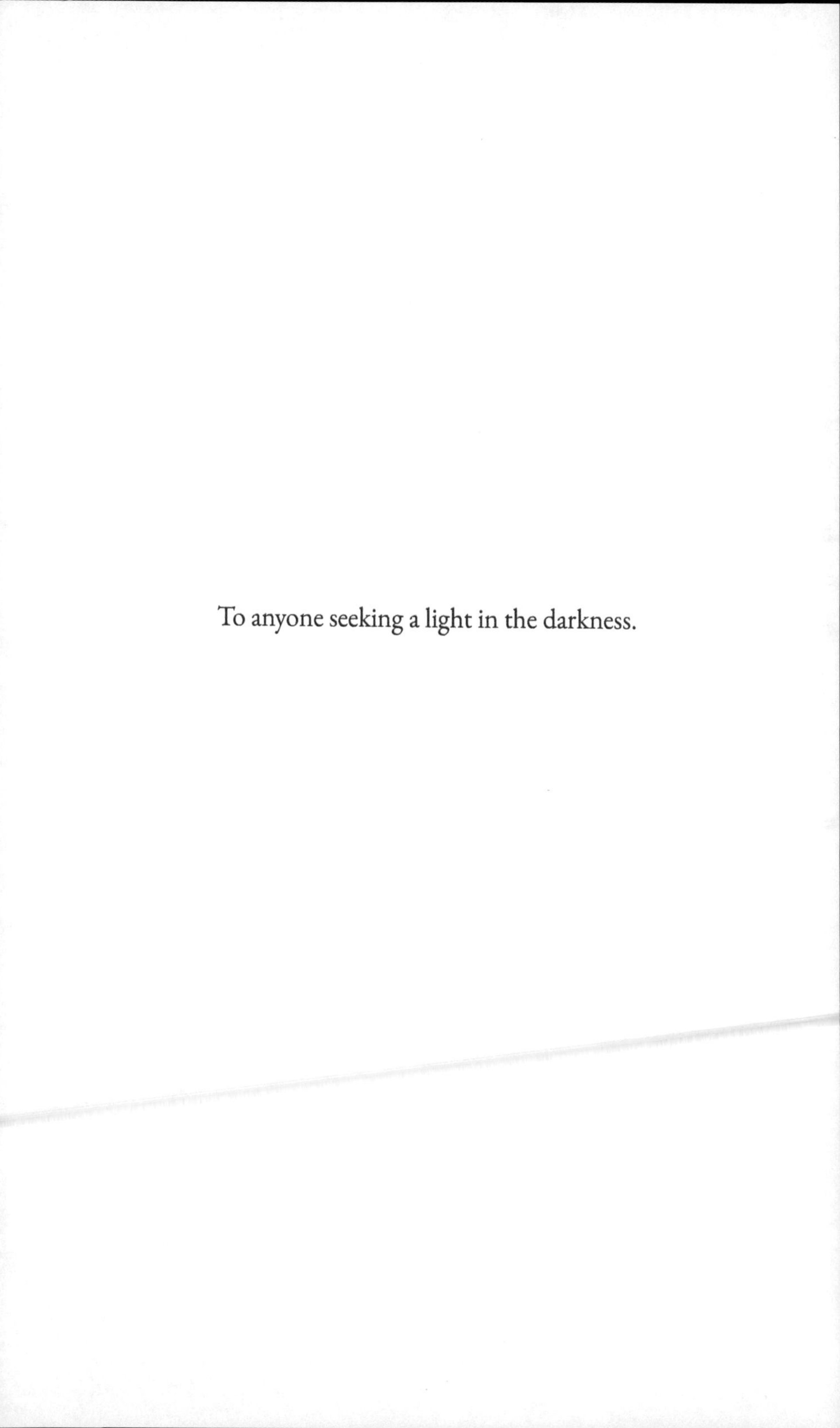

To anyone seeking a light in the darkness.

Beware the bells of violet blue,

a flower sweet and lovely too.

To hear the bluebell's haunting tune,

means death will come to follow soon.

CHAPTER 1

Katrin

I was not prepared to meet Death at the tender age of twenty.

At the time, I was convinced the only way I would leave this life was kicking and screaming, that whoever came to claim my soul would need to drag me to the Afterworld and bar the way back. I couldn't comprehend how anyone passed peacefully, or that still others *yearned* for death.

Naive thoughts of an entitled mind.

They ran rampant as I darkened the corner of the sunlit drawing room, wishing I could drown out the vexing noise.

The bluebells were ringing again.

Like all the times before, my mother gave no indication she also heard them.

No one ever did.

Could they truly not hear them? Or did we all suffer from the same shameful silence, too concerned by what others thought to speak up when something was amiss?

I stalked to the window, determined to find the source of the phantom chimes. Those pesky little flowers needed to be pruned.

Ornate bronze hooks held back the brocade drapes, providing me a clear view of the manor's lush gardens. They blossomed with asters, chrysanthemums, and coneflowers. Almost every color of the rainbow sprawled before me in artful patterns: pinks, purples, oranges, and yellows.

Noticeably absent was blue.

Though unsurprising, the absence of the late spring bloom failed to explain the persistent ringing.

Suppressing a shiver, I balled my hands into fists and squeezed my eyes shut. Darkness greeted me like an old friend, its comforting embrace somehow muffling the haunting melody.

I sighed, and the scene on the back of my lids transformed. The darkness shifted, swirling and pulsing like living shadows. As though sensing my attention, it expanded, preening like a peacock before its mate. It welcomed me, enticed me with promises of peace and quiet.

An escape.

An eternity.

My eyes shot open, frantically searching the sunny drawing room for any trace of shadows, wishing I could claw off those that marked my skin. I would take the incessant ringing over the beckoning dark.

"Katrin."

I jolted at my mother's voice and turned toward where she sat at the other end of the parlor. She stared back, concern pinching the space between her brows. The needle in her hand hovered forgotten over the cloth she'd been embroidering.

"Do you hear that?" I asked, though I already knew the answer.

The ringing had grown distant, but I couldn't shake off the chill that permeated deep into my bones. Even the sunlight felt cold on my skin.

She angled one ear toward me, suspicion evident in the purse of her lips. Her brown eyes darted around the room as she listened then shook her head. "I don't hear anything."

I nodded in understanding, willing my lips to curve upward. Smiling was such an effort anymore, but I managed it for an instance.

Mother's gaze softened, and she gestured toward the envelope clutched in my hand. "It won't bite."

I sniffed. "That's what you think."

I'd all but forgotten the invitation that had arrived shortly after lunch. Though nearly an hour had passed, I still hadn't opened it.

I brought the offending paper up to eye level, holding it up to the light like I could reveal the secrets within. There was no danger of it sprouting teeth and attacking me, but letters like this caused a different kind of pain. One that cut deeper than the eye could see.

I offered my mother another smile and sat at the small writing desk by the window. Satisfied, she returned to her needlework. My breath came easier the moment her eyes left me. The weight of her expectant gaze never failed to affect me.

Nearly one and twenty and I still yearned for my parents' approval.

Tucking my hair behind my ear, I swept my gaze over the calligraphic flourishes and gilded touches. It seemed only I could sense the cruel mockery of social grace hidden beneath the finery, the taunting approximation of common courtesy that made me squirm.

I flipped the invitation over and traced the familiar wax seal. I'd been expecting this announcement for weeks, but that didn't make it any easier to swallow. I slipped a finger beneath the flap and hesitated. If I never opened it, I could remain in blissful ignorance. I didn't need to know that life was continuing on without me.

As though sensing my indecision, my mother looked up. The heat of her stare branded me from across the room, and I shook off my morose thoughts. Nothing bothered me more than sinking into my own melancholia, though lately I'd noticed it happening more and more often.

Straightening my spine, I tugged the seal free, gasping as the thin edge of the paper passed through my skin. A small line of blood pooled along the surface, bold against the pale backdrop. I held my hand out to my mother as though a papercut would prove my point. She rolled her eyes and turned her focus back on her work.

Sucking my wounded finger, I pulled the card free and skimmed the sprawling text.

The words *cordially invited* and *wedding* struck me like a dagger to the heart.

My stomach dropped.

It was exactly as I'd feared.

I blinked to dispel the excess moisture from my eyes before my mother could remark upon it.

"Remind me to respond with my deepest regrets," I said, tossing the card atop a pile of similar notes.

Mother *tsked*. "That's the third invitation you've declined this season."

"And I expect there will be many more." My tone was more defensive than I intended, but I had no interest in continuing the conversation.

"You and Miss Taryn used to be so close, though."

"Yes, we *used* to be. Before..." I trailed off, glancing down at the darkened fingers of my left hand. Mother knew exactly what had transpired to make me the social pariah I was today, watching as all my former friends debuted, courted, and married. All while I remained tucked away from everything I'd once known.

With a twitch of my head, my chestnut waves fell forward to cover the left side of my face. I drew my knees up and wrapped my arms around trouser-clad legs, pointedly ignoring the warning glare from the other side of the room. Proper fashions and manners meant nothing to me now. There was little point to any of it when I refused to leave the manor.

"She is to marry Lord Tanner," I said.

My mother straightened at that bit of news. There was a time I had been favored for Tanner's hand. Our parents had discussed the possibility at length. I'd even begun to practice writing my name as Lady Katrin Bellvue.

"You should consider attending at least one of those events," said Mother, gesturing to the stack of discarded invitations. "Maybe not that particular one, but it would do you some good to keep up appearances."

I tilted my head to regard her through my curtain of hair. "What appearances would those be, Mother?"

Her eyes widened at my icy tone. "I only meant that it's been some time since you've had to observe any kind of"—her eyes traveled the length of my body from my legs to my unkempt hair—"propriety."

"They only invite me because of Father."

"Now, Katrin. That's simply not true—"

"Is it not?" I yanked my hair back from my marred face and gestured to the dark whorls that discolored half of it. "You think I don't know what they say about me? Even servants talk, Mother. They call me cursed. They worry I've some contagious disease that will infect them all like the plague. You think all these merry couples desire to have the 'marked one' at their wedding?" At her answering silence, I rushed on. "I haven't seen or heard from any of these people in years, but no one can afford to snub the Duke of Felwyck outright by omitting his daughter from their guest lists. And so, we shall continue this game wherein they invite me to their luncheons and balls, and I respectfully decline."

Mother sagged, and I felt a tinge of guilt at my directness, but this was an argument we'd had time and again.

A pragmatist in a family of optimists, my capacity for hope had vanished with every inch of skin claimed by shadow. There was only one thing keeping me going, and it wasn't the promise of future social engagements. I just needed all the right pieces to fall into place. Even then, chances were slim that all would work out in my favor. As much as it pained me, someone had to prepare my family for the harsh eventuality my future held.

I strode to my mother's side. She looked up at me with glassy eyes as I perched upon the arm of her chair. Holding her stare, I clasped both of her hands in mine.

"I know you wish for me to have a normal life. Trust me, I want nothing more than to have my own season, attend luncheons and balls, and court the finest men of the kingdom. There is nothing I wouldn't give for the chance to live the life that was stolen from me the day I was marked, but this is my lot. This is the hand I was dealt." Pulling back my hair, I bared my ruined face to my mother. Though she didn't glance away as most did, the pity that transformed her features had me pulling back. "I may not have a chance at winning, but at least I'm still playing the game." My cheery tone belied the heaviness that had washed over me.

Mother tilted her head, considering me. Her eyes traveled over the shadowed side of my face and finally returned to mine, steel resolve blazing forth.

"Oh, Katrin. You are not in the game. You are watching it unfold from behind a curtain."

I stood, letting my hair fall back over my shame. "If Taryn wishes to see me, she may call on me privately. I've no interest in becoming a public spectacle. No more than I already am, at least."

Knowing this conversation could go in circles for hours, I turned and stormed out of the parlor. Mother called after me, but I put one foot in front of the other until I was certain she hadn't pursued me.

All the while, the bluebells rang.

Chapter 2
Katrin

The light tinkling sounds followed me down the hall, their gentle chiming at odds with the ominous fate they foretold. Death was coming for me.

I'd told no one, though most of the town had long suspected my ill fate. I doubted anyone would believe that the clock counting down toward my expiration was nearing its final hour.

Almost eight years had passed since the dusky shadows first tainted my fingertips, and I still had more questions than answers. Though now they covered most of the left side of my body, I hadn't believed the townsfolks' rumors and ramblings until the ringing had started a few weeks earlier.

It had begun as innocuous sounds that could be written off as the *clink* of silverware or the *jingle* of coins in a purse. Over time, the bells had grown louder, increasing in frequency and fervor until it had become the clamor it was now. For days, the bluebell's melodic notes had crawled so deep into my ears, they clawed at my sanity.

I clapped my hands over my ears and hummed the first tune that came to mind. Bustling servants gave me a wide berth which wasn't altogether unusual. However, the quizzical glances thrown my way were quite a change from being ignored.

Tucking my elbows in close, I scurried into the grand foyer with no particular destination in mind. I would stop when the ringing did.

Rather than silence, however, the sound of someone pounding brought me to a halt. I froze, torn between my curiosity and the urge to run.

The butler appeared from a connecting hallway and crossed the space, paying me no mind. I watched, still rooted in place, as the slim older man opened the front door.

A fierce onslaught of bells swarmed me, every peal landing like a physical blow. With the view barred, and the cacophony effectively overpowering any words spoken by our visitor, I retreated to the farthest reaches of the foyer.

My head throbbed in rhythm to the chimes. They assaulted me from every angle. I doubled over, clutching my ears, but the ringing had infiltrated my mind. When my eyes snapped shut, the tempting darkness was there. I wrenched them open and gasped as time slowed, and my nightmares became reality.

The sky darkened as shadows poured into the house like fog rolling over a hill. They seeped through the windows and pooled on the floor, a churning river of storm clouds.

I wanted to scream, but a quick glance around confirmed no one else was seeing what I saw. Even as it snaked around the servants, weaving between their legs and billowing before their faces, they did not react.

With each person the darkness passed, my stomach sunk lower and lower until I could no longer deny that the shadows were heading straight for me.

I scrambled back, slippered-feet struggling for purchase on the marble floors. The darkness advanced, and I slammed into something hard and unyielding. My breath escaped in a puff of fog—a contrast to the raging shadows licking at my toes.

Was my mind projecting the icy chill in the air too?

Tremors wracked my body. The shadows were upon me. They'd overtaken my legs. I pressed into the wall like I could disappear through it, but its solid wood and plaster refused to grant me passage.

I closed my eyes, seeking the comforting dark within. These shadows seemed benign now compared to those engulfing me.

It's not real, I told myself. *It's not real.*

But if it wasn't real, why had my skin turned to gooseflesh wherever the shadows touched? Why did I feel like I was being pulled under, on the verge of drowning?

I gasped as the icy tendrils reached my neck, feeling like any breath might be my last.

A door *clicked* shut and warmth flooded me. I opened my eyes and blinked at the sudden return of sunlight.

Life resumed its usual pace. The bluebells had quieted to a gentle murmur. There were no shadows beyond those naturally cast by objects in the sun. Nothing crawled or seeped or threatened.

The only thing out of place was me.

I dusted myself off from where I lay sprawled on the marble floor, grateful for the trousers that offered me some dignity as I rose. My lungs heaved, still convinced I was dying. I bared my teeth, unable to manage the tight-lipped smile I wished to adopt.

Every head in the foyer had swiveled to look my way, varying degrees of concern or confusion etched across their faces. My hand lifted in a stilted wave as I crossed to the main door.

The butler stood with one hand still gripping the handle. In the other, he held a small envelope not unlike the invitation I'd received earlier.

"Is that for my father?" Thankfully, my voice betrayed none of the emotional turmoil I felt at being the center of attention. I strode as confidently as I could with my limbs still trembling and plucked the message from his hand. "I'd be happy to deliver it for you."

The butler bowed, and the room resumed motion.

No one gave me a second glance as I slipped into my father's study.

I closed the door behind me with a sigh, glad to escape the bustle of the foyer. My ears buzzed with the absence of sound. No hint of those damned bells remained, but even in their absence, the memory of them lingered. A ghost whose silent screams echoed in the corners of my mind.

Father never permitted the windows to be open in this room. Though the heat in the summer made it nearly unbearable, it wasn't worth risking his precious books to the elements. And so, this room had become my refuge of late.

A large oak desk and matching chair dominated the space. Book shelves lined the far wall from floor to ceiling, each volume carefully organized by subject, then author, then title. The fireplace to my right sat unused for the season. Even the ashes sat undisturbed.

Small mementos of his travels adorned the mantel like a visual timeline of his life: a miniature ship in a glass bottle, a jewel encrusted dagger, a long-dead rose. Sometimes, I would walk the length of it and wonder what might occupy a shelf of my life.

The only things I could think to represent my memories were shadows.

The small area before the fireplace and a slim walkway toward the desk remained the only bare surfaces. The rest of the room was a monument to eight years of fruitless research. Towering piles of medical journals, religious scrolls, scientific texts, and, atop them all, ancient tomes of myth and lore. Each layer chronicled my father's obsessive search for answers. Most were completely useless.

After all the research, the countless visits to doctors, witches, mystics, and priestesses, the tinctures, bloodletting, and exorcisms, we were no closer to curing me. The only explanation that rang true was the one he refused to believe: I was doomed.

Stepping around the precarious stacks, I crossed to the desk where my father sat, a dragon amongst his hoard.

Hunched over yet another book, he had his head propped on one hand and marked his progress with the other, sliding a finger along each line of text.

His hair had grayed in recent years; I once joked that he was losing pigment while I was gaining it.

He hadn't laughed.

I cleared my throat, and he jerked upright. Ice blue eyes scanned the room and quickly found me amidst the chaos. I shrunk under the weight of that gaze, though it was not unkind.

"Katrin." His voice was the hoarse croak of one recently awoken, and I wondered how long he'd been in here.

"This just arrived for you," I said, placing the envelope on his desk. "Would you like me to ring for some water?"

He waved away my question and reached for the message. With sure fingers, he ripped it open, pulling free a small, folded paper. His eyes moved slower over the note than they had the book, a deep crease forming between his brows.

When he finished reading, he crumpled the paper into a ball and tossed it over my shoulder. I watched as it sailed into the cold ashes of the fireplace, kindling for the winter fire. Turning back, I saw not my father but the Duke—a man whose personal desires could not keep away the duties of the title.

"Lord Rencourt has died," he said without preamble.

His face betrayed no emotion, leaving me lost for how to respond.

I didn't know the man, though I'd heard his name a time or two. Had he passed peacefully, or had he fought until his final breath?

As unfortunate as the news was, the relief I felt was instant. I had a plan, and, for once, it seemed fate was on my side. Thoughts flew through my mind. There was so much I needed to do before nightfall. I needed to pack. I needed to prepare.

I whipped my head to my father as the realization settled.

I needed to say goodbye.

Father, misreading the look of horror that transformed my features, sighed and placed his hands on his hips. Then he turned, surveying the room as though truly seeing it for the first time. "It's here, Kat. It has to be. We're missing something, but we'll figure it out. Don't you worry."

I nodded but couldn't force my lips into their usual placating grin. His empty promises had grown tiresome. I finally knew the truth, but how did you tell your father you were dying?

If everything went to plan, hopefully I could save us both the heartache.

"Do you remember the old woman, the medium we saw in Wynhallow?" I asked.

My father changed in an instant. "You mean the quack?" he spat. "What a complete waste of time and assets. I should have pressed charges. That fool belongs in a cell."

I twined my fingers together, watching as light and dark wove together, the shadowed half of me a constant reminder of my burden. "What if it wasn't a scam?"

"Don't be absurd, Kat. You're not dying."

"But nothing else has been able to explain my mark. None of the doctors or scientists. None of the books or journals. And lately, I've been hearing these bells." My hands clutched the sides of my head, tugging my unbound hair. "What if I really was marked by Death, and there's nothing I can do to stop him coming?"

"You're not dying!"

The window rattled in the aftermath of his outburst. I looked away, hurt that the man I trusted to protect me refused to believe that this inexplicable ailment could have an unbelievable cause. I didn't need to see the broken man desperately clinging to false hopes.

"You're not dying," he said again, as though repeating it could make it true. "Not if I have anything to say about it."

He offered his arm, and I wove mine through, allowing him to escort me from the room without another word from either of us. He likely thought he'd convinced me, but I knew arguing further would be pointless. I wouldn't change his mind, and he couldn't alter my plans. Tonight, I would leave, and if all went well, I would save us both the pain of my death.

CHAPTER 3

Katrin

The bells resumed the moment Father opened the door. I clamped my hands around his arm to keep from covering my ears. My smile was a brittle mask plastered on so often I feared it would crumble away to reveal the scared, angry girl beneath.

My father's lips continued to move as we strolled down the hall. Between the noise from the bells and his mustache impeding any chance at lip reading, I was clueless to everything he said. I mimicked his facial expressions and nodded whenever he paused.

For once, I was grateful of society's preference for silent women. I couldn't have answered if I wanted to. Even without the bells, I was finding it increasingly more difficult to maintain the ruse of a happy daughter.

My father didn't seem to notice though. He prattled on, unknowing that his words fell on deaf ears.

After several minutes of one-sided conversation, I pulled my arm from his and made a vague excuse to leave.

Now that my plan was coming to fruition, I needed to prepare. My mind whirred as I thought about all that I would need before tonight. Thankfully, the shift in focus muffled the damned ringing. With a slightly clearer mind, I tallied the short list of necessities. Traveling light was my first priority, especially since there was no way to guarantee success. Still, if I *did* succeed, I didn't want to be left with nothing.

My first stop was my parents' chambers. On my way, I concocted a story for my intrusion that proved unnecessary. The rooms were cold and empty upon entry, the servants not yet turning down the beds. My parents shared a large calling room from which branched off separate sleeping quarters.

Between the two rooms sat a small safe containing my mother's jewels and a meager portion of our wealth. Father had recently invested in a new keyless safe. This one required only the proper combination of numbers to open. Luckily, I knew the correct code already. It was tomorrow's date, my birthday.

The irony was not lost on me as I turned each of the dials until they showed eight-zero-eight and pulled the lever. The date that had been important enough to protect their valuables would soon be remembered as the day their daughter ran away from home.

The money inside was used only in situations when bank notes would not do. My father's title went a long way toward ensuring confidence in business deals. So much so that these coins were rarely touched. I hoped that would remain the case for the next several hours as I stashed a substantial amount in my pockets.

Guilt hurried my steps as I raced to my room and deposited the gold into one of my many purses. Using my vanity chair as a step-stool, I hid the bag above my wardrobe. It joined my secret collection of choice reading material and a dried rose that had been given to me by Tanner on my thirteenth birthday before everything had changed.

I picked up the rose, remembering everything I'd thought it meant. The future I'd dreamed for us on the promise of a single bloom. It crumbled as I held it, wasting away like my dreams.

Crossing the room, I opened a window and threw the remnants of the flower out. I spit after it for good measure, slamming the window closed as the symphony of bells crescendoed yet again.

I inhaled slowly, drawing my mind back to the task at hand. When I exhaled, the ringing had lessened to a manageable decibel.

I grabbed a rucksack and headed for the kitchen. Though I wanted to have provisions on hand just in case, I had no idea what I needed. It had been years since I left the manor, and even then, I'd never worried over food. The dresses I packed were more important, especially when there were servants to oversee all the meals.

The kitchen was bustling in preparation for dinner when I entered, but most of the staff ignored me. The others gave me dirty looks but let me be.

I found an empty waterskin that my father used while hunting and filled it from the large cauldron of freshwater meant for cooking. From there, I snuck down to the root cellar and gathered what food I could fit into my sack. Dried meat, cheese, apples. My hand hovered over the potatoes, but I didn't dare bring anything that required cooking. I had no idea what conditions would be like if I even made it that far.

Task completed, my focus waivered, allowing for the cacophony of bluebells to overtake me. The unfortunate truth that poked holes in my mental barrier was that Death might come for me at any minute. My plan may fail. I could be struck down where I stood, but at least it was better than waiting for Death to come to me. At least, I was trying.

Slinging the rucksack over one shoulder, I returned to the main kitchen area, head downturned against the barrage of noise. I muttered under my breath in an attempt to bring my focus back to the present.

"A better life, no more shadows, someone to love me, a family of my own," I named all my reasons for fighting, for wanting to stay alive. "To see the world, to try new things..." The list went on with each new dream drowning out more of the bells.

My steps grew lighter, less hurried as I found that peace within myself. I still kept my head down to hide my muttering, but it was working. A smile ghosted across my lips seconds before I collided with a soft yet immovable wall.

I windmilled my arms to catch my balance as I careened backwards, my peaceful mantra coming to a sudden stop. Dishes clattered to the floor, food flying in all directions, but I managed to stay on my feet. The head cook glared at me from where I'd walked into her, mouth moving faster than a hummingbird's wings.

The ringing resumed with a vengeance, but I didn't have to hear her to know what she called me. *Demon.*

Her lips pulled up in a snarl as they shaped the word over and over.

I shrank under her hateful stare. My chest hollowed with every strike of her venomous words. Clapping my hands over my ears, I elbowed past her and fled to the sanctuary of my room.

CHAPTER 4
Katrin

Nothing I did for the rest of the evening managed to drive away the ringing. Every time I tried to focus, the cook's hateful face would appear.

That night at dinner, I gripped the scraps of my sanity in one hand and my fork in the other. Again, no one made mention of the invasive song that nearly sent me to my knees. My parents conversed in quiet tones I strained to hear over the din. Even those serving appeared unaffected.

Perhaps Death wasn't coming for me after all. Perhaps I was to be driven mad by botanical bells.

I glared at the open window and winced as an onslaught of sound accompanied the refreshing breeze.

The news of Rencourt's death had sparked an ember of hope I'd thought long extinguished, but that fire waned the longer I waited. The sooner I could make my excuses and retire to my room, the better.

I'd changed into more socially acceptable attire for dinner. Though my stays had been loosely laced, I struggled to draw breath. Between the fabric crawling up my neck and the dark depths of my skirts, I was reminded too much of my earlier encounter with the drowning shadows.

If I was more distracted than usual, my parents took no notice, too busy going over their plans for my birthday celebration the next day. The small feast was a far cry from the elegant soiree a person of my status could expect on such an occasion, but I'd insisted we keep the event informal and the guest list small. It was one thing for me to decline their pity invites. I couldn't expect the same courtesy from everyone in town.

I was to be one and twenty, but I still felt like the thirteen year old girl who'd woken one morning to find her fingers dusky with shadow. Though years had passed since I'd removed myself from society, I constantly worked to conceal my mark. Even now, I sat with my body angled away from the candlelight, my hair swept in front of the left side of my face. I flexed my hand, certain I could see the blemished skin beneath the gloves I'd donned. Though I regretted the high neckline and long sleeves in this heat, without them, I was too exposed.

When the next breeze blew through, I leaned forward and blew out the candle in front of me, plunging me further into shadow.

Mother's gaze flitted my way and I stared back, daring her to comment. Her lips pursed, but she turned her attention back to Father without a word.

And so, we continued in a manner that perfectly encapsulated the past eight years of my life with my parents eagerly planning for my future, and me struggling to endure the simplest of day-to-day tasks.

When the plates were finally cleared, I pushed back my chair, drawing the eyes of both my parents.

"I think I'll retire so I'm well rested for tomorrow's excitement." Judging by the confused glance that passed between them, I may have shouted.

My father's response was lost to the bells. When he nodded, I gave a quick curtsy and ran from the room. Only after I'd fled the room did I realize I'd wasted my one chance to say goodbye.

I almost turned back. My footsteps faltered in their hasty retreat, but I clung to the hope that I would see them again.

One day.

***

Three hours later, I regretted my choice to forgo farewells.

The sun had set, and the manor was quiet. My parents had presumably retired for the evening, and most of the servants had settled in for the night. Meanwhile, I trembled with unspent energy.

I'd spent some time gathering what I thought I'd need into a small satchel then paced the length of my room until I'd scored a path in the hardwood. My mind raced with all that could go wrong, but when I weighed each potential outcome, I came to the same conclusion. If I stayed, I'd only prolong the inevitable. This was my last chance to alter the course of my destiny.

Death was coming for me. The recent onslaught of bluebells had confirmed it. It might not be tomorrow, but it would be soon, and I refused to go willingly.

It was a fool's hope, but I'd rather be a fool than a pawn. At least the fool had a choice, though my plan tonight was more of a last resort. Hard decisions came easier when the alternative was death.

I slipped through the house unnoticed, accustomed to wandering the dark corridors. Without a candle, I was just another shadow evading the dappled moonlight.

My fingers skimmed over familiar surfaces, the textured walls, the oiled banister. I'd committed every inch of this house to memory but had the inexplicable desire to leave pieces of myself embedded within it. I feared all evidence of my existence would be erased with my departure and I desperately needed a tether to this world.

Time was not on my side.

I itched to trace the entire manor, but my plan required urgency. Though I'd planned to exit through the kitchen, my feet carried me away from the servant passages, finally stopping when I reached the grand foyer.

Hours earlier, I'd stood in the same spot and watched as sunlight turned to black. I shivered in memory, checking every corner for a hint of anything unnatural, but the darkness of night was tame in comparison to those creeping shadows.

As before, I retreated into the safety of my father's study. This time, I crossed to the other side of the desk, careful not to topple any of his towering piles of books.

I sat in my father's chair and gazed over the organized chaos. All this work and we'd had the answer years ago. All that time wasted because he refused to accept the hard truth. We all had.

Reaching into my satchel, I removed a page I'd torn from one of his texts. My father had quickly discarded the book of ancient myths, but a particular bit of lore had caught my eye.

The legend told of a wicked creature that followed in Death's shadow, a dark figure that collected the souls of the recently departed and ushered them to the next world. No one had ever met the Ferrier of Souls and lived to tell about it, but that was precisely what I intended to do.

I flipped the page over and reached for a quill and inkpot, scrawling three words above a chilling illustration of the Ferrier.

She was right.

No matter how hard I tried, I couldn't muster the energy to write something more soothing. It would be hours before my parents learned of my parting, longer still for my father to retreat to his study and see my note. It wouldn't ease his suffering, but at least he would know I left of my own volition.

My eyes roamed over the ink sketch. It showed a hooded figure with no discernable face, only darkness. In one hand, it bore a scythe. The other hand curled into claws encircled with wispy shadows eerily similar to those that marked my skin.

A sense of foreboding tingled the back of my neck.

Like it or not—and I very much did not—the Ferrier was perhaps the only creature who could keep me safe. I only needed to convince him I was worthy of his protection.

I yanked the glove off my unmarked hand, placing it beside my note. One day, I'd reunite the pair.

I didn't look back as I walked out the room and through the front door. Though I nearly stumbled at the silence that greeted me. The bluebells had finally ceased.

Perhaps this was a good plan after all.

Chapter 5
Katrin

This was a terrible plan.

Two hours into my journey, I was hot, lost, and bru-
tally reminded that the most physical activity I'd done in the
last five years was walking the gardens with mother before tea.

I had half a mind to hitch a ride on the next passing carriage.
There were only two problems. First, I had no idea where I was
going, and, second, the roads were empty.

Father's book had been vague on the details surrounding the
Ferrier. I knew only that I needed to stand at a crossroads after
dark and offer two coppers to the wind—whatever that meant.

I came to an intersection and stopped. Was this the crossroads I was meant to find? How was one to know?

It looked like any other connecting road. All around me lay
overgrown meadows that stretched to distant hills in the east. Far
to the west lay Gwyad Forest, the solitary tree at my back a mockery
of its expansive arbors. The roads themselves were nothing but

packed dirt trails carved by frequent travel. If I looked closely, I could trace the various marks made by foot, hoof, and cart wheel.

I shivered despite the oppressive heat and burrowed deeper into my cloak. Though lightning coursed through my veins, my eyelids grew heavy. I fought the urge to sit as my throbbing feet joined with my aching back, each providing a convincing counterargument that grew harder to ignore with every step. If I sat, sleep would claim me, and I didn't know if I would rouse again. I'd been waging war for eight years, and this was my last stand. Tonight, I would either leave with the Ferrier or wait for Death to claim me.

The full moon painted the landscape in cool, muted tones, the eerie picture accompanied by an unnatural silence that pricked at my nerves. It was only magnified by the absence of the blue-bell's ringing. Not a single animal sang their nocturnal song. There were no howling wolves or hooting owls. Not even a single cricket chirped among the tall grasses.

The stagnant air felt like the calm before a storm. I resisted the urge to remove my cloak as sweat beaded on my brow and drew winding paths between my breasts. I hadn't changed from my dinner clothes and regretted every bit of clinging silk and itchy lace. Covering myself had become second nature, but it was still an effort not to strip down to my chemise. As freeing as it might have been to greet the Reaper as a harlot, I didn't need him getting the wrong idea about my proposition.

My vision blurred. I pressed a hand to my stomach like it could calm the roiling within. Digging through my satchel, I pulled out a canteen and took a deep swig. The tepid water did little to calm the unease churning in my gut, but it did stop the world from spinning long enough for me to stumble over to the lone tree. I leaned my back against its solid trunk, wishing I could find the relief of its shade during the dead of night. Instead, I pressed my palms against the rough bark to ground me as I breathed in and out, willing my nausea to recede.

A welcome breeze kissed my flushed skin, and I sighed in gratitude at the short respite. Goosebumps rose along my arm as the wind snaked through my sweat-soaked clothes. The leaves rustled overhead and I closed my eyes, allowing their symphony to calm my growing anxiety.

A sudden gust swept through the clearing, whipping my hair in all directions. I squeezed my eyes tighter as strands stung my cheeks. My cloak flapped wildly around me, but under the cacophony, my ears latched onto something *other*.

Hoofbeats.

My eyes snapped open. Turning my head from side to side, I sought the source of the sound that had fallen abruptly quiet.

The wind raged around me, shaking loose the leaves of the tree. They danced in a never-ending whirlwind that pulled me in all directions.

With all the grace of a newborn deer, I wrangled what I could of my hair, holding it in one fist at the base of my head. I scanned the roads, searching for the approaching party, but not even an echo remained to hint at their whereabouts.

On impulse, my eyelids fluttered shut and the sound returned immediately. Closer now, as though they had never disappeared, a team of horses raced toward me.

Again, I looked out, only to find the roads once again silent and empty.

The wind was now a tempest, forceful and mighty. It urged me into motion, pushing me until I stumbled away from the tree. The gale carried me to the middle of the crossroads and held me firmly in place.

Against every instinct, I closed my eyes. The ground trembled beneath my feet, and I wobbled on unsteady legs. My heartbeat matched the erratic rhythm of the horses' gallop. Gravel crunched beneath hoof and wheel. If I had to guess, I'd wager there were four horses pulling a carriage, and all the while, the persistent wind tore at my hair and clothes.

My mind urged me to flee, but the wind would not relent.

The Ferrier walked between worlds, this I knew. I had come to the place where the lands of the living and the dead were said to merge to meet him as he made his crossing, but I never expected that he would arrive unseen. It was a weakness I couldn't afford, not as his invisible steeds raced straight for me.

I thought back to all I knew of the Ferrier. None of the legends had mentioned this, though maybe the veil would lift as he closed in.

Squinting through one eye, I peeked toward the direction of the horses.

Still nothing.

I huffed out a breath, certain I was missing some key piece of information. My time was running out until the horses were upon me.

Perhaps this was my death that had been foretold all those years ago. Would he pass me by, or was I always doomed to die trampled by unseen steeds? Had I unwittingly walked into fate's hands just as I endeavored to escape it?

At that moment, I wished I'd remained the pawn—that I could wipe my hands of all the poor decisions that had led me here.

Only Death called the Ferrier, and only to Death would he answer. He came for all souls, and each paid a price.

A price.

My hands raced over the knot at my satchel. Though my fingers were clumsy, I managed to open the bag as the galloping reached a crescendo. I thrust my arm in, blindly patting around, unwilling to risk opening my eyes and losing the only knowledge I had of their approach. I found the two small objects and squeezed them tight.

Trembling from head to toe, I willed strength into my arm and raised it toward the invisible party. No matter how hard I tried, the coins remained clenched within my fist.

The hoofbeats grew louder, more insistent, their tempo increasing like an execution drum, tolling the last seconds of my life. They were nearly upon me, so close I could hear their ragged breaths.

I braced for the impact but finally managed to pry my fingers open, throwing the coins forward.

The phantom horses halted.

Even the wind stopped, the chill on my skin the last remaining evidence of its existence. My ears rang in the absence of such noise, the silence pierced only by the dull *thud* of my two coins hitting the ground.

I exhaled, my whole body deflating in relief, though my heart continued to race with the knowledge that I was not yet out of danger.

A blast of hot air teased my still outstretched hand, and I cracked one eye open, jumping back at the sight of the massive black horse before me. Three others accompanied the beast, each as large and imposing as the first.

But none held a candle to the wicked creature holding the reins.

CHAPTER 6
The Ferrier

Death called and I answered.

CHAPTER 7
Katrin

Atop a gleaming carriage of ebony sat a man cloaked in shadow. At least, it had the vague shape of a man. Darkness writhed around him like a living shade, the figure beneath little more than a formidable shape swathed in night. At his side, a long, curved scythe glinted in the moonlight, a shining beacon of death.

A large cowl covered the reaper's head, concealing his features completely. Though I couldn't see his eyes, I could feel his gaze like icy claws raking across my skin. I refused to flinch under his scrutiny. For once, I had nothing to hide.

"What cause have you to keep a reaper from his duties?" asked the Ferrier, his tone indifferent and condescending. If he was surprised at being halted by a mortal woman, he did not show it.

I stiffened at the sound of his voice, shocked by how human he sounded. With all the rumors surrounding this creature, I'd expected the screams of a banshee or the growl of a beast. Though cold, the rich, silkiness of his words drew me in like a siren's song.

I straightened my spine and lifted my eyes to the approximate area of his own. "I've come to bargain with the Ferrier of Souls." My words slipped over one another in their reluctance to leave my mouth, but their meaning was clear.

The Ferrier's attention slid away from me, and I sagged like a spell had been broken. "I do not bargain with the living."

I bristled at the finality in his tone. He likely intended the words to cow me, but I merely brushed them off and dared a step closer. Smoothing back my windswept mane, I angled my head so the moon highlighted the markings on my face.

As accustomed as I'd become to covering myself and my mark, I might as well have been standing before him naked, even as I remained fully clothed.

Baring the ruined side of my face, I cleared my throat pointedly, trying and failing to capture the Ferrier's attention once more. The horse nearest me nickered, and I had the vague impression that it was laughing at me. I shot the massive creature a baleful glare but gave it a wide berth as I scurried past, planting myself directly in the Ferrier's line of sight.

The second his attention returned to me, he froze. Even the shadows that surrounded him ceased their constant motion.

He did not speak, but I felt his gaze tracing my mark from my hairline to my collarbone.

"As you can see, I have been marked for Death." My voice cracked on the words that had brought me so much pain and heartache. I lifted my left hand, splaying my darkened fingers as further evidence of my shame.

The Ferrier remained silent, but he didn't turn away again. Taking that as a good sign—or at least, not a bad sign—I approached the carriage. My eyes never wavered from the reaper, though he made no move to stop me. Dirt crunched under my feet, but it was a soft purr compared to the persistent roaring in my head that screamed for me to abandon this mission and retreat. Yet, I could not allow this chance to slip through my fingers. I *would not*, not when I had come so far.

The wood was smooth and surprisingly warm beneath my feather-light touch. Until that moment, I could have been dreaming. My mind had been known to conjure such images for lack of true adventure, but this carriage—this man—was wholly real before me.

I swallowed thickly as I turned my face up to the dark creature that held my life in his hands. Even close enough to touch him, my vision could not penetrate the shroud of darkness to see the man beneath. He was an enigma, and though I knew I should be wary, the mystery called to me. I was overtaken by the sudden urge to reach out and touch the reaper's cloak, a desire so repulsive I nearly recoiled.

Keeping my hands firmly planted on the rail, I changed tactics. "Surely you can see that I have barely begun to live. It is nigh my twenty-first year on this world—"

"And I have taken souls far younger than yours."

"And do you feel nothing for those you pry from their mother's arms?" I countered. "Do you not suffer an ounce of grief? Are you so heartless?"

The Ferrier leaned forward, and I found myself mirroring the action like we were two school children sharing secrets. My heart raced. In fear? Anticipation? I didn't know, but I rose up on tiptoes to catch his next words.

"If you hope to appeal to my humanity, you will be disappointed."

My heels slammed to the ground as dismay landed heavily upon my shoulders.

The reaper continued as if he hadn't dashed my plans against the road. "I have not been plagued by such weaknesses in over a century. I am a courier, nothing more. It is not my place to weave fate's thread as my own nor question Death's plans."

Frustration mounted in me like a wave. For years, I'd been told that there was nothing to be done for my *condition*. That I had no choice but to sit back and watch my life fade away into nothing. I'd kept my voice pleasant—albeit a little pleading—thus far, but now, it exploded out of me. "Perhaps you should question Death's plans. I know I do. I question everything! What does this mean?" I waved my shadowed hand for effect. "Why is this happening? Why *me*?! And *you*! You who see countless wasted lives, will you do nothing when the chance comes to save one?"

My breath sawed out of me, but the Ferrier sat unaffected by my tirade.

"I am no knight in shining armor," he replied evenly. "I can neither heal you nor remove you from harm's way."

"I am not sick," I spat. "I have reason to believe Death will claim me soon. I'm certain we can come to an arrangement that is agreeable for both of us."

The Ferrier cocked his head. "Why does Death seek you?"

I shrugged. "It is just one of my life's great mysteries." My mother would have been appalled at my tone, but my well of patience was dry.

I stared into the depthless black beneath his hood, daring him to see the earnest truth in my eyes.

"What is it that you want from me?" the Ferrier asked.

Though his words promised nothing, I stuck my foot in the door he'd cracked. "Take me with you to your home between worlds. Hide me from Death and keep me alive until I can find a cure for this curse."

He barked a laugh. "Only a fool would promise something so vague. It could be years before you solve your little problem. Decades, if you figure it out at all. The Between is not a sanctuary to harbor those afraid to die."

Adjusting the reins in his hands, he turned toward the road. Panic overtook me. I lunged for the carriage, planting my feet on the small step and holding on for my life. He would not be able to brush me off so easily.

"Until the day of my twenty-second birthday, then," I cried out. "On the eighth day of the eighth month, one year from today, you will return me to my family unharmed." I'd spent the hours before I'd left cultivating the ideal phrasing for such a bargain, one that would grant me everything I desired with no loopholes to fall victim to.

"What is your name?" he crooned.

I'd been warned against giving my name so freely. There was power in names, but I could win nothing if I didn't show my hand. Freeing one hand from my white-knuckled grip, I dipped into a shallow curtsy befitting my station. "My name is Katrin Fil'Owen."

"And what do you offer to bargain, Miss Fil'Owen?"

"Ten gold pieces—"

The Ferrier chuckled, dark and humorless, the sound reigniting my body's desire to run.

I cleared my throat, doing my best to look down my nose at him though he towered over me from where he sat atop the carriage. "Ten gold pieces for *every* day you keep me safe, paid when the year is up. Plus a good-faith deposit of three hundred and fifty gold pieces."

He was silent for a long time. So long I feared he would say no.

"You are offering me four thousand gold pieces to keep you from Death for one year."

I nodded. Finally, I had his attention.

What use the Ferrier had for gold, I could only guess, but legend claimed he took two silver coins from each soul as payment for safe passage to the Afterworld. It was a tradition that loved ones honored by placing a silver coin in each hand of their dearly departed before the death rites. When someone suffered a loss, the townspeople would litter the bereaved doorsteps with copper coins to alleviate the financial burden of the so-called 'death tax'. That kindness meant one less thing for the mourning to worry about, but it still begged the question of why. What did the Ferrier of Souls need with all those coins?

"Show me," he said.

I hesitated only a moment before stepping down from the carriage and reaching behind my back to untie the sizable coin pouch.

It is said that to meet the Ferrier, the living must journey to the crossroads on foot. I'd done exactly that, praying that no thieves would cross my path as the jingle of hundreds of coins accompanied my every step.

My feet still ached from bearing the weight of nearly four hundred coins, but it was worth every second of agony to see the way the reaper stilled when I revealed the gleaming treasure.

His actions confirmed what I had already guessed. For whatever reason, the Ferrier wanted the money. My relief was temporary as the dark figure descended from his perch in a swirl of darkness. I jumped as he reappeared before me somehow taller than he'd seemed in the driver's seat.

"What say you, Ferrier?" I'd laid it all out. Every request, every bargaining chip. He would either help me, or I would die.

I glanced back down at the small fortune between my hands. It was a meager price to pay for a life. I only hoped it would be enough to entice the reaper.

The Ferrier's gaze burned along my body, assessing. "You're sure about this?"

I nodded, standing tall under his blatant scrutiny. He would not find me lacking.

And perhaps he saw the truth in my eyes, saw that I stood at a breaking point, one I would not rise from if he turned me down. No matter what he'd said, it would take a foul creature to look into the eyes of an innocent and sentence them to death. Though I'd promised myself I would not give up until the Ferrier acquiesced, his next words knocked me off-kilter.

"Very well. You have yourself a deal, Miss Fil'Owen."

I recovered quickly, dropping my chin to hide the relief that lit up my features. A leather-clad hand stretched toward me, barely discernible from every other dark part of his body. It was perhaps the most foolish thing I'd ever done, but I took the Ferrier's outstretched hand without pause, only then realizing that he'd offered his left, forcing me to do the same. The smoke and onyx flesh of my marked hand blended with his darkness, making it hard to distinguish one from the other.

The leather gloves were supple, a stark contrast to the strength I felt contained within them. His grip tightened, not hard enough to hurt, but enough to hold me in place as his shadows sprang to life. I watched, captivated while they twisted around our enclosed hands like a serpent claiming its next meal. In a blink, our arms had disappeared into their darkness, only the oddly comforting pressure of his fingers let me know they remained.

Just as quickly as they had appeared, the shadows dissipated, leaving only our joined hands exactly as they had been. Though no words had been spoken, I got the sense that something unbreakable had been forged. I had drawn a line in the sand, and he'd pulled me across. There was no going back—no undoing what had been done.

"I have delayed too long, Miss Fil'Owen." The Ferrier gestured with his free hand, guiding me toward the awaiting carriage.

"Katrin, please. Or Kat, if you prefer." I had no idea why I'd just offered my nickname to the Ferrier of Souls. We were hardly on a first-name basis, but I hated being addressed so formally. It reminded me too much of the life I was meant to have.

Miss Fil'Owen was a lady of fine standing with a long line of suitors and a substantial dowry. *Kat* was a forgotten girl who hid from the world and had just traded her entire dowry for a year-long sentence in the world between.

The Ferrier made no remark at my request as he helped me into the coach, but it mattered not what he called me so long as he kept his word.

I paused on the step and turned to look into the dark depths of the reaper's cowl. Even inches apart, I could see nothing of the creature beneath. I hesitated, my hands itching to pull back his hood, to know something about the man behind the title.

Not that it would have changed anything.

Perhaps the shadows hid a disfigurement similar to my own. Perhaps, as rumor claimed, he was nothing more than a skeleton reanimated by magic, though I certainly hoped that was not the case. I could respect his desire to remain hidden when I'd spent much of my life doing the same.

Once inside, the door shut swiftly behind me. I whirled, watching through the small window as the Ferrier disappeared to the front of the carriage.

Tears came unbidden, an insistent stinging behind my eyes that threatened to spill over. I blinked them back, refusing to cry over something that was literally saving my life. After all, this was my chance to step out from under the dark cloud that had followed me since I'd first found the marks upon my fingers.

Finally, I would have the chance at a normal life. I just had to make it through one year with the most terrifying creature I'd ever known. One year and I could return to my family and live the life I'd always hoped for.

The carriage shifted, and I toppled onto the tufted velvet cushion as the horses sprang into motion. I forced myself to face forward, though everything in me yearned to glance back. There was no use reminiscing about the life I'd led until now. Those memories were nothing but ripples in a pond, and I had just thrown an enormous stone. Even if I'd only prolonged the inevitable, it was sure to make a great splash.

Chapter 8

The Ferrier

She was a pretty thing—entitled yet clever.

And Death wanted her.

For what she offered, I'd play this game through to the end.

She was a pretty thing.

CHAPTER 9

Katrin

The carriage bounced and swayed as it headed into Fel-Twyck, the cantering horses becoming a dull roaring in my ears. I watched the familiar landscape pass by without a hint of nostalgia. Yes, it was my home, but lately, it had been more prison than manor. It didn't matter that it was a self-imposed sentence. No one but my parents had balked at my departure from society.

The mark had been easy to hide beneath sleeves and gloves at first, but as soon as the affliction had climbed my neck, I became the scorn of the town. The social effects had been worse than the shadows themselves to the point that by the age of fifteen, I was mostly sequestered to the estate.

Children can be particularly cruel, and my father pulled me out of school before we even knew what ailed me. I'd had a private tutor for my studies and rarely made an appearance when guests visited. Even those I saw regularly treated me differently—my parents included. Either I was a delicate flower to be protected at all costs, or I was infected with a highly contagious illness that was sure to kill any who came in contact with me.

Though I hoped for considerable changes upon my return, I also feared what my future would look like then. Would I be cast out once again? Would I still be *other*? Would I go from being the girl who was marked by Death to the woman who cheated him?

It was a risk I was willing to take. Any life would be better than the one I'd lived these last several years. At least on my return, I would no longer have to bear the constant threat of Death.

The carriage rolled to a stop, pulling me from my morose thoughts. I recognized the dwelling immediately as that of the Rencourts. Black drapes had been drawn over the windows, signifying their loss. I owed thanks to the late Lord Rencourt. Without his death, I would never have been able to summon the Ferrier. I hadn't known the man personally, but I still felt a pang of sympathy at the thought of his family living on without him.

I didn't want to think about the possibility of one or both of my parents passing while I was gone. Our relationships were complicated, but they loved me, and I them.

The Ferrier stepped down from the carriage, and I made to follow, making it as far as opening the door before his voice floated back to me on a phantom wind.

"Wait here."

Fearing what would happen if I disobeyed him this soon into our arrangement, I closed the door and settled in to wait.

I watched, unsure how he planned to enter. It was customary to leave one window open for the reaper to enter, but I couldn't picture this hulking man climbing through such a small opening.

His shadows writhed around him, billowing like clouds of smoke as he neared the house. One moment, he stood outside the Rencourts' home. The next, his shadows engulfed him. When the doorstep cleared, the Ferrier was no longer there.

My eyes darted around the street, seeking his dark form. I gasped when he walked past the window *inside* the building. Somehow, his shadows had transported him into the house. He disappeared into the darkened halls for only a few minutes before reappearing with the spirit in tow.

There was nothing particularly distinctive about the soul. I assumed it was old Lord Rencourt because who else would be walking out of their home escorted by the Ferrier of Souls? And they *were* walking, not floating as I may have expected.

Perhaps when I returned from my year away, I could spend my life correcting the myths of death. So far, the few I'd known had proven inaccurate, aside from the coins, that is.

The pair approached the carriage, and I froze with the realization of what would come next. Sure enough, the Ferrier opened the door, bringing me face-to-face with the ghost of Lord Rencourt—or rather, his soul.

In the moonlight, his form had a faint shimmer. He was corporeal but not fully there, either, like he'd left some vital piece behind and brought only the most reduced version of himself.

Lord Rencourt stared at me open-mouthed, clearly not expecting to share his ride to the Afterworld with anyone else.

I searched my mind for something to break the mounting tension in the confined space.

"Good evening." It was better than nothing, but truthfully, I didn't know what one was meant to say to the recently departed. *I'm sorry you died* seemed uncouth even with the best of intentions behind it. "I'm—uh—Katrin Fil'Owen."

Recognition flashed in Rencourt's eyes, and he finally accepted the seat across from me.

His knee bumped mine, and I jumped at the contact, shifting my legs to one side to cover up my embarrassing shock. I'd still expected him to pass right through me.

"Lady Katrin, is it? I reckon all those rumors were true, then. I'm sorry. It's always a shame when Death comes for one so young."

It was odd that I was considered too young to die but old by marriage standards.

I opened my mouth to correct the soul, but movement from the reaper caught my eye. He shut the door with a *click* and brought a single gloved finger up to where his mouth might be, a clear enough warning to hold my tongue.

Clearing my throat, I returned my focus to the spirit before me, his head tilted to one side as he awaited my reply.

"Thank you. Yes," I said, feigning sorrow. "It was a tragedy."

My response proved enough for the dead, and he lapsed into silence while I snuck occasional glances at my temporary coach mate.

He wore a dark tweed suit, likely the best clothing he'd owned as that was customary for death rites. If I had to guess, I'd have put him about ten years older than my own father. His hair curled slightly around his ears and what might once have been chestnut brown was now a charming cinnamon sugar. Though a full beard covered most of his face, I had an unobstructed view of ice-blue eyes—wide with curiosity not horror.

His demeanor struck me as odd. I'd anticipated a wailing specter being dragged away to the Afterworld, but Rencourt wasn't weeping or moaning, nor did he seem anxious or fearful. I couldn't fathom accepting death so calmly. After several minutes of biting my tongue, the questions practically bubbled out of me.

"Are you not afraid, Lord Rencourt?" I blurted out.

Rencourt frowned at my outburst. He didn't look at me, rather his gaze settled somewhere over my shoulder as though the answer could be found written on the carriage walls. When he finally looked my way, he smiled.

"No, I'm not afraid, Miss Fil'Owen." Even his voice was calm and soothing. "Are you?"

I ignored the question. "But why aren't you afraid? Do you know what comes next? What to expect in the Afterworld?"

He shook his head. "Of course I don't. No one does, but I reckon there's not much to be done for it now, is there? It is not the end of all things, but rather, the beginning of something new. I look forward to what the next world shall bring and hope that I will see my loved ones again on the other side."

I chewed my lip, unable to refute what he said, and unwilling to dampen his good spirits even if I could. I surely didn't share his enthusiasm for new beginnings, especially since my relocation was only temporary. Though the possibility of death had been a constant presence in my life, I'd never come around to accepting the inevitability. As such, I'd never really contemplated what I'd find in the Afterworld. It wasn't *my* world, and that was all that mattered.

The moon had fallen behind the tree line when the carriage finally slowed to a stop. I glanced out the window but was unable to see beyond the dim glow of the coach's lanterns. I had no idea where we were, but that was to be expected given how infrequently I'd left my family's estate.

"Guess this is it." Rencourt patted his legs once as though signaling the end of a friendly gathering instead of a shared carriage ride to the Afterworld.

In the blink of an eye, the Ferrier was at the door, pulling it open on silent hinges and stepping aside to allow Rencourt to pass.

I remained seated, anticipating the order from the Ferrier.

As his feet touched the ground, Rencourt turned to look at me.

"Aren't you coming?" he asked.

I started to shake my head, but the Ferrier saved me from needing to concoct an excuse.

"Miss Fil'Owen will be departing elsewhere."

If Rencourt found the Ferrier's reply odd, he didn't question it. Together, he and the Ferrier headed away from the carriage. Within a few steps, they faded from view, lost to the dark.

CHAPTER 10
The Ferrier

Souls like this made the job easier—enjoyable even. My silence went unnoticed by the prattling Lord Rencourt who continued to tell me all his favorite memories even after we'd reached the point of departure.

A loving wife.

Healthy children.

A long life.

I smothered my pang of jealousy as he faded away into the mists. Those feelings had no place within me. I'd dug my grave, and now, I had a mysterious little human to share it with.

Chapter 11

Katrin

The solitude struck me all at once, the reality of what I had done crashing into me with the force of a cannonball. Alone in the dark in an unfamiliar place, I felt the noose of anxiety slip around my neck. My breathing grew labored, my hands clammy.

I pressed back into the seat, seeking the contact of something firm and steady—something to ground me—but the plush, velvet cushions did little to assuage the panic clawing its way up my throat.

I wanted to scream.

I wanted to cry.

I wanted to throw open the door and bolt after the Ferrier.

But I did none of those things.

Melting off the seat, I became a puddle of sweat-soaked fabric and trembling limbs. I squeezed between the two benches, drawing my knees up to my chest, and there I waited.

An eternity passed before the steady *crunch* of gravel alerted me to the reaper's return. At least, I hoped it was him. I had no way of knowing from my position on the floor and no chance to look without revealing myself.

I tried to quiet my heaving gasps, forcing calm, measured breaths through my nose.

The footsteps paused on the other side of the door, and every muscle in my body tensed. If it was the Ferrier, would he look in and think I'd left? Who else but he would be out here in the middle of the night?

Whoever it was, they made no sound as I contemplated all of this.

A thought occurred to me that made my blood freeze in my veins.

What if Death lurked outside the door?

It had to be after midnight and that meant it was officially my twenty-first year. I could have traveled all this way, paid all that money, just for Death to find me anyway. Unless the Ferrier had summoned Death. He could have pocketed the money and sold me out.

I'd been a fool to trust that one so close to Death would be willing to protect me from it.

My labored breaths turned to hiccupping sobs, tears flowing uncontrollably as I curled in on myself.

The door to the carriage flew open, but I didn't have the breath to scream. I scrambled away from the approaching darkness with renewed vigor. If this was the end, I wouldn't go without a fight.

Still on the carriage floor, I backed away until I came up against the other side.

A shadowed limb separated from the main body. Drawing one leg back, I delivered a swift kick. The creature recoiled, hissing in pain.

Seizing my opportunity, I reached up to unlatch the door behind me. I had only a moment to consider the wisdom of such a move when it swung open. My legs flew up and over my head as I plummeted, landing in a heap on the hard-packed earth. I managed to protect my head, arms taking the brunt of the fall. My hands stung and one elbow throbbed in protest as I struggled to stand. My foot caught on the hem of my dress, and I would have gone sprawling into the dirt a second time if two solid arms hadn't snaked around me at the last minute.

A scream escaped my lips as I was hauled upright. One of the arms disappeared from my middle only for a hand to clamp over my mouth.

I bucked and kicked, but nothing could dislodge my captor. My muffled cries sounded pathetic to my own ears, but I didn't dare go quietly.

"You'll wake the dead with that mouth, Miss Fil'Owen."

At the sound of his voice, all the fight drained out of me. I stilled in the Ferrier's arms, unable to completely relax in such a vulnerable position, though some part of me wanted to melt into his arms.

Knowing he couldn't see my face or read my expressions, I took the moment to marvel at the strength wrapped around me. He'd plucked me from the ground like a tiny child and I still felt dwarfed by his massive frame. His muscled chest rose and fell against my back, his warm breath caressing the top of my head.

I could almost close my eyes and picture myself in the arms of a lover.

My body jolted at the comparison. This was not some townsman come to rescue me. The Ferrier was an agent of Death, not some paramour I'd run off to see.

I twisted, and he finally saw fit to release me. I hoped he couldn't see the blush rising to my cheeks as I turned to face him.

"Do you want to tell me why you ran? Backing out of our deal so soon?" His voice betrayed no emotion, and his hood remained firmly in place, obscuring my view of his face.

If I hadn't just felt his thickly muscled frame wrapped around me, I might have thought the legends were true and he was only an animated skeleton beneath those robes.

"I thought you might be Death come to claim me." It felt foolish now, saying it aloud, but the fear had been real. I still felt the electricity of it coursing through my veins.

The Ferrier turned as though taking in his surroundings for the first time. "We have passed into the shadow realm. Death is often too preoccupied with the dead and dying to visit those in between, though it happens. You will know when Death is near."

"How will I know?" I whispered.

Deciding our conversation was over, the reaper held out his hand for me. I accepted his help back into the carriage, reclaiming my seat on the velvet cushion as he shut the door.

The opposite door remained ajar, and I stared at the point where Rencourt had disappeared, presumably to enter the Afterworld. Before I knew it, the Ferrier had crossed to the other side of the vehicle.

"He's really gone then?" I asked.

The reaper turned, following my line of sight, then nodded. "He is journeying to the Afterworld as we speak."

I frowned. "You do not ferry them there?"

"I take them as far as The Beyond. From there, they must travel alone."

"How long will it take him to get there?" I didn't expect him to answer. If I were the Master of Shadows, I'd certainly have better things to do than answer the questions of a silly, little girl, but the Ferrier surprised me again.

"There is no guarantee that he will, though I suspect he has a fighting chance. Each path is different, each fraught with its own obstacles. For some, it may take minutes. For others, years."

"And what of those that never make it? What happens to them?"

"They remain between."

I thought he was being intentionally cryptic, but talking seemed to ease my remaining nerves.

"And is it always like that?" I asked.

The Ferrier sighed, a sound so human I momentarily forgot where I was.

"Like what, Miss Fil'Owen?"

"So—" Biting my lip, I searched my mind for the right word. "Easy"

I shrugged, dissatisfied with the word choice, but unable to conjure a better replacement.

"No," he said. "In fact, it is very rarely 'like that.'"

With that final, mysterious answer, he closed the door. It latched with a finality that drew me back to the present situation. I tipped my head back, closing my eyes as I listened to the Ferrier take his seat and set the horses in motion.

For a brief moment, he'd been surprisingly forthcoming with answers to my questions. I cursed myself for again forgetting to ask his name and endeavored to do so when we next stopped.

Chapter 12

The Ferrier

I'd almost let her go. Her fear had been a sharp reminder of the monster I'd become. Never mind that she'd relaxed when she learned it was me. Decades had passed since I was human, since I inhabited the world of the living, but she was my ticket to freedom.

As I'd headed back to the carriage, I'd reflected on all she must have left behind—all that would be lost to her if I failed in this task.

And it was an impossible task.

Luck—or perhaps fate—had put her in my path. If anyone had something to prove against Death, it was me. This woman would either be a jackpot or a fantastic bargaining chip. Only time would tell.

Chapter 13

Katrin

It was nearly dawn when the carriage finally stopped, judging by the soft light gilding the horizon. I'd nodded off once or twice during the ride only to be jostled awake by the rough terrain. Exiting the carriage proved quite the feat as my quaking legs threatened to buckle beneath me at every step. I hadn't known what to expect of the Ferrier's home. He could have dwelled in a dark cave deep under a mountain, and I would have been expected to stay with him. The Between was as much a mystery as the Afterworld. Though I'd prepared for the worst, I couldn't stop my sharp intake of breath as I beheld what was to be my home for the next year.

The very world around me was drained of color—of life, frankly. A dense fog blanketed the area, turning the sky a sickly shade of gray. The bony limbs of skeletal trees jutted up at odd angles. Given where I was, I couldn't help but compare them to the hands of giant beasts clawing their way from the depths of the Earth.

I glanced down, noting the myriad of cracks that spiderwebbed across the landscape. Spinning, I traced the winding pathways.

Patches of dead grass sprouted up at random intervals. If this was a web, then I was the fly. The only living thing here beside the spider.

The creature in question was busy tending the horses, and I stepped away to make the most of his distraction.

A foreboding wrought iron fence surrounded us, though the gates stood open for now. I wondered if he would close them while I was here. If this place would be a prison, or if I'd be free to come and go as I pleased. Not that I had anywhere to go.

I heaved a sigh of frustration, and one of the horses echoed my sentiments.

"If you're in such a hurry, you can wait within." The Ferrier gestured to the other side of the horses.

Though he'd mistaken the target of my frustrations, I knew a dismissal when I heard one. Adjusting my satchel over my shoulder, I stepped around the carriage and paused in awe as I finally acknowledged the sprawling manor house.

Three stories tall and at least twice as wide as my family home, the dark behemoth towered above me. It stretched into the fog in both length and height. Spires pierced the low-hanging clouds like needles in a bolt of fabric. Arched windows dotted the crumbling stone facade, the shape echoed in the gables and dormers. Creeping vines snaked over the entire structure, threatening to make it one with the ill-maintained garden.

I hesitated at the black door, my hand hovering over the iron handle. Every etiquette lesson played in repeat at the back of my mind. *A lady should always wait to be announced. Always knock before entering. A guest should never let oneself in.*

All of it was completely irrelevant to this situation. Still, it felt wrong to enter the Ferrier's home before him, almost like I was intruding upon a sacred space. As far as I knew, no other living person had ever stood here. I had no idea what I would find on the other side of the door, but rather than trepidation, my body thrummed with excitement. I'd already accomplished the hardest part of my plan. All that was left was for me to see where I would be spending the next year of my life.

"If you are waiting for the butler, there isn't one."

Startled, I glanced back to where the Ferrier still cared for the horses. His hood remained up, and though he appeared to be focused on the task at hand, I could have sworn I'd heard a hint of mirth in his words. Had he been watching me this whole time? Of course, he would. He might have claimed to harbor no human emotions, but these small glimpses of his personality said otherwise. It made me all the more curious to find out what lurked beneath the dark cowl.

"Arse," I muttered, pushing open the door.

Though the world outside had been dreary, I had to pause on the threshold as my eyes adapted to the tenebrous interior of the house itself. The stagnant air assaulted my senses with the saccharine scent of rotting flowers. My eyes watered, and I swallowed thickly against the urge to gag, holding my sleeve to my nose like a makeshift mask.

I breathed in the scent of home, of wildflowers and cedar that was already beginning to fade from the fabric. Waving away the depressing notion, I forced my feet forward. The floorboards creaked with each step, the sound echoing in the cavernous foyer. I halted where the murky light from the doorway ended. To my unadjusted eyes, I appeared to stand on a precipice before a plunge of unimaginable depths. Though the logical part of my mind tried to tell me that the likelihood of there being a bottomless pit in the middle of this veritable palace was slim, the louder voice in my head was reminding me of how little I knew about the Ferrier and this place.

Refusing to ignore the more insistent—albeit less sane—voice, I stayed exactly where I was and watched as the objects around me slowly began to take shape.

A threadbare rug stretched before my feet, its pattern indistinguishable in the low light. An upholstered bench and a small table were the extent of the furniture that I could make out. Several doorways branched off from the room and to my left, a sweeping staircase spiraled up and out of sight. A large wrought iron chandelier dangled above it all.

In a flash, I was blinded again. I squinted against the sudden brightness as every candle, sconce, and chandelier sparked to life. A loud bang had me spinning to find the Ferrier standing behind me, the door at his back now firmly closed. Though the room glowed with newfound light, shadows continued to snake around his black-clad form.

For a moment, we only stared at one another. At least, I thought he was staring at me. He remained motionless while facing my direction, and I could only assume his thoughts mirrored my own. This was our new reality. For the next year of our lives, I would be here, invading his space and demanding his protection. And for what? A mere pittance of a reward.

I hoped he wasn't having second thoughts because there was no way I was returning home to wait for Death.

"Neat trick," I said, gesturing to the lights around us. "I wasn't aware you could control light, or is it flame?"

"Darkness is mine to control. I can call it." The Ferrier lifted a hand and darkness fell. "And I can take it away."

My eyes stung at the sudden return of the light. I turned in place, finally able to take in the sheer majesty of the Ferrier's home.

"This is where you live?"

"Allow me to make one thing clear, Miss Fil'Owen. I do not *live*. I do not age. I merely exist. This manor is where I choose to reside during my time between harvesting the souls of the dead. It is not a life."

I blinked at the dramatic assessment of his situation. I was no expert on social skills, but his were non-existent. "So, this is where you *exist*?" There was no hiding the note of teasing in my voice, and I had to question my sanity at the choice to mock the Reaper.

His focus remained fixed on me. I squirmed under his scrutiny and turned my attention to the grandeur around us. Though shrouded in a gloom that matched its master's countenance, the manor boasted an understated opulence that put my family home to shame.

Two enormous windows flanked me, draped in pleated, damask curtains that pooled on the floor. My fingers itched to push them aside, some innate part of me already longing for the sweet caress of daylight. The many flickering candelabra and sconces did little to improve the somber mood of the place.

The Ferrier had not moved when my eyes found him again, and I wondered what he saw when he looked at me.

Did he see a young woman with unruly brown hair and an up-turned nose? Did he see someone filled with hope for the future?

Did he see a soul worth saving? Or did he—like everyone else—see the shadows that marked my skin and nothing else?

Whereas most people I knew were repulsed by my mark, I could see how they might call to him. Had he seen something of himself in those shadows? Would my shadows be his to control like all others?

I blinked, hoping that realization was as far-fetched as it sounded. Surely, if my shadows fell under his command, he would have already tested that power. Right?

The silence thickened with unanswered questions.

"Well, then..." I trailed off, unsure what the proper social etiquette was for engaging in conversation with the demon you're paying to save your life.

My words hit their mark, breaking the reaper from his trance. He shook his head as though dispelling an errant thought. The human gesture settled my nerves, making me braver than I had any right to be.

"Aren't you going to take that off?" I asked, indicating his cloak.

He tilted his head to the side in a distinctly inhuman motion. "Are you so eager to see what lies beneath?"

"It can't be any worse than this?" Tucking my hair behind my ear felt like being possessed by someone else. I never made a show of revealing my mark, yet I'd done exactly that twice now for the

Ferrier. Each time, I grew more amazed at his lack of reaction, even if *this* time I'd been hoping for some acknowledgment of my attempted levity.

Perhaps I'd offended him. I'd meant it as a joke, but I didn't care what he looked like. I only wished to know the man beneath the faceless demon veneer.

I opened my mouth to apologize for my insensitivity, but it snapped shut as the reaper stepped forward, tugging at the edges of his hood. It was only as he neared that I realized he was keeping the light from penetrating his cover as he stepped closer to the candlelight—closer to me.

"Understand, Miss Fil'Owen—"

"Call me Kat," I interjected, immediately regretting my outburst. "Please," I amended, but the damage was already done.

Disdain rippled off him like the shadows that pooled between our feet. I bit my tongue, and the coppery taste of blood filled my mouth.

"Miss Fil'Owen."

I flinched at the Ferrier's emphasis of my proper name.

"We are not friends. This is not a holiday. It is a business arrangement." His voice was a growl I felt deep in my belly. "As such, there are certain expectations I have for this situation."

He paused, and my head bobbed in agreement. I was at his mercy. Whatever rules he had for this arrangement, I had to accept or face the reality of returning to my cursed life.

Seemingly satisfied with my complacency, he rattled off a series of commands in a clipped tone. "No leaving the grounds. Should you decide to annul our agreement, you may go at any time, but my protection extends only to the gate. Stay out of my way. I have no interest in small talk or braiding each other's hair. You may move about the manor as you wish so long as you do not interfere with my work. You will not accompany me on any other missions."

"I can't come with you? What about Death? What if he comes for me when you're not here?" I looked around as though I could conjure him by name alone.

"You are at best a distraction, at worst a liability. Death has no reason to come here, other than to see me. Since he knows when I am away, he will have no cause for being here when I am not."

"He can't... sense me?"

"He can sense you in the way that he can sense all that are mortal. Your impending demise would call to him like a siren song, but here you are no closer to death than I. Your soul is in stasis."

"But I'm marked by Death. Surely, that means he has some awareness of me."

"To my knowledge, you are the only person Death has ever marked. I don't know what cause he had to single out someone like you."

I heard all the words he didn't say. Someone *ordinary*. Someone *unremarkable*. I'd wondered the same thing. *Why me?*

It would seem the Ferrier was as confused as me.

"Until we know more about his motives for marking you, it is best that you remain at *Tyr Anigh*." The foreign words rolled off his tongue. "Do you have any questions?"

"What am I to call you?" I crossed my arms over my chest and stared right into the depths of his hood.

He seemed to hold my gaze, though I could see nothing of the eyes I stared toward. When he spoke, his voice had lost its fire. "I am the Ferrier of Souls, Master of Shadows, Right Hand of Death. You may refer to me by any of those titles."

I cocked a brow. "Truly?"

"Have I given you any indication that I am a jester, Miss Fil'Owen?"

I seethed at his persistent use of my surname but held my tongue. We still had three hundred and sixty-five days to spend together. It seemed pertinent to avoid any unnecessary strain on this tenuous partnership. One wrong move and the Ferrier might decide to renege on our deal and send me packing. I had no idea how binding his promise to me was. For all I knew, he had summoned his shadows to twine our hands together for show.

Until I could trust his word, I would have to be on my best behavior.

"Oh, Mighty Hand of Death! Wouldst thou be so magnanimous as to show this lowly mortal to their room?" So much for my best behavior.

As the Ferrier turned away, I tried to picture him fighting back a smile under all that darkness, but his voice betrayed no hint of amusement.

"Most of the living quarters are on the third floor. You're welcome to choose any that suit your needs."

"And where is your room?" The question was out before I could think better of it, but I didn't dare try to take it back.

"Why? Planning to drop by for a visit?" he purred.

"Of course not," I sputtered, cheeks heating at the insinuation. "I simply wanted to make sure I didn't choose yours by mistake."

"Mine will be the one that is locked." He turned, effectively dismissing me as he strode toward the next room.

Chapter 14
The Ferrier

This was a mistake.

Already, I regretted agreeing to the entitled brat's terms. An entire year of this for a bit of gold? Fine, a lot of gold. Almost one hundred years as the Ferrier and I was no closer to paying off my debt to Death. A couple silvers for every passing was nothing compared to the worth of a soul, but four thousand gold coins? That would help, and if it didn't, perhaps Death would trade her soul for mine.

That's if he even remembered the girl. I couldn't see what he would want her for. Sure, she was pleasing enough to look at, but Death only suffered those who followed orders. Miss Fil'Owen didn't seem to fit the bill.

I walked with no destination in mind other than putting distance between me and the girl. The shadows I'd left in my wake would watch over her and report back to me. Already those nearest to me whispered of her movements.

She was climbing the stairs.

Good.

Maybe if she slept I could forget she was here and carry on like nothing had changed, like she hadn't rearranged my entire existence.

Chapter 15

Katrin

The stairs creaked as I ascended, white paint chipping off with every brush of my hand along the banister. Tattered, lace curtains hung by the windows doing nothing to keep out the watery sunlight. I stopped at one such window and peered out over the grounds. Though I knew the sun had fully risen, the thick fog surrounding the manor remained impenetrable. If it weren't for the occasional protruding branches and glimpses of the ground, I could almost believe we floated among the clouds.

My legs burned by the time I reached the third floor, the lingering exhaustion reminding me that it had been almost a full day since I'd last rested. I paused at the top of the stairs, bracing one hand on the wall while the other firmly gripped the banister.

A wave of dizziness washed over me, and I paused long enough to pull the waterskin from my bag. After several deep swigs, I felt well enough to continue.

Doors lined the long hallway that stretched out on both sides of my feet. Each appeared identical to all the others. Stark-white frames surrounded each of the ornately carved wood doors. The walls between were decorated with faded floral wallpaper. Flickering sconces cast shadows over the areas where it had peeled away, revealing a cream and green striped pattern beneath.

The sun had been weak on my journey up the stairs, but here, darkness reigned once more. Not a sliver of natural light illuminated the dim corridor.

Foreboding traced icy fingers up my spine, freezing me in place. The candles flickering in amber glass sconces failed to dispel the strange shadows that clung to the walls and ceiling. I stared, certain they were moving. They shifted and whirled in opposition to the dancing candlelight.

I scrubbed my eyes with my palms. When I looked again, the shadows were still. Perhaps this place was haunted. I shook my head, forcing my feet into motion. It had been a long night. I would not be cowed by some trick of the light—not when rest was so close.

This was *The Between* after all. There was sure to be a number of inexplicable phenomena in the place between life and death. I couldn't lose sleep over moving shadows.

Even so, I stuck to the small patches of light as I approached the first door to my left on silent feet. Though the entire manor gave the impression of being utterly abandoned, I pressed my ear to the door to be sure no one waited inside. The last thing I wanted to stumble upon was some minor demon or spirit the Ferrier failed to mention.

The wood was cold against the shell of my ear. I suppressed a shiver as I held my breath, listening intently for any noise beyond its intricately carved surface. When I was certain no one waited within, I opened the door, wishing I'd had the wherewithal to procure a taper as it swung open to reveal an equally dim bedroom.

After growing up in a bustling household full of servants, family, and guests, the utter silence of the Ferrier's manor unnerved me. Even the whisper of my dress brushing the floor seemed to fill the space with ghostly sighs. I raced across the room, hurrying for the window I suspected to be on the opposite wall. Managing to avoid almost all of the near-invisible objects within, I exhaled in relief when my outstretched hands met heavy, draped fabric. In one jerking motion, I flung open the curtains.

The same murky light seeped in, but it was a welcome reprieve from the dungeonesque hallway beyond.

I spun, searching every corner and crevice for lurking shadows. Satisfied that the room contained only natural shadows and those plaguing my own body, I turned my focus to the simple—albeit elegant—contents of the room.

To my right was an unlit fireplace. Evidence of its last use lay in a heap below the andirons. A small door led to a privy chamber, which I was very glad to see, having known very little about the bodily functions of demons. I'd worried I would need to procure my own chamber pot. A large, four-poster bed sat to my left. A matching trunk and wardrobe—the latter empty—completed the set. Linens that may once have been white adorned the bed, emitting a cloud of dust when I sat upon it.

I coughed and sputtered, choking on the glittering remnants of days past. The air in the room felt stagnant as though it had not been used for some time. It was no wonder, given the current master of the home. Unless the Ferrier brought his work home with him, he'd hardly have an occasion to host guests, which made it all the more curious that he chose to *exist* in such an impressively large home. I hadn't seen any servants or caretakers either.

The Ferrier didn't seem the type to need constant companionship or even regular socializing, but it must have been a lonely existence in The Between. The next year of my life would be the same. Was it too much to ask to be lonely together?

I returned to the window, prying it open until the fresh scent of pine and hay reached me. The air outside was just as still, but I hoped it would go some way toward airing out the room. In the morning—the *later* morning—I would give this room the cleaning it deserved. Until then, I would have to make do with what I had.

After some searching, I found clean linens tucked away in the trunk. I'd never had to make my own bed before, but I made quick work of stripping the bed and eventually wrestled the clean sheets into an acceptable state.

By the time I finished, all my anxiety had trickled away, a hollow ache left in its place. I'd been wrung out and left to dry like a soiled shirt. In one night, I'd left my family, gambled away my dowry, and made a deal with a demon. I'd given up everything for this one chance at getting my life back. In a year, I'd have it all back, or I'd be dead.

I left the curtains open but locked the door. It felt ridiculous given the Ferrier's ability to walk through walls, but I took comfort in hearing the lock *snick* shut regardless. Though I laid down with every intention of remaining alert, the moment my head hit the pillow, I fell into a deep sleep.

***

I woke with a start, heart stuttering at the sight of my unfamiliar surroundings. Every muscle in my body tensed, preparing me to fight or run, whichever would keep me alive. My eyes scanned every corner for a threat before the events of the previous night came flooding back to me.

It took my body far longer than my mind to register that I was safe. Over twenty years of waking up in the same room of the same house and my heart refused to accept anything different. It pounded out a furious rhythm, threatening to jump from my chest and save itself if it came to it. I pressed my hand against my ribs like I could hold it in, but the adrenaline pumping through my veins refused to be so easily tamed.

I breathed in through my nose and exhaled heavily, willing my shoulders to drop, my fists to unclench, and my pulse to steady. After repeating the exercise several times, my muscles finally relaxed.

Flopping back on the bed, I stared at the crumbling plaster ceiling. Light still shone through the window, and I hoped it meant I'd only slept a few hours and not an entire day. I sat up, rubbing the sleep from my eyes. A heaviness had settled into my limbs, and my movements were sluggish.

I debated returning to sleep, but my rest had been fitful at best. Nightmares plagued me just like they had in the world of the living. Sometimes I'd watch life pass me by from behind the bars of a cage, growing old while those around me experienced all that the world had to offer. Those dreams left me with an enduring sullenness, but they weren't as bad as the ones where Death came for me.

When he'd drag me kicking and screaming into the Afterworld, and I'd wait for someone—anyone—to save me, but no one came.

No one ever came.

Sighing, I swung my legs over the edge of the bed, resigned to shake off the fear that had haunted me for years. I had done it. I'd saved myself. I'd found a way to escape my fated demise, and all I had to do was endure a year in The Between. A year with the Ferrier.

Well, that and find a way to stop Death from hunting me.

I rose, wishing I'd had the foresight to bathe before I collapsed into bed. A thin layer of sweat and grime caked my skin, and I longed to be rid of this dress. The thing was, I hadn't packed another. For all my planning and all my confidence, I'd brought very little aside from coins and food. I guess I thought I'd either fail miserably or I'd have bigger things to worry about than clean clothes.

While I did have bigger things to worry about, I wasn't eager to dive into them just yet. I pulled an apple from my sack and took another swig of water. I would run out of water before I ran out of food, so that would need to be my first priority.

I cracked open the door and froze as shadows darted away from the spear of sunlight that breached the gloom. My throat constricted, and I slammed the door shut.

Now, I knew I wasn't hallucinating. These shadows were alive. Well, maybe not *alive*, but capable of independent movement at the least, possibly even sentient.

If the Ferrier had control over darkness, did he control these shadows as well? Were these his minions?

It made perfect sense now. He'd left me seemingly alone when, in actuality, he'd only left me at the mercy of his shadow creatures. They probably reported back every move I made to their dark master.

I pressed my palms to the solid wood like this small barrier could keep them out. Sure, they avoided the light, but what would happen when night inevitably fell?

Grabbing the old sheets from the haphazard pile on the floor, I stuffed them between the door and floor. Hopefully, it would be enough to barricade any errant shadows. Perhaps, if I was lucky, they would leave with the Ferrier at night when he returned to the world of the living.

I could wait until night fell to explore the manor.

I returned to the bed and emptied the contents of my bag. If I portioned out the food, I had five, maybe seven days at most. The water would only last me one or two.

The privy contained only the commode, no water pump, but that didn't mean there wasn't one somewhere in this house. If it came to it, I thought I remembered a well outside by the stables. For all I knew, it was dried up.

Leaning back against the headboard, I took a bite of my apple and questioned if I'd suffered a temporary bout of insanity when I'd left home last night.

Chapter 16
The Ferrier

Rest did not find me that day or the next, nor—to my eternal surprise—did Miss Fil'Owen. I'd guessed her to be someone plagued by insatiable curiosity if she'd done enough poking around to discover how to hail a reaper. Though I waited for the sound of footsteps outside my door, none ever came.

My shadows kept my curiosity piqued with whispered updates. They told me which room she'd selected, when she appeared to rest, and when she awoke, opening the door for only a moment before retreating back inside. I suspected she'd seen my shadows and been afraid to proceed, though she'd shown not an ounce of fear since we'd made it to The Between. In fact, she'd shown little fear toward me at all, only when she'd mistaken me for Death.

She was a strange one.

I didn't miss the way her markings resembled my shadows almost as if she were marked for me and not for Death. The notion was absurd. More likely, Death or Fate had foreseen this moment and marked her specifically to toy with me. No other explanation made sense. What could the king of the Afterworld want with a human woman?

As dusk fell, I gave up my fruitless attempts at sleep and stalked to the other wing of the manor. I'd not intended to visit her but soon found myself standing before the door to the room she'd chosen. The shadows I'd assigned to her reported no recent movement. It would seem she was content to remain within, which was fine—great, actually. And yet, my hand raised to knock, hovering mid-air as I warred with myself.

She was not my problem. Except she was.

"This is ridiculous," I muttered and knocked.

My brows rose as a muffled curse sounded from inside.

"Don't come in!" she called.

Soft footsteps approached. I leaned forward as though drawn to her proximity through the wood. There was another person in my prison. I was at once intrigued and repulsed by the idea. She halted on the other side of the door but made no move to open it.

"Are we to converse through walls for the length of your stay?" I joked and immediately regretted the playfulness in my tone.

"I'm—I'm indecent."

I jumped away from the door like it had caught flame. My entire body thrummed to life, awakened in a way it had not been in over a century.

Indecent, indeed. The very word was indecent. It conjured to mind lacy underthings and glimpses of forbidden skin.

Apparently, I'd been alone far too long.

I cleared my throat and recovered some of my composure. "I am leaving. I'll be back before dawn. Don't get into trouble."

I turned without waiting for a response, but the sound of her shaky exhale found my ears nonetheless.

Chapter 17

Katrin

Like the day, the darkness here was muted, incomplete. Night fell and the sky turned to dark gray, the fog too thick to be pierced by the moon or stars. I was coming to find there were no opposites in this low-contrast world, nothing so simple as black and white or good and bad. There could only be more of something or less. In the night, it was more dark than light. I was more alive than dead. The Ferrier was more arse than not.

He'd clearly come over here to show he knew which room I occupied. What benefit that knowledge offered, I didn't know. Perhaps it was a show of power, but I didn't get that impression. I was grateful that he let me know he was leaving. The manor, *Tyr Anigh*, seemed less intimidating with him gone. I'd peeked my head out long enough to confirm the living shadows still lingered in the corridor and decided exploring was not in the cards for me that night. Their amorphous bodies ebbed and flowed around the flickering light of a candelabra. While they appeared harmless, I didn't like the idea of them reporting all of my movements back to the Ferrier. Not that I had anything to hide.

The hours ticked by slowly with nothing to occupy my time. I dozed a bit, waking to a still darkened sky. Hunger gnawed at me, and I recalled that I'd eaten very little at dinner the night before and only an apple since. I forced down a bit of cheese and meat, wishing I had some bread to go with it. Despite my intent to ration, my waterskin was nearly emptied by a couple gulps after my meager dinner.

Still hungry, I tucked away the rest of my provisions, determined to make them last, even if they'd be pointless to save without more water.

I stared out the open window, wondering if I'd traded one type of prison for another. This one was temporary, at least, though it may only be a stay of execution. The task of finding a cure was too daunting to take on in the late hours of my first night here. I didn't know where to start. The only example I knew was my father's failed research attempts.

Exhaling heavily, I drew my gaze to the landscape beyond the window. Very little pierced the fog surrounding the manor. If I squinted, I could picture the walled-off land as an island surrounded by calm waters. The occasional tree limb broke the surface like pieces of a shipwreck. It was like nothing I could have imagined, stretching farther than I could see. A vast, secret world between life and death.

My room was just as dark as the world beyond with no candles to light, but I was no stranger to the darkness. I allowed my thoughts to drift as the horizon slowly lightened.

True to his word, the Ferrier returned about half an hour before dawn broke. He tended to the horses as he had the day before with quick, practiced motions. I waited to see if he would remove his cloak, but even without my presence, it remained a constant shroud.

His head tipped up as though sensing my attention. I darted back from the window, but couldn't tell if he'd spotted me. I suspected my room had the only open window, making it easy to pick out among the many pointed arches. My breath caught in my chest. Though he'd done nothing of ill-intent since I'd met him, everything about him radiated danger.

The playful confidence I'd managed on little sleep had fled after the day's rest. I trembled as I recalled what I'd said to him. It was a wonder he didn't hand me over to Death then, but I'd felt the strength that hid within those robes, and I knew if anyone could keep me safe, it was him.

When I glanced back, he had gone.

I watched the sun rise like spilled milk across the sky. Though it did little to lighten my mood, it was enough to illuminate the interior of the moody mansion. I needed answers and I wasn't getting any on this side of the door.

With a fortifying breath in, I eased it open. The creeping shadows retreated from the light, those who had ventured closer springing away with haste. I held the door firmly between us as I peeked out.

The darkness shifted and whirled, stark compared to the natural shadows of the hall. If I didn't know better, I'd say they were observing me in return. Possessed by a sudden surge of bravery, I slipped my hand through the narrow opening. The shadows paused their motion as they focused on me.

Before I could think better of it, I waved to the shadow nearest me. I felt every bit a fool until a small bit of shadow separated from the main body and proceeded to mirror my movement.

Definitely sentient, then.

I gave the shadows a vulgar gesture, sticking out my tongue for maximum effect as I swung the door wide open.

They scattered as the weak light permeated the hall, clearing my way to the door across the hall. With nothing better to do, now seemed as good a time as any to explore the other rooms.

As I searched the other rooms, I left their light to merge with the first until the third floor practically blazed with the filtered sunlight.

After exploring several identical rooms, my stomach growled its discontent. It was time to find some real food and, hopefully, water.

Unfortunately, after nearly an hour of searching, the kitchen proved useless. I knew as soon as I walked in and saw the empty hearth, but that didn't stop me from looking through every cabinet and pantry for a crumb of bread or vegetable. Aside from a couple bundles of dried herbs, there was no food to be found.

Did the Ferrier even need to eat? Probably not, but I did. At least, I thought I still needed to eat, and my rumbling stomach seemed to agree.

A stray shadow scurried beneath a table, startling me as I stepped from the room. I sighed but couldn't hide the faint smile that twitched at the corners of my lips. If I looked closely, I could pick out another of the Ferrier's shadows hiding in a dark corner beneath the stairs.

While part of me loathed their spying, I could admit their presence dulled the sharp edge of loneliness.

A thought occurred to me, and I shook it off as nonsense. Then, I looked around, remembered where I was, and thought better of ignoring my gut instinct. Facing the shadow closest to me, I bent down until I was eye-level with it. It shrank under my direct focus.

"Can you show me how to get outside? To the garden?" I pointed to the nearby window in case it couldn't understand my language. In all my wandering, I'd found myself in the belly of the manor. While I was certain to find my way out again, this way would both expedite the process and confirm my suspicions about the shadow's capabilities.

The shadows seemed to converse with each other silently. As they discussed, I thought about how they reacted to the light. It was possible any light was harmful to them.

"If you can't, I understand," I added, not wanting to cause them pain.

As though a dam had broken, the shadow beneath the table oozed out. The amorphous shape entered the light without any ill effects, though it appeared more transparent. It hovered in front of me about waist high as though giving me a chance to change my mind.

Tentatively, I reached out a hand, expecting to encounter some resistance. It passed right through the shadow, a slight chill the only sign that it was there. The shadow reciprocated the movement, reaching toward my face. This time, I was surprised to feel something cold and solid touch the tip of my nose. I jerked away and laughed, slightly uncomfortable, but also amazed at the marvelous creature.

"You weren't hiding from the light at all, were you?" I asked. "You were hiding from me."

The shadow bobbed, which I took for assent, and headed out the door. As I followed, the second shadow creature eased into position behind me. Maybe they weren't spies. Maybe they were guards. The thought brought a smile to my face as we traveled through the dim corridors.

We reached an exit that was different than the one I had first entered through. The world beyond the glass-paned doors looked just as unwelcoming as it had when I'd arrived, but if there was food to be had, I was determined to find it.

Both shadows passed easily through the door. It took me some time to force it open, and I cringed at the squeal emitted by the rusty hinges.

The silence in The Between was remarkable, like the dead of winter when no creature dared to stir. Only here, not even the air moved.

I, however, was a walking clamor.

Brittle, brown grass crunched beneath my feet as I stepped outside, skirts swishing with every step. I sniffed and rolled my eyes at the noise.

For years, I'd perfected the art of being unnoticeable. I'd practiced standing in a crowded room and forcing the attention away from me—drawing in on myself until I became indistinguishable from the furniture around me. Fading away had been preferable to derision, hatred, and outright fear I'd seen reflected in the eyes of those around me—those I'd once considered friends.

I halted, struck immobile by the memory. Self-pity was a plague, one I refused to fall victim to. Squeezing my eyes shut, I willed away the images of my past and the accompanying resentment. I was here after all. I was changing my fate. And then I'd return to those people that scorned me. I'd let them see the woman that became of the girl they shunned, and then I'd leave forever. Somewhere in this vast world was a better life, a better place for me. If I could track down the Ferrier of Souls, I could find my paradise too.

Tilting my chin up to the sky, I opened my mouth and screamed. The cry that poured from me was eight years of pain, eight years of silence, eight years of pretending I was fine when all I wanted to do was rage. It crashed through the silence like a thunderclap.

My knees buckled, and I collapsed to the ground in a graceless heap, utterly spent.

I gasped for air, but breath was not all I'd expelled. With a single sound, I'd let go of everything I'd been. It was the farewell I hadn't let myself make. Goodbye to my old life. Goodbye to the cursed destiny I refused to accept.

Now, I sat, an empty vessel ready to be filled, a blank page with endless possibilities.

The shadow guards, who had scattered at my sudden outburst, creeped back into my periphery.

I stared at my hands, one light and one shadowed. Part of me had hoped the shadows would disappear when I'd made my bargain. If I'd changed my fate, why was I still marked?

The sound of approaching footsteps startled me into motion. I scrambled to my feet, hiding my affected hand behind my back and angling my face away out of habit. The steps were unhurried, deliberate, and they were getting closer.

For a moment, I considered the time it would take to rush back into the manor, but then I remembered. I was through with hiding. With a deep breath in, I turned to fully face whoever neared. If it was the Ferrier, he'd already seen the worst of me. I'd assumed we were the only two in The Between, but maybe that assumption had been wrong.

A shiver coursed through me, but I held firm, even as a man dressed in black stepped around the corner of the stable.

CHAPTER 18

Katrin

The man in black zeroed in on me from across the way, eyes darting over my form. It was hard not to notice the way his gaze breezed past the shadows on my face, marking them, but not recoiling as most would.

I dared a step forward, taking note of the pitchfork propped over one shoulder. A stable hand? Foolish of me to assume there were no servants at the manor, but I hadn't encountered any inside the house. He must have heard me scream and come to investigate. What did it say about this place that he hadn't hurried at the sound of apparent distress? Were screaming maidens a common occurrence?

"I'm sorry. I didn't realize anyone else was here." My voice was little more than a croak.

In one smooth motion, the man flipped his pitchfork off his shoulder and plunged it into the ground. He crossed one leg over the other and leaned onto the protruding handle. The look on his face suggested he had better things to do. "Miss Fil'Owen—"

I startled at the sound of my name. "Aside from the four horses, yours and mine are the only souls here."

I stepped back, horror following swiftly on the heels of realization.

"You're the Ferrier." I hadn't intended to say the words aloud, and the man made no sound in confirmation or denial. He only stared at me, one eyebrow cocked in amusement.

There was no way that this man was the same person who appeared from nothing and controlled the darkness, but as he turned, I noticed the ever-present shadows eddying about his feet.

My eyes slowly glided up his form, taking note of every detail that had been hidden from me the night we met. He was clad fully in black, but it did little to conceal the thick muscles that pulled at the fabric along his long legs and broad chest. The leather gloves still covered his hands. In fact, every inch of skin was covered except for his neck and face. And what a face it was.

He had a strong jaw dusted with stubble and dark eyes that bored into my very soul, all framed by nearly black hair with a gentle wave.

I realized I'd been staring and quickly averted my gaze, finding a sudden interest in the stark ground.

Somehow, I'd felt more hidden while he was cloaked. I itched under his scrutiny, tilting my head to force my hair over my mark.

He'd already seen it, of course—at least the part of it that consumed my face and hand—but I'd been able to show him without fear of seeing the judgment and disgust reflected back in his eyes. I wasn't sure I was ready to deal with those looks again.

A dark chuckle drew my focus back to him. Apparently, my discomfort amused him.

I huffed in annoyance. Here was this beautiful, strong, magical man, and I expected him to protect me, to see me as a person with value. I'd been naive in thinking of him as my savior.

I remembered his words from the night before when he claimed he was no knight in shining armor. He was right. Standing before me was a demon in human form, a veritable prince of darkness.

I was suddenly very aware that I was an unmarried woman staying alone in the home of an unfairly attractive man. And it *was* unfair. This wasn't my life. It was no life at all. The Ferrier had said so himself. I was only meant to hide away here, beneath Death's nose, until it was safe to return to my utterly normal life.

"Is something wrong, Miss Fil'Owen?" He regarded me curiously, arms crossing as he abandoned his pitchfork to step toward me.

It felt like an attack. My hackles rose and I resisted the urge to bare my teeth at the perceived threat.

"I just didn't expect you to look so—" I stopped myself before I could tell the blasted Ferrier of Souls that I thought he was attractive. Heat rose to my cheeks, but my foggy mind failed to fill in the blank with a more appropriate descriptor.

"Ruggedly handsome?" he asked, a mocking smile turning up one corner of his mouth.

"Human," I spit out, pouring every ounce of indignation into my answering glare.

He sighed, shoulders drooping with the motion. "It may shock you to know that I was once human, Miss Fil'Owen."

"Please, call me Kat. And what are you now?"

"Other."

I waited for more, but he didn't elaborate. I let the subject drop.

"I was looking for food," I admitted, oddly ashamed of having basic human needs. "And water?"

"And you thought you could scream some into existence?"

I didn't try to hide my eyeroll.

He pointed over his shoulder. "There is a well there, but there are water pumps throughout the house. You'll find no food here."

Crossing my arms over my chest, I glared at him with all the fire I could muster. "Clearly. So what do you intend to do about it?"

He brushed the dirt from his shoulder where the pitchfork had been. The gesture was so casual, it enraged me further. "I fail to see how it's my problem."

"You agreed to keep me alive for a year." My hands balled into fists, but I kept them tucked beneath my arms.

"I agreed to keep you from Death for a year," he said, raising one finger for emphasis.

"Semantics. Either way, you can't just let me starve. That would just as surely deliver me to Death's door as your carriage." I'd grown up in the lap of luxury, so I was hardly on the verge of starvation, but that didn't mean I could go an entire year without food.

"Strictly speaking, I cannot deliver you to Death's door. I can merely show you the way there."

"You're quite infuriating, do you know that?"

"I've been told I'm quite charming actually."

My sharp retort died on my tongue as the edges of the world darkened. I blinked in an attempt to clear my vision, but my head was fuzzy. A bout of dizziness struck me. I swayed, thrusting out my arms for balance. My right hand made contact with something solid, and I grappled for the strength to hold on, my fingers refusing to do what my mind commanded. My knees buckled, and I braced for impact as the ground raced up to meet me. Or was it the other way around?

I collided but not with the ground. Something soft yet unyielding halted my fall, and I knew it was the Ferrier before the dark spots could fade from my sight. As the world came back into focus, I found myself once again in the Ferrier's arms. His proximity was all the more arresting without the hood and cloak. I leaned into his strength, breathing in the faint smell of ozone and pine. The sense of falling intensified as I glanced up to find him peering down at me, an inscrutable expression on his face.

My feet found the ground, and he stepped away, keeping his hands braced on my shoulders until I got my balance. I caught myself still leaning into his touch as his fingers slipped away. Balling my fists in my skirts, I fought the urge to chase after the sensation, knowing it was my extended seclusion and not any sort of desire for the Ferrier that had me yearning for his touch.

"I'm fine." I stepped back, waving him off though he showed no sign of following. "I don't know what's come over me. I ate before I left my home, and my water should have been plenty for two days."

"This is the third day you've been here, Miss Fil'Owen."

I did the math in my head. "No, it's only the start of my second day."

The Ferrier shook his head, and I gaped. The first time I'd slept, I'd awoken and thought it was later the same day, but I could have been mistaken. I rearranged my mental timeline to account for sleeping an entire day and realized I'd missed several meals instead of the few I'd thought.

"I haven't needed to eat for years. I assumed whatever life-extending properties this place possesses would extend to you as well." A line appeared between his brows. "Apparently, I was wrong." Glancing at the sky, he sighed and scrubbed a hand over his mouth. "I cannot enter the world of the living until sundown, but I'll try to grab some provisions when I'm out tonight."

"When *we're* out."

"Not happening."

I crossed my arms over my chest. "Fine."

"Fine," he echoed.

I glared at him. "Are you ever going to tell me your name?"

Rolling his eyes, he turned back to the stables. "It's of little consequence. I've already told you what you may call me."

"I am not calling you 'Master of Shadows,'" I called after him. "If you won't tell me, I'll just have to make something up! I think Ferry has a nice ring to it, don't you?"

The man in question threw a particularly vulgar gesture over his shoulder before he disappeared from view.

Laughing, I returned the gesture, an act my mother would be appalled by, and left to track down one of the water pumps.

Chapter 19
The Ferrier

Hooking the last of the horses to the carriage, I watched as the last of the sun's pale light dipped below the horizon. Another night, another soul. But first, I had other plans.

The cursed woman had found something else to occupy her for the remainder of the day, but my mind wouldn't let me forget the feel of her body pressed to mine. The morning's interaction replayed in a constant loop inside my head, and my body thrummed with barely-restrained energy.

I had to admit she had courage, but she was also foolish and entitled and utterly maddening. I'd barely escaped our early encounter without calling the whole thing off. Still, I admired her tenacity in the face of such circumstances.

What Death wanted with her, I didn't know, but I had more than one debt with him and this vow would go a long way towards settling both.

First, I needed to keep her alive. Somehow, I knew that feat would be more difficult than expected.

With the sun fully gone from the sky, my shadows crowded in around me, and I exhaled in relief. They'd come with the position—the shadows, the power. I was ashamed to admit that I'd become accustomed to their presence. I found comfort in their shroud, in disappearing from the world. Though, I couldn't say the same for the cowl and scythe of the Ferrier uniform.

I grabbed the latter as I mounted the steps, settling into the driver's seat. I'd make a quick trip to procure food for Miss Fil'Owen, and then I'd complete my task.

With one command the carriage burst into motion, the beasts at the front needing little direction to understand my desires.

I'd never bothered to name them, the four black horses. They were titans in their own right. Enormous steeds of unknown power, they were as old as me, if not older still. I suspected they'd been at their job for a very long time.

We raced through the open gate and again my thoughts tugged back to the woman I was leaving behind. I wondered if she regretted her choice to come here. When we'd arrived, I'd left the gate open behind us as a way out. If she took her chance, I wouldn't pursue. She'd find her way back to the world of the living easily enough. After all, she didn't belong here. The Between seemed amenable to her presence, at least for now, but she was still a living being. We would see how a year in The Between would affect her.

I shook off thoughts of her, growling as I urged the horses faster.

Skeletal trees whipped past, stray branches reaching for my cowl. With one hand holding the reins, I took up my scythe and struck down those closest to me.

We crossed into the land of the living like stepping through a door. Only a sliver of moonlight lit the landscape. The oppressive heat of summer had not yet relented and the scent of a recent rainfall lingered in the air.

We passed by the crossroads, which were blessedly free from bargaining maidens. The soul I needed to collect lay to the west, but I steered the horses to the east, toward Felwyck.

I passed unnoticed by houses and lone travelers who would know me only as a cool breeze at the back of their necks. Only the recently deceased and those who met me properly at the crossroads could see me, but a hand of Death was not so easily hidden from the other senses. An intuitive few might guess at my presence, but it would be of little consequence. I was either coming for them or I wasn't. Like Death, there was no hiding from me in this world. Unlike Death, I was not so blinded by confidence as to believe that my quarry wouldn't think to escape this world entirely to flee me.

No, Miss Fil'Owen was not the first to attempt such a thing, but, to my knowledge, she is the first to do so with any measure of success. Who's to know if there are others though. Only those who failed would be found out.

Perhaps there were others like me who had harbored fugitives from Death. And to what end?

I would endeavor to ask one of my colleagues if I thought they could be trusted.

A great house rose before me as I crested a hill. Not so great as *Tyr Anigh*, but a proud home nonetheless.

I didn't question how my magic knew the exact location of Miss Fil'Owen's home, but somehow, I knew it was hers without a doubt. There was an essence of her here like a memory held by those she'd left behind. People often underestimated the power of the human mind. Those grieving could conjure images of loved ones so strong, they believed they were looking at a ghost. The truth was, aside from the first few nights after passing, there were very few souls who did not leave for the Afterworld. Those who didn't roamed the bridge between until they could either face their trials or fade from time forever.

The memory of Miss Fil'Owen lived on here, even though she hadn't passed.

I took in the stone walls, the mullioned windows, the manicured lawns. Perhaps I should have been calling her *Lady* Fil'Owen.

Of course she'd had an easy life. No one living in the slums would have had the means to escape her curse as she had, nor, likely, the desire to.

Who wouldn't want to return to a life of luxury?

I halted the carriage on the cobblestone path outside the front door. The horses nickered and stomped, impatient to continue on to their task.

"I'll be quick," I reassured them, unsure when I'd begun talking to the horses as though they could understand me. Whether they could or not, they quieted, seemingly content to allow me this detour.

Leaving the scythe, I leapt to the ground and called forth the shadows. Some sprang off the walls, others slithered up from the cracks between the stones at my feet. Still more flew down from the soffits and gables. They swarmed, engulfing me in rippling darkness.

The sweat on my brow cooled and the tension in my shoulders melted away. Power flooded me as I pressed forward, becoming one with the night. Nearly blinded, I gave myself over to the shadows. They ushered me through the door like I was less than air. I blinked as they peeled away revealing a grand foyer boasting plush rugs and ornate wallpaper. Twin curving staircases arced up from each side, meeting in the middle behind a crystal chandelier.

If I'd had any wits about me, I would have asked the girl the layout of her house before setting off to raid it. Unfortunately, it proved quite difficult to keep my thoughts straight in her presence. Every encounter with the woman seemed to upend my plans.

I sighed, banishing Miss Fil'Owen from my thoughts.

A door opened to my left, and I watched as a hunched man entered, pushing a laden tea cart that rattled with every step. As he neared me, he stopped and turned his head. His gaze slid over me, and he shrugged before continuing on his way. He left through a door on the other side of the foyer.

I knew if I followed, I'd find the kitchen, but I needed to find something else first.

I headed up the staircase on the right to the second floor where I expected to find the bed chambers. My footfalls echoed in the cavernous room, but I made no move to dampen my steps. No one would hear me anyway. No one ever heard a reaper.

At the top of the stairs, I was greeted by a large painting in a gilded frame, a portrait of three people. I recognized Miss Fil'Owen instantly. Though she appeared quite a bit younger than I knew her to be and had none of the shadows marking her face, her upturned nose and full lips were unmistakable.

Young Katrin sat before an older couple—presumably her parents, the lord and lady of the manor.

Her father was an older gentleman with white hair and a kind smile. Her mother appeared quite a bit younger than her husband, but that was not uncommon, especially among those of propriety. The girls had matching chestnut brown hair, Miss Fil'Owen's in two plaits while her mother's was swept up in a fashionable coiffure. Each parent had a hand resting on one of their daughter's shoulders, and she beamed between them, her smile so large her eyes had become half-moon slits.

I'd seen nothing of the like on the current Miss Fil'Owen. Gone was the joyous naivety of youth.

Had the shadows upon her skin taken it or had the people around her?

It was a mystery I didn't need solved. She was a means to an end—a temporary house guest. After a year, she would return to her perfect little life, and I would be one step closer to freedom.

Several rooms branched off from the hallway on either side of the portrait. Gathering the shadows again, I passed into several chambers before discovering the one that had been Miss Fil'Owen's. A heavy black shroud had been pulled over each of the windows in her room, not unlike my own dark cowl. A customary tribute to the dead, it signified the absence of light after loss.

I didn't know how Miss Fil'Owen had left things with her parents. Perhaps she had run away without explanation, leaving her parents to assume the worst. Or maybe she had told them of her intentions and they still believed Death took her. Either way, it was clear they mourned the loss of their daughter, even clearer still by the sleeping form of her mother on the bed. Unlike the portrait, silver threaded through her chestnut hair and fine lines creased the corners of her eyes and mouth. Upon closer inspection, twin trails of salt blanched her cheeks, stemming from swollen eyes that remained pinched as if pain. She held a small doll clutched tighter to her chest.

Grief was one of the worst parts of my role as a ferrier. Oftentimes, I could fetch a soul and escape without coming into contact with the survivors, but on days like this, the grief seemed inescapable. The sheer magnitude of it rendered me immobile.

To love was to hurt. I knew that as well as any.

I gathered what I'd come for and left the lady to her anguish, melting into the shadows the same way I'd arrived.

Chapter 20

Katrin

I spent the day in a daze, wandering the corridors and exploring whatever doors would open for me. My encounter with the Ferrier had left me hollow. I didn't know what I'd expected to find beneath his hood. A skeleton? A demonic beast? Whatever I'd thought, it hadn't been *that*.

Now, I was sharing a house with a man who appeared deceptively young for how long he'd walked the worlds. Not only that, but he was an—arguably—attractive man, who happened to be saving my life all while claiming not to be a savior.

It would have been better if I'd never seen him without the reaper uniform.

I'd watched him leave and had promptly lit as many candles as I could find. The manor blazed to life, and I carried a candelabra with me to light more as I went.

I'd been wandering the floor beneath my bedroom and found more bed chambers like my own. Those on this floor were much grander in both size and elegance. I had half a mind to move all my things down a level.

After so many similar rooms, I had low expectations for the second to last door at the end of the hall. In my mind, I'd formed arguments for why I needed to move to one of these larger rooms. There was no reason for me to traipse up three flights of stairs in a near empty house, especially one this size.

I'd fully convinced myself of the practicality of my choice when my fingers grasped the doorknob and stilled.

The knob wouldn't turn.

It was locked.

That could mean only one thing—this was *his* room.

Instinct told me to run. I yanked back my hand like I'd been scalded, stumbling away from the door until I collided with something solid. My hands splayed on the wood at my back, seeking the reassurance of something sturdy to ground me. I darted glances at the nearby shadows, expecting them to sound the alarm at my near intrusion.

My lungs heaved. I took a deep breath in through my nose and exhaled through my mouth. The Ferrier was not here. There was nothing to fear from a locked door. I repeated the breathing exercise until my heart rate returned to normal. My shoulders gradually retreated from my ears as the tension in my body melted away. I leaned back and before I knew it, I was falling. It happened so quickly, I was only able to brace for impact before I landed unceremoniously on my backside.

I glared up at the offending door, my expression quickly shifting to one of shock as I took in the rest of the room.

Unlike the others I'd entered, the windows here were bare. No curtains or other dressings kept out the light, and though there was only filtered moonlight coming in through the window, the whole room glowed with ethereal radiance.

Rolling to my side with a groan, I quickly made my way to standing. Every other chamber I'd encountered had been furnished, but sparse, with nothing to set it apart from the bedroom beside or across from it. This space looked as though someone still lived in it. From the vast array of personal effects, I could surmise it was not the Ferrier. Dainty embroidered pillows lined a bed complete with a lace canopy. A goldenrod yellow dress lay draped over the mattress, waiting to be donned. The door to the wardrobe was slightly ajar, revealing more finery hanging inside.

For a moment, I feared the occupant would walk in on me exploring their private chamber. A closer inspection revealed a fine layer of dust coating every piece.

On the wall hung a portrait of a handsome couple. Unlike most oil paintings I'd seen where the couple faced toward the artist in stiff poses, this portrait showed the pair in profile, gazing into each other's eyes. The woman, a fair-haired beauty with rosy cheeks and a pouty mouth, looked adoringly up at the broad expanse of a man with long dark hair and a square jaw.

Their love radiated from the canvas, warming the room without the need of the fireplace.

Had this been their home? Had the Reaper ferried their souls only to return and claim this magnificent dwelling for his own?

I imagined the manor bursting with life. Children squealing as they ran down the halls, narrowly avoiding servants and guests alike. Sunlight streaming through the windows while fires roared in every hearth.

It was a tableau I dreamed for myself many times, but maybe it was better this way. At least now I didn't have to hide in my own home, shrinking into the shadows as I slowly turned into one.

This room was a happy memory for someone, but it only reminded me of the life I hadn't yet lived.

I spared the painted couple one last glance and turned to leave, extinguishing all the candles I'd lit along the way. The Ferrier could keep his darkness.

Chapter 21
The Ferrier

After shaking off the brief encounter with the lady of the house, I located a servant's staircase at the back of the house and followed it down to the kitchens.

I had no idea how much the young woman could eat, nor when I'd be able to source more food. With harvest being around the corner, I assumed her family could spare more than most. I grabbed an empty sack and stuffed it full of bread and potatoes. I found a couple early squash and some eggs and passed them to the shadows for safe keeping. Securing the sack, I handed that to the shadows as well. Like all things, it disappeared in a blink, leaving only shifting darkness behind.

I'd resented the shadows when I'd first taken up the mantle of Ferrier. To say I had done so unwillingly was an understatement, and those shadows represented all that I had lost—all that was taken from me.

Eventually, I recognized them for the asset that they were. Now, they were like a second skin, as one with me as Miss Fil'Owen's own shadows. I melted into them once more, content to deliver my bounty and answer the incessant pull of a soul in need.

My shadows, it seemed, had other plans. They deposited me back in the main entryway, slipping away to darken the corners while I watched them in bewilderment.

"What are you doing?" I hissed. Straightening to my full height, I infused every ounce of authority into my voice. "I command you to return."

The shadows stilled, becoming indistinguishable from the natural shadows in the room. Whatever the reason, they were refusing to take me through the door.

I could open it, though I liked to interact with the living world as little as possible. Opening doors and rearranging furniture was how whispers of ghosts started.

My fingertips brushed the handle, and I heard the unmistakable sound of someone in the next room. Sure enough, candlelight flickered from the partially open entryway into what appeared to be a study.

With my hand fully grasping the handle of the front door, I slowly turned it and waited for the inevitable squeak that I'd be unable to conceal without help from the shadows. Instead, a large shadow peeled off the wall and barreled into me. I staggered back from the blow, trying to wrap my brain around being assaulted by a shadow. They'd always appeared less corporeal, more akin to smoke or steam, but this had felt like being struck by a man twice my size. It knocked the air from my lungs.

Squaring my shoulders, I reached for the door handle only to be shoved back again. A third shadow swooped down from the ceiling, and I ducked before it could knock into me. *What was happening?*

A great force struck my back, propelling me forward. Before I could find my feet, another one shoved me. I stumbled, careening into the study door. It flew open with a *whoosh* of air, sending papers flying and candles flickering.

I froze in the midst of the mayhem, staring at the man seated at the desk.

The years had not been kind to the lord of the house. His shoulders curved forward, the downward tilt of his head revealing thinning hair. He took a small sip of the amber liquid he clutched in one hand, pursing his lips in distaste as he set the glass down.

"Have you come to take me as well?" he asked his drink.

I stood still, unable to move for fear of creating a larger disturbance. *Did he know I was here?* If he did, he'd be the first such person I'd ever encountered, though I'd heard stories of the sighted.

The lord's eyes lifted, sweeping the room. His cloudy gaze passed over me, and I breathed a sigh of relief. Whoever the old man thought he was speaking to, he could not know it was I who stood in before him.

"I'm not proud of myself. I've made choices I regret, but everything I did was to keep her safe—to keep her from you."

This wasn't the first time I'd wished I could communicate with the living—though I could for a price. Nor was it the first time I'd been mistaken for Death. Still, there was something about this man that had me wishing I could offer some comfort, and perhaps it was only his personal connection to Miss Fil'Owen, but I knew better than to get involved.

I retreated a step, thinking to slip from the room like the phantom I was. Seeming to sense my departure, the old man leapt to his feet with an unexpected burst of speed.

"Take me!" he bellowed, wild eyes frantically seeking me out. He stumbled in his haste to round the desk, only to fall to his knees, hands clenched in a pleading gesture. "Take me in her stead. Surely, the years I've collected are worth more than those she's yet to see. I would trade my life in an instant if it meant she could live."

I'd heard enough. Storming from the room, I abandoned all pretense of subtlety as the lord's pleas grew louder and more desperate behind me. I spared a withering glance for the shadows that had caused this mess before wrenching open the door and striding out.

The horses snorted their disapproval at my sudden arrival.

Slamming the door shut behind me, I took a moment to assess the rage building inside me. I didn't need the horses turning on me as well, but the old man's words had unearthed memories that were best left buried. With a deep breath in, I unclenched my jaw, shifting it side to side to work out the ache that had formed. I tilted my ear toward my shoulder until it elicited an audible pop, repeating the same action to the other side until my shoulders sagged in relief.

Finally, I lifted my hood into place, watching my shadows coalesce around me.

"These *people* are not my problem. Try something like that again, and I will abandon my position as Ferrier." I kept my voice lethally calm, knowing the shadows were more sentient than most knew. "I do not care if my debt will go unpaid, or I'm driven mad by the unanswered call to souls in need. I will leave this place to be overrun by ghosts until those people you seem to care so much about are nothing but haunted husks that don't know how to escape their own Hell. I have nothing to lose but myself, and I'm not certain I'm worth the trouble at this point."

The shadows eased toward me, seemingly cowed by my outburst. Though part of me wished to leave them behind, they held all my loot from the visit. I would not be making another trip to this manor any time soon. The shadows rippled away as I mounted the carriage, merging in my wake to create a small cloud of darkness around the carriage.

I felt a tug toward the wayward soul that was my quarry for the evening, but decided to deliver the food to Miss Fil'Owen first. I didn't need her passing out again in my absence.

My leather gloves creaked as I took up the reins, holding them with more force than was necessary. Without a word, the horses sprang into motion, hurrying us back to The Between.

Chapter 22
Katrin

Somehow, I hadn't anticipated evading Death would be so boring. Honestly, I'd had very little hope my last ditch effort to save myself would work. I thought I'd be fully immersed in the Afterworld by now, or at least anxiously awaiting my departure in my family manor.

I thought of my parents, going on with their lives in my absence. If I could have spared my parents the pain of waking to find their only child gone, I would have, but it would have only prolonged their inevitable heartache.

Hopefully, they had gotten my note. I'd been vague about my intentions, not wanting either of them to follow me. Perhaps there was a way to get word to them that I was safe—that I hadn't passed to the Afterworld. I would have to ask the Ferrier, which was a trial in itself. It hadn't been difficult to sway him to my side at the crossroads, but ever since, he'd been far less accommodating—even if he was currently procuring me food. For some reason, seeing him without his Ferrier cloak today had made it harder to accept his supposedly lost humanity. Now, I was a confused ball of emotions, fretting away in a cold kitchen while I awaited my not-savior's return.

I'd explored more of the manor, got lost a few times, and stumbled across a ballroom, a salon, a wine cellar, a greenhouse full of dead plants, and a library whose books looked well on their way toward crumbling to dust.

There was still an entire wing left to explore, but hunger had eaten away at my curiosity. I'd run to my room for a small bite to eat then returned to the kitchen to stew.

Few of the Ferrier's shadows remained, most having accompanied him on his outing. The ones that stayed floated around the corners of the room as though making their presence known. I had no doubt these strange creatures could hide away or blend in with the shades of the house. Instead, they'd chosen to let me know that I wasn't alone, and for that, I was grateful.

I smiled at the one closest to me, and it appeared to perk up at the attention, puffing up in size. It rolled toward me like a storm cloud, and I resisted the urge to flinch from its approach. When it came within my reach, it stopped, bobbing benignly as though in wait. With slow, cautious movements, I slid my arm off the table, extending my unmarked fingers toward the shadow. My eyes flicked up, seeking approval from a nonexistent face. The shadows inched closer, and I watched, transfixed, as my hand was engulfed in darkness.

The cold hit me first. It was a chill unlike any I'd felt before. A chill of death. Even my first brush with the shadow upstairs had not been so frigid.

I nearly jerked my hand away at the unwelcome sensation, but then the darkness shifted, dancing and weaving through my fingers. My right arm appeared and reappeared while it flowed around me like a flowing river. As it coursed up my arm, I couldn't help comparing it to my marked side.

I looked at each of my hands disappearing into darkness and gasped. Just as quick, the shadow retreated back to the corner, chastened.

"I'm sorry," I croaked, trying to calm my heart that threatened to beat from my chest. "I just..." I trailed off feeling foolish for speaking to a shadow, but also for the words I was about to utter. I'd just seen myself fading away into nothing like a real-life nightmare.

The worst part of my curse wasn't that I had to die, though I wasn't excited about that part either. I wasn't through experiencing all that the living world had to offer. No, the worst part was losing myself—becoming nothing. When the little parts of my identity slipped away, I constantly had to redefine who I was, until I was existing only within the tiny box approved by the rest of the world. That box had grown smaller and smaller over the last eight years, and even now, without it, I didn't know how to keep myself from disappearing completely.

I'd already lost so much of what I was: student, peer, lady, intended, friend. They were words that no longer defined me, each shadow on my skin marking another bit of me carved away by fear.

Laying my hands flat on the table, I stared from one to the other. The mark hadn't changed me, so much as it had other people's opinions about me. But without their mirrors to stand before, I was looking for me in a sea of shadows. It didn't matter that the mark had remained. People would always see me for what I lacked. I was a glass vase, invisible but for what I could offer others.

I was still staring at my hands when the Ferrier appeared. He materialized out of the shadows, and if I hadn't already been so thoroughly spooked, I may have jumped out of my seat.

His hood was thrown back, giving me a clear view of his face. For a moment, he looked familiar, like someone I knew in a dream. I shook off the strange sensation as I took in his tense jaw and the downward slope of his brows. My whole body went on alert. He stood casually, hands tucked into unseen pockets, but everything about him radiated danger.

Our eyes met, and I bit down on the overwhelming desire to flee, knowing there was nowhere I could run where he couldn't find me.

"What's happened?"

"Are you alright?"

We spoke at the same time, and I ducked my head to hide the smile that snuck onto my lips.

"Nothing has happened," I assured him. "I was merely contemplating my existence when you stormed in."

He looked around as though questioning my choice of location for such thoughts, but shrugged it off. "You'll find that is a common pastime in The Between." His mouth turned down in distaste. "And I did not *storm* in."

I smiled fully this time, oddly pleased to have gotten under the skin of such a terrifying creature. His tone was brusque, but I brushed it off as impatience. He'd taken time away from his task to find food for me, and I could only be grateful. My stomach made its appreciation known with a loud growl that he mercifully ignored.

With a wave of his hand, a vast shadow swept the table, leaving a small banquet in its wake. Bread, meat, cheese, eggs. My mouth watered at the sight of the potatoes. He'd done well, better than I'd expected of a man who hadn't eaten in years.

I briefly considered where he'd acquired it all. So much food was sure to be missed. Deciding I'd rather not know, I willfully ignored the moral dilemma and swallowed my pride.

"Thank you," I told the Ferrier, hoping to soften some of his icy demeanor.

He inclined his head, looking anywhere but at me. Finished with me, he turned and strode for the door. "I've taken the liberty of fetching some more of your clothes as well, Miss Fil'Owen. I've sent them to your room—"

"Wait!" I scrambled to my feet, closing the distance between us as he continued toward the exit. "You went to my home? Did you see my parents? How are they? Why didn't you tell me you were going to my home?"

"Because I didn't want you to come along."

I stopped short. "What? Why? It's my home."

"Yes, and you left it. You really think the best place to hide from Death is exactly where he expects you to be?"

I hadn't considered that. He'd mentioned my home, and every nagging thought I had about leaving my parents returned tenfold. I could, however, see the logic in his decision, even if I didn't like it. "Fine. What of my parents?"

The Ferrier regarded me, and I searched his face for the answers he withheld.

"What is it you want to know? Do you want to hear how they are mourning your departure as if you had died? Or that they've moved on completely as though you'd never existed? Neither answer would ease your worries, likely they would exacerbate them."

"You act like those are the only two options."

"Are you so eager for news of your former life, Miss Fil'Owen? Or should I call you *Lady* Fil'Owen?"

I bristled, hating the formal title. "Just Kat is fine."

"Please allow me to make myself clear, *Miss Fil'Owen*, I will not be addressing you so informally. Not now nor any time in the future. We are not friends. We are... temporary allies."

"Well then, my dark ally, I thank you for your continued assistance toward our mutual goal. However, in the future, I would appreciate not being kept in the dark, as it were." I shot him a wry look. "Particularly regarding matters involving my life and family."

"The life and family you abandoned?" It was his turn to return the sardonic expression.

I huffed, a rebuke on the tip of my tongue, but he had already faded away into the shadows.

Stomping my foot, I released a roar of frustration. The remaining shadows scattered at my outburst, and my cheeks reddened in mortification. "Why is he so irritating?" I ask them, hands curling into fists at my sides. "I'd like to punch him in his frustratingly beautiful—"

His *face.*

He *had* looked familiar, but not from a dream, I realized.

I flew through the doorway. Rooms blurred together as I raced through them, an endless display of neglected opulence and flickering candlelight. My lungs burned by the time I reached the stairs, and I cursed my pathetic endurance as I began the trudge up to the second level.

A surge of icy cold engulfed me. The world turned black, and I screamed as my feet left the floor. My hands scrabbled for purchase, unable to find anything through the inky black.

Just as quickly as they'd come, the shadows fell away, depositing me upon the landing of the second floor. I whirled and caught the last of them scattering to the darkest corners.

"Thanks for the lift."

Snatching a candelabra from a small table, I silently thanked my past self for leaving a few tapers lit when I'd left. I took my time retracing my steps to the end of the hall, stopping at the door opposite the Ferrier's rooms.

I scrubbed my hands down the front of my skirts, wiping the perspiration from them. If what I suspected was true, it changed nothing—meant nothing. Yet I couldn't help the anxiety that bubbled up inside of me at the mere thought of unraveling part of the mystery of the Ferrier.

The door swung open at my touch. I held my light high, keeping the shadows at bay as I entered. My footsteps didn't falter as I crossed to the painting. I already knew what I would see, but when I saw the Ferrier's face, it was like the entire painting had been made anew.

No longer were these strangers. Well, I had no idea who the woman was. Some former lover, I assumed. Perhaps even his wife? But here was the Ferrier, human, alive, and *happy*.

How did one go from *this* to being the Master of Shadows?

Did that mean this enormous manor had been his? I'd assumed it had belonged to the couple in the painting long ago and that the Ferrier had taken it over as his residence when they'd passed. Clearly, I had some part of the story wrong if the Ferrier was the owner all along. He was still here, even after life—or a normal lifespan.

I looked at the woman again, the beautiful woman teeming with joy and life. What had happened to her?

My little adventure had created more questions than it answered. Now, my curiosity was thoroughly piqued.

Everything I knew about the Ferrier told me to leave well enough alone, but I knew I couldn't just let all these unknowns lie if I were going to spend an entire year living with him. I itched from all the questions burning inside me.

Knowing I'd find no respite from my own nosiness, I decided to wait for the Ferrier's return and confront him about what I'd learned. It was lucky that he'd brought food because my hunger was the only thing that kept me from tearing apart the room for further clues to his past.

CHAPTER 23
The Ferrier

Miss Fil'Owen had been right about one thing on the night we'd met: some souls weighed more than others.

Everyone greeted the reaper differently. Some, like Lord Rencourt, came peacefully. He'd likely known about and accepted his impending death long before it happened.

Many wept at the loss of their life. Others raged. Those that died in anger were often the most difficult to ferry, physically. They would run, hide, refuse to leave their living home. It was a race against the sun, but only the rare spirit required multiple days to shepherd.

Then, there were the souls that clawed at my defenses. The mother who never got to meet the baby she'd brought into the world. The soldier barely old enough to hold a weapon. The father leaving behind his wife and five children. Even knowing there was more after death, it doesn't lessen the burden of separation between worlds.

Tonight was no better. I could still feel the imprint of the boy's tiny hand in mine, could hear the tears he held back as he asked for his mama. The truth was, I had no idea what lay on the other side. I'd never been to the Afterworld, never asked questions I feared the answer to. Most of the time, I was content to exist in ignorance, but sometimes a little boy would look to me for reassurance I could not give and the silence would taste like char in my mouth.

Whenever I collected children's souls, I kept my hood down, not wanting to frighten them.

He had been so small.

I didn't understand the rhyme or reason of death. Even after so many years, it remained as mysterious and random as it had felt when I was alive. I'd only ever questioned Death once, and I had paid the ultimate price for it.

When I returned to *Tyr Anigh*, it was nearly dawn. The interminable fog surrounding the place had lightened from storm cloud gray to the color of wood smoke. It was exceptionally thick on this day, heavy as the dark thoughts that plagued me. The upper floors of the manor had disappeared into the mist entirely like a mourning shroud hung over the world.

It did not bode well for the day to come.

I unbridled the horses and left them to roam. Like me, they required neither food nor sleep but seemed content to haunt the estate most days.

I hung the scythe in the stable beside the pitchfork and shovel like it were any other tool and not a symbol of everything I hated.

The sun rose as it always did with no birdsong to welcome it nor golden rays to announce its appearance over the horizon.

I could not remember the last time I'd felt the sun's warmth upon me. My skin had paled to a nearly translucent shade reminiscent of bone. It was no wonder the living portrayed me as a walking skeleton. What was I if not a corpse kept animated by Death's magic?

On days like these, I missed the numbing effects of good company and ale.

I expected Miss Fil'Owen to be asleep, which was probably for the best. There was no reason to subject her to my current mood, even if I did enjoy provoking her. Her fire was unexpected yet not unwelcome—a rare trait for one raised to simper and comply.

Upon entering the manor, I was surprised to see the shadows I'd left behind to watch over the girl. They hovered in the foyer like a pair of dark specters, making no move as I closed the door and hung up my cloak. I turned back and finally noticed the third figure seated on the bench beside the stairs.

Miss Fil'Owen glared at me from her position between my dark sentinels, resembling a fallen angel, beautiful and cold.

"My lady." Unable to help myself, I bowed, finding pleasure in the ire that flared behind her eyes. "I thought you'd have retired for the evening—or morning, as it were." Could this be about my lack of answer about her parents earlier?

I wanted her to know the truth, but I didn't want to cause her unnecessary suffering. She didn't need to know the full repercussions of her actions just yet, nor was I of the right mind to deliver the news. My dark disposition had followed me home.

She must have realized, for her face changed in an instant. The inner corners of her brows tipped up, the downward turn of her mouth softening into something akin to pity.

I looked away before her compassion could draw forth my wrath.

Her voice was a light in the dark, reaching out to calm my inner demons. "How was your—" She faltered searching for the right word, finally landing on "—trip?"

With that one word, the memories of my night flooded back to me. Reality struck me like a bolt of lightning to the chest. I was the monster and Katrin the victim. She might have borne marks that resembled my shadows, but at her core, she was everything I wasn't.

And she didn't belong here.

"I thought you'd be asleep." The bitter taste of regret coated my tongue, giving my words more venom than I intended.

A flash of hurt transformed her features before she schooled her face into something cold and aloof. It was a skill known by courtier and demon alike. I hated that I'd forced her to mask herself, but it was safer this way. Cordial but separate.

"I couldn't sleep."

Her answer was brusque. I looked down at her arms wrapped firmly around her middle and knew she was lying.

That was fine. She didn't owe me any truths. Her secrets were hers to keep. Fate knew I had plenty of my own.

"I wouldn't know anything about that." So much for cordial. "You could at least have bathed after I'd gone through the trouble of fetching your garments."

I mentally berated myself as she lifted her chin, fixing me with a glare that would put Death to shame.

"Your disgust is noted. Perhaps if you answered my questions *honestly* instead of waltzing around them, I'd have found it in me to bathe and dress for polite society. As I seem to be in the company of a heathen, I think it perfectly suitable for me to maintain my present state of filth."

Her chest rose and fell with rapid pants. I'm ashamed to admit I found the sight oddly captivating. I tore my gaze away, fists clenched at my sides.

"Fine. Do whatever you want." I called the shadows to me, unwilling to continue this petty back-and-forth.

"I intend to!" Her answering shout pierced the darkness that enfolded me just before I was swept away.

CHAPTER 24
Katrin

The Ferrier's words had hurt, but it wasn't anything I was unaccustomed to. At home, they'd called me cursed, tainted, infected, but those words didn't wound nearly as much as abandoned, ignored, and disappointed.

My shadow guards brushed along my arms, apologizing for their master's curt dismissal.

"It's fine," I sighed, and it was. I hadn't come here seeking friendship. Frankly, I hadn't expected any pleasantries from one that referred to himself as the "Right Hand of Death." No, this situation was far from what I'd thought it would be, but I didn't hold my breath in hopes of him changing his stance on our conditional alliance.

One of the shadows brushed my arm again then appeared to gesture toward the stairs. I didn't know if it was offering to carry me up or insinuating I should follow after the Ferrier. Either way, I wanted to be as far from him and his dark mood as possible.

I shook my head and chewed on my lower lip. If anything, our sad attempt at a conversation—well, *my* attempt and his adamant refusal—had reminded me that my time here was temporary. I needed to find a cure. I needed to return to my life.

With the sun giving life to the mist beyond the windows, the dark rooms and eerie corridors became abandoned relics once more, aged and empty, but no longer haunted.

I retraced the steps of my earlier wandering and headed for the library. Upon first inspection, it had seemed like all the tomes within were written in some ancient script unknown to me, but I thought it as good a place as any to search for clues to the manor's mysterious master. The only other place I was likely to have any luck was currently occupied by the man in question. Though it was likely to be one of the few times the room was unlocked, I didn't fancy a venture up two flights of stairs to barge in on someone who'd just insulted me for asking about his night.

But *I* was the fool. It had been only days ago that I was hiding my trembling hands in my skirts as I stood before him. What had happened between now and then? Was I so much a product of my upbringing that an alluring face and sculpted form would have me ignoring everything I knew about this man?

Apparently.

When I reached the library, I paused before the great double doors, one hand resting on the bronze doorknob. In the silence, my mind replayed every word of our conversation like actors rehearsing the same scene over and over again. I pressed my forehead to the wood and squeezed my eyes shut like I could force out the memories

"Stupid. Stupid. Stupid." I punctuated each word with a knock of my head against the door. *Thud. Thud. Thud.*

He'd warned me that he was no longer human. He'd told me, in no uncertain terms, that he no longer suffered such weak emotions.

In less than a week, I'd forgotten. Had I imagined our similarities? Created parallels between us where there were none?

He was not my mirror. He was an agent of Death, and I would be wise to remember that.

Exhaling, I pushed away my train of thought and opened the doors to the exquisite room beyond.

The Ferrier's library was unlike anything I'd ever seen. Easily double the size of the ballroom, several rows of enormous free-standing shelves stood like giant dominoes awaiting their fall. A rolling staircase sat at the end of the bookcase closest to me, providing access to the highest shelves. The entire room glowed in blue, green, and amber hues courtesy of the sunlight coming through the stained glass windows on the far wall. Several iron chandeliers hung between the rows of books with lanterns capping each end. There were multiple seating areas, some with large wooden desks and others with plush sofas and chairs. Somehow, the overall effect of the cavernous room was cozy, inviting.

My guards flitted off to a darkened corner as I walked up to the first shelf. Inhaling the scent of aged paper and leather, I ran my hand over the worn spines. The words beneath my fingertips were foreign to me as they had been upon my earlier perusal.

I moved to the next shelf and the next, waiting for something familiar to stand out among the nonsense. If this library was as old as I suspected, it was possible every text within was written in the same language. If so, I was out of luck.

Five shelves into my search, I had to stifle a yawn as exhaustion finally settled over me. Not wanting the trip to have been in vain, I grabbed a random book off the shelf and carried it to one of the tufted sofas by the unlit fireplace.

I all but collapsed onto the cushion, releasing a cloud of dust that I batted away as I coughed. My eyes watered, and I waited for the dust to settle before glancing at the book I'd chosen.

It was a hefty tome, as many of them were, with a dark leather cover embossed with letters I recognized in patterns I didn't. I traced my fingers over the details, mindful of the cracks where the leather had dried. The spine creaked as I pried it open, but the vellum pages within appeared in good condition aside from their slight discoloration.

I flipped through the pages with gentle hands, careful not to tear any. The words remained a mystery, but there were illustrations every few pages that appeared to depict people of importance. Their faces meant nothing to me, but I thought they might have been rulers of another land or another time.

I didn't mean to fall asleep. My body, it would seem, had other plans. Next I knew, I was being nudged awake by a persistent blast of cold air. I shivered and drew the book that was still clutched in my hands over my chest. As if bolstered by my movement, the breeze became a typhoon that hauled me upright. My eyes popped open, only to be met by complete and utter darkness. Before I could scream, the shadows parted, drifting back into the general form of my two sentinels.

I melted back onto the couch, relief turning my bones to liquid as my mind caught up to my body's wakefulness.

The doorknob rattled, and I sprang upright again. I had approximately two seconds to decide how to prepare for the Ferrier's entrance—because who else would it be?

If I stood, it would look like I had risen *because* of his presence, which was not the response I wanted to portray. As such, acting casual seemed the only option worth considering.

Faster than I would have thought possible, I tore open the book and hefted it in front of my face.

The door opened, and I fought the impulse to watch him enter the room. Keeping my nose down, I pointedly ignored the draw of his dark force, going so far as to slide one finger along the page as though I were skimming the text.

His boot clad feet stopped within my field of vision and my heartbeat intensified. I pulled the book closer in case he could see the pulse of it through the fabric of my dress.

"You slept in the library?"

"What? No, obviously not. I've just been reading." I looked at the book with unseeing eyes, all of my focus going to the man on the other side of the cover.

"I didn't realize you could read Old Demonic, Miss Fil'Owen."

"I was perusing it for interesting pictures."

"It's upside-down."

Slamming the book closed, I glared at the Ferrier. "You startled me. I was about to head down to the kitchens to break my fast."

It had been a mistake to remain sitting. I felt like a petulant child craning my neck to look up at him. I pushed up to standing to emphasize my point about preparing to leave, but the Ferrier still towered over me.

"Yes, of course. You must have been drooling in anticipation of your next meal."

My hand flew to my chin, swiping at nothing as my fingers came away dry. The Ferrier smirked—actually *smirked*—and I wondered if his shadows were fast enough to protect him from a book launched at his head.

"You can't lie to me," he said, gesturing to his two shadows that had remained by my side.

I glared at them sidelong. The traitors. "Fine, I fell asleep here. It was a bit chilly upstairs today. Some kind of bitter frost radiated from the second floor."

Was that color staining the Ferrier of Souls' cheeks? For the first time since I'd seen his face, his mask of cold indifference had disappeared, perhaps without his knowing. His throat bobbed as he looked away, a muscle feathering in his jaw as he schooled his features.

"Did you have need of me, oh great Shepherd of Souls?"

"I wanted to apologize for my part in our interaction this morning. I was not myself." He paused as though reconsidering. "I was not the version of myself that I wish to be."

Tipping my head to one side, I weighed his words against what I knew of the Ferrier. His stance was relaxed, hands in his pockets, expression blank as I openly scrutinized him. Here was a man who had lost everything to work for Death.

Or had he given up his life willingly?

Therein lay the difference. Was this someone who had walled off all trace of his humanity to protect himself? Or someone who possessed so little of it to begin with that he'd willingly sacrificed that part of himself for powers of darkness?

Considering what I knew of people, I was hesitant to relinquish my suspicions, but I knew I'd find no answers by pushing him away. "I am sorry if I said something to offend you."

A corner of his mouth tipped up. Not a full smile, not even a smirk, but acknowledgment of my words just the same. "No apologies necessary, Miss Fil'Owen. Some nights my duties are more trying than others."

I supposed that explained his mood swing this morning. "Do you want to talk about it?" I ventured.

"Decidedly not."

Right. Well... "While we are on the subject of things said this morning, you mentioned bathing." He opened his mouth to speak, but I held up a hand. "I did stumble across the bathing chambers on my self-guided tour. However, I'm embarrassed to admit we had running water back home. I'm afraid I don't..." I trailed off, ashamed to finish the thought.

His face lit with understanding, quickly concealing the hint of shock that arched his brows. "You don't know how to draw yourself a bath?"

I cast my eyes down, certain this was the height of humiliation. Forget falling on my arse in the rain outside of school and having to endure the entire day with a mud-stained backside. Revealing to the Ferrier of Souls that I was too pampered to know how to bathe myself had my insides turning to melted wax.

The Ferrier's eyes gleamed with mischief as the smirk reappeared on his lips. "Are you asking me to help you bathe, Miss Fil'Owen?"

My toes curled, and I was suddenly very aware of our proximity. Though it seemed inconsequential, I realized I'd made no effort to hide my shadows around him. I resisted the urge to duck my chin, staring defiantly back into the Ferrier's dark eyes, but his gaze never strayed to my marked side.

My face heated at his unwavering attention. I couldn't tell if his question had been in jest, but I did truly need his help if I had any intention of bathing in the next year.

"I am asking for your assistance in *running* a bath," I clarified. "I assure you, I am quite capable of cleaning myself."

He chuckled and something stirred deep in my belly.

"Grab something clean to wear and meet me at the bathing chambers. I'd be happy to assist you."

The Ferrier turned and strode from the room, darkness following in his wake.

CHAPTER 25
The Ferrier

My shadows were restless. They sensed my desire to pace and fidget even as I willed my body to calm. I leaned against the wall outside the bathing chamber, arms and legs crossed in what might be seen as a casual gesture but was really the only way I saw fit to constrain the energy winding its way through my veins.

I'd regretted my outburst this morning the moment the words had left my lips, but she hadn't pursued me, hadn't returned to her room at all. I listened all morning for the sound of her light footsteps, for news from my shadows that she'd retired. All for naught. She'd slept in the library to avoid the monster of the house.

I'd lashed out, but I knew better. It wasn't her fault she'd been here when I needed space. It wasn't her fault I would suffer this task for eternity unless my debt could be paid. *She* was helping to pay that debt. I should be grateful for her presence, not punishing her.

When I'd finally worked up the courage to seek her out, I'd nearly come undone at the sight of her sleep-mussed. It brought me no small amount of joy to vex her, to stoke that fire of hers that thawed a part of me that had been frozen far too long.

Then she'd mentioned bathing and my mind had immediately conjured images of her slipping off her clothes, her chestnut waves fanning out around her as the water obscured her more intimate areas.

My shadows grew still, alerting me to Katrin's approach before I could sense her. I swallowed thickly. When had I started thinking of her as *Katrin*?

She appeared around the corner before I could wrap my brain around the change.

"Miss Fil'Owen," I said more for my peace of mind than to welcome her.

"*Lord* Ferry," she sighed, trudging down the hall with her arms burdened by a heap of dark cloth.

As she neared, I gestured to the clothing in her arms. "Allow me."

I crooked two fingers, and one of my shadows sprang forward to relieve her. She cocked a brow at it before handing over the bundle.

"Are they your slaves?" she asked. Her fingers stretched toward the one that held her clothes.

"I don't care for that word."

"It doesn't matter if you like it if that's what they are."

I considered the idea. "No, they are not slaves. Not exactly." I glanced at the living shadows that haunted my steps. "I hardly notice their presence anymore. Not like you do, I mean. They're like the fingers of my hand. I know they are there. I use them regularly. In fact, I would sorely miss their usefulness were I to lose them, but they aren't at the forefront of my mind if that makes sense. In some part, they are an extension of me, of my power as the Ferrier. Our relationship is symbiotic. I do something for them, and they do things for me."

She squinted at the shadow, tilting her head to one side as she regarded it. "Are they sentient?"

"If you'd have asked me before you arrived, I'd have said no. They are more alive with you here. I'm not positive to what extent they can think for themselves, but they seem to have emotional responses to stimuli." I watched as the shadow turned an approximation of a head to mirror Katrin. "And personal agendas," I added, remembering the way they'd shepherded me into her father's study.

I opened the door to the bathing chamber. Moist heat wafted into the hall in curls of steam as I motioned for Katrin to enter first.

I inhaled as she brushed past, and her scent struck me. It was no secret that she'd traveled for some time and wore the dirt of the road upon her, so I hadn't been lying when I said she needed to bathe. However, my motives may have been more selfish than they seemed.

Her scent drove me mad. She was lilacs and warm summer breezes, and I wanted more than anything to scrub the aroma from her skin, to replace it with everything that was ordinary and between. So that every time we shared space, I could breathe without remembering all I'd traded away.

The shadows lingered after she entered. Even eyeless, I felt their stares—their judgment—like they knew my thoughts. I raised a brow in their direction. If they had something to say, they would need to acquire the power of speech.

I followed Katrin into the bath, and the shadows swooped in after.

Logs crackled and popped in the hearth, the fire I'd started while waiting now roared to life. I wore only a light tunic and trousers, but even that was too much. Sweat collected on the back of my neck and ran in rivulets down my face and chest.

A large clawfoot tub sat before the fire. I was certain that in my life it had been white with copper feet. Here, it was a black monstrosity that swallowed the light of the flame. A small table lay next to it, laden with all manner of soaps, oils, combs, and towels.

Katrin stood facing the fire, the warm glow a stark contrast to the dark markings on her face. I'd never seen anything like her mark. I had no idea if it was truly a mark of Death as she thought. It did nothing to hide the gentle curve of her cheekbone or the arch of her brow as she turned my way.

"Aren't you meant to be showing me how to do this?" she asked.

Chastened, I strode to where she stood. The compact chamber felt smaller still by the presence of the shadows which seemed to take up no space and fill half the room at the same time. I let them be if only for the futility of asking them to leave. For what reason would we need space or privacy? I would only show her how to fill the tub, and then I would leave.

I stepped up to the large cauldron hanging beside the fireplace.

"The water pump is here," I said, gesturing beside me. "All you need to do is fill the pot and put it over the fire to heat." It took several seconds for the water to pour forth. Moving the lever up and down, I waited until the water began to flow then gestured for her to try.

She struggled at her first attempts but eventually managed to fill the cauldron. I showed her how to use the iron poker to swing it over the fire.

"You'll need to do this several times to fill the tub, so it's best to get the water piping hot lest the bath cool before you get in."

"And how do I get the water from the pot to the tub?"

"I'm sure if you ask nicely your shadows will do it."

She squinted at me in surprise. "They'll listen to me?"

In response, one dark form separated from the rest. It twined around her legs like a hungry cat, turning transparent in the flickering light of the fire. She giggled as it danced around her, ruffling her hair and winding through her fingers.

I nodded as the shadow retreated, rejoining the darkened corners of the room. "They appear quite fond of you."

She hummed thoughtfully and sat on the lip of the tub.

We lapsed into silence as we waited for the water to heat. When it was near boiling, I showed her how the poker became a hook that she could use to pull the cauldron from the flames. Once it was out of the fire, I beckoned the shadows to empty it into the tub.

Katrin observed without comment and rose to start the process again.

I should have left once I verified her confidence with the process. She had no further need of me. Instead, I leaned against the wall, content to observe her while she wasn't fearful or arguing with me.

"How did you do this before the shadows?"

I straightened. "Pardon?"

"This was your home, right? Before…"

I heard the words she'd left unspoken. "Before I turned into the monster that steals children from their mother's arms?"

She flinched as the words struck their blow. I couldn't seem to keep my tongue from cutting.

"Before you became the Ferrier."

I didn't ask how she'd figured it out, focusing instead on her first question. "Before *Tyr Anigh* was lost to The Between—" *and me with it,* "—there were hundreds of people staffed here, including those who would run the baths."

"What happened to them all?"

Though her gaze remained fixed on the pot of water, I had a sense that she was more focused on my words than the state of her bath.

"I killed them."

Her head whipped to me, mouth parted, eyes searching mine for the retraction I could not give.

"You killed hundreds of people?" she whispered.

And there it was, the fear that lurked beneath the surface of our encounters. The proof that I was the monster I claimed to be.

The truth tumbled from my lips unbidden. "It was not by my hand, but rather a result of my actions that they died."

A line formed between her brows. "I don't understand."

"No. I suppose you wouldn't."

I sprang to my feet, effectively cutting off the conversation. The water was nearly boiling as I pulled the pot from the fire. Again, my shadows poured it into the tub.

This time, when she made to rise, I held out a hand to stop her and took up the pump myself. Her gaze branded my back as I worked the lever up and down.

I yearned to see inside her mind. She'd taken up permanent residence in my own.

With every pump another question sprang to mind. Up, down. *What was she thinking?* Up, down. *Did she finally see the monster with whom she'd bargained?* Up, down. *Was this the final straw?* Up, down. *Would she leave?*

These questions compounded in my mind, forming a wall I couldn't breach. It joined the many others I'd built up over years. I was a veritable fortress. Solid and impenetrable. Cold and unfeeling.

I pumped and pumped until a pair of delicate hands, one pale and one shadowed, froze me in place. Her touch was feather light, but it struck me like lightning, igniting every nerve.

Neither fear nor loathing contorted her face. The inner corner of her brows tipped up and her mouth was a hard line, but she didn't balk at the contact with my fevered skin. Warm brown eyes met mine and held, unwavering, until they flicked to the floor and back again.

I glanced down and noted the puddle beneath our feet.

"This would be so much easier if you had power over heat instead of darkness." She chuckled, but the attempt at humor was lost on me as I fought for composure.

Coming to my senses, I pushed the cauldron over the fire which *hissed* its discontent as water splashed onto it.

"Death has power over fire. At least, the current one does."

"I thought Death was cold. Wait. Did you say the *current* Death?" Katrin asked, returning to her seat on the tub.

I leaned back against the wall and sighed as a chill skittered over my neck. Pulling more of my shadows to me, I let their cold ease the tension in my shoulders.

"People talk about the cold touch of Death, but what they feel are the Shadows of Death." I gestured to those holding space around us. "Death is a title, a position like any other. He is King of the Afterworld. The current king—Behryn—has fire magic."

Her face contorted as this information warred with what she'd already thought about him.

"It's not as pleasant as it sounds, I assure you." I shifted at the memory of those flames upon my skin.

"So, this King... Behryn? It is his mark I bear?" Her darkened fingers traced over the matching skin of her face.

"It would appear so." I had no evidence to the contrary, but neither was I convinced of this fact.

"Why shadows? Why not burning embers or fever?"

I shrugged. I truly hadn't given much thought to her marks. "Perhaps because fevers are not as visible and burning embers would cause permanent damage. Death has a flair for the dramatic. I'm sure he thought to mark you with darkness until it claimed you completely."

We lapsed into silence again, the crackling logs the only sound between us. The shadows rushed forward to empty the cauldron. With the bath now two-thirds full, it was past time for me to leave.

"Enjoy your bath, Miss Fil'Owen." Pushing off from the wall, I headed for the door, ready to put this entire day behind me.

"Wait!"

Against my better judgment, I did. She faced me now, though she didn't meet my eyes as I turned. Her hands bunched the fabric of her skirt, eyes downcast as she wrung the material again and again. She'd captured her bottom lip between her teeth, and I had a sudden vision of my mouth replacing hers, of nipping her full lip and kissing away the pain.

I stifled a groan, cursing my body for preserving the worst parts of its humanity.

"I could use some assistance with my buttons." She turned, displaying a long, tidy row of black buttons. "If you wouldn't mind, oh mighty shepherd."

My fingers flexed as I considered her request. It was innocent enough. Of course, the shadows could provide her all the assistance she needed, but I'd stayed this long. Part of me had been longing to touch her since I'd found her half asleep in the library.

She glanced over her shoulder when I didn't immediately respond, and it was my turn to avert my gaze.

This was a mistake, but apparently, I was making a lot of those lately.

I crossed to her in the span of a breath. Brushing her hair over one shoulder, I was struck again by her intoxicating scent and resisted the desire to breathe in deeply. My hands trembled as I reached for the first of the delicate buttons. With a push of my thumb, it slipped free from its loop and I moved on to the next one.

I'd found a rhythm by the tenth button. At the twelfth, she inhaled a stuttering breath, and I wondered if she'd been holding hers like I had.

"I don't suppose you'd see fit to tell me your name now," she said and my fingers stilled.

"And why would I do that?"

Goosebumps rose where my breath met her exposed skin.

"Surely, you can't expect me to continue referring to you by your title after you've practically undressed me." She laughed though her voice was high-pitched and breathy.

My hands fell away. "So that is your game." I'd been a fool, but so had she. She'd taunted the monster. My arm snaked around her middle, pulling her flush against the hard evidence of my arousal. I nudged her head to one side with my cheek and inhaled up the length of her exposed neck. "If you think you haven't driven me mad since the very moment we met, you are mistaken. If you think I haven't wanted to strip you bare and learn all the places those shadows touch, you are mistaken. If it weren't for that smart mouth of yours—" I broke off in a growl and stepped away, the distance between us like a cold shower. She swayed in the absence of my support, but I resisted the temptation to reach for her.

"What is so wrong with me knowing your name?" Confusion wrinkled the space between her brows, but it didn't detract from her beauty.

The differences between us couldn't have been greater. "It humanizes me. Never forget that I am a monster."

"A monster wouldn't be so affected by the souls he encounters. A monster would not have bargained with a crazy woman hailing him from a crossroads. I think you want to be the monster because then you don't have to try to be a better person."

"Better than waiting for someone else to solve my problems. The shadows can assist you with anything else you require."

Before she had a chance to turn, I called my shadows to me and vanished into their cold embrace.

Chapter 26

Katrin

I crumpled to the floor, trembling in a puddle of skirts but not from fear. My body was on fire. Every inch of me felt electric—alive. My heart beat wildly, and I panted for breath as if I'd run to my room and back. I touched the skin on my neck where I could still feel the ghost of his touch. Even the memory of his hard body pressing into mine made me shudder.

"So much for that," I muttered into the now empty room. My attempt at nonchalance extended only as far as my words. It took several tries before I peeled myself off the floor. My legs were too shaky to stand, so I settled for sitting on the lip of the tub again.

After several deep breaths, I was able to stand. I couldn't believe the effect he had on me. No, it wasn't him, surely. It was being touched by someone. The same would be true of anyone willing to look beyond my shadows.

The steam battered my already flushed skin, and I hastened to complete the job the Ferrier had abandoned. Reaching behind my back, I swiftly unfastened the remaining buttons. I'd gotten myself into the dress, I could get myself out, but I'd seen an opportunity and ran with it. Unfortunately, I'd pushed too far.

For a few minutes, the Ferrier had been different, not exactly forthcoming, but far more open than I'd known him to be. I thought I'd managed to chip away at some of the walls he'd built around himself, only for him to disappear again.

What was it about his name?

I froze, holding my dress up as I remembered where I was. The room might feel empty, but my two shadow guards lingered near-by. The Ferrier had mentioned that they were an extension of his power, but to what extent? Could he see me through them?

The idea seemed preposterous, but I couldn't shake it.

I cleared my throat and searched the shadows for the living ones. "Do you mind waiting outside?"

Two forms detached from the wall to my right. They glided by in a rush, ruffling my hair as they passed, and slipped through the crack beneath the door.

My gown slipped to the floor, followed swiftly by my petticoat. I made quick work of undoing my stays and finally pulled my shift over my head.

Fully nude, I walked over to the large mirror that hung on the wall. I ignored the state of my hair, assessing my mark for any places it may have expanded in the days since I'd checked it. While it hadn't disappeared upon my bargain with the Ferrier, I had hoped that being here would at least halt its progress across my body. Looking now, it would seem that hope was also in vain. New shadows stretched across my abdomen, snaking up toward my breasts. My fingers touched the mark, but, as always, it felt no different than the unmarred places of my body, which were becoming fewer and fewer.

A tear traced down my shadowed cheek. I swallowed past the lump in my throat and balled my hands into fists, wishing I had the power to rival this King Behryn.

I'd intended to bathe quickly and be done with it, but the soothing warm water had other plans. By the time I pulled the plug to drain the tub, the sun had set. I dried, dressed, and plaited my wet hair back before stepping into the hall.

There was no sign of the Ferrier. With nothing better to do, I decided to head back to the library. Perhaps I'd be able to uncover more clues without the fog of exhaustion hanging over me.

A chill skittered over me, and I knew without looking back that my two shadow guards flanked me. I pivoted to face them but continued walking backwards.

"Do you have names?" I asked the shadows. It was foolish, but I was tired of referring to them as simply shadows. I wanted to differentiate *my* shadows from the rest of the Ferrier's gloom.

The shadows, being shadows, said nothing in return.

Squinting, I glanced back and forth between the two, seeking any defining characteristic that set one apart from the other. They weren't identical, but their constantly morphing forms made it difficult to pinpoint the differences.

The one on the right appeared smaller and less dense while the left one was larger but more opaque. The left rolled like a thundercloud, but the other spilled like water down the hall.

"I will call you Storm," I told the left shadow then turned to the right. "And you, Inky."

Inky and Storm seemed to swell with pride at their new monikers. I smiled, feeling like I'd finally accomplished something after days of sitting on my arse.

"Have you always possessed a preoccupation with names?"

I realized too late that the Ferrier's deep, rich voice sounded from behind me. Colliding with him felt like hitting a wall, and he made no move to catch me as I stumbled. I recovered swiftly, crossing my arms and glaring at him as my mind fought to latch onto the words he'd said.

"I'll have you know that it is perfectly normal to wish for something to call those around you. What is strange is refusing to give your name to someone who lives in your house and with whom you have a magical contract." I raised my brows, daring him to respond.

One corner of his mouth tipped up, and I counted that as a point in my favor.

I looked away from his face, noticing the pitch-black robes for the first time. "You're leaving?"

"The dead do not collect themselves, Miss Fil'Owen."

"Might I accompany you?" Another night alone in the manor was the last thing I wanted.

"No." He turned away, stalking down the hall.

I hurried after him, taking two steps to keep up with each of his. "Please, I'll—"

"No."

"What if I hide in the carriage without you knowing?" Though I dreaded meeting another dead soul, two days into my stay I was already restless.

"Your guards would inform me."

We'd arrived in the main foyer, and I collapsed onto a nearby chair. "You mean my captors?"

This drew the Ferrier up short. He turned, giving me his full attention. "You are not a prisoner here. I have sworn to keep you from Death. Right now, the safest place for you to be is here. If you've reconsidered your choice to avoid him," he pointed to the grim world beyond the window, "the gates are always open. You need only walk until the fog clears."

"Truly?" I locked that knowledge away lest I need it someday in the future.

"Thinking of quitting after only a week?"

"No, I just... I thought our vow was more binding than that. Does that mean you can walk away at any time as well?"

"I vowed to keep you from Death until a year has passed or you leave of your own free will. In exchange, you swore to provide the agreed upon payment for fulfillment of my duties at the end of the term. No more. No less. You are the only one that can end it."

My eyes unfocused as I chewed my lip. In the aftermath of our trek through the manor, I'd grown quite warm again. Using my hand as a fan, I hoped to find some relief, but I only grew more flushed.

"Has it gotten warmer in here?" I asked.

The Ferrier whipped his head to me, eyes wide. "Hide her."

Inky and Storm sprung from their place along the wall and scooped me into their cool embrace. They were surprisingly solid as they pressed me into a corner. Stretching in all directions, they formed a wall between me and the Ferrier. I opened my mouth to protest, but a cold touch against my lips told me I should remain quiet.

I bucked against their hold, and the shadows shifted, a small transparent opening appearing at eye level. It was still shaded, but through it I could see the Ferrier pacing. He stopped as if sensing my eyes on him.

In a flash, a blazing inferno sprang to life in the center of the room. A searing blast of heat penetrated my wall of shadow, and I turned my face away. The fire was gone as quickly as it ignited. In its place stood a man.

No, a demon.

He faced away from me but stood tall, shoulders thrown back and head held high. Even without the circlet on his head, he radiated haughty grace. Gold trimmed the edges of his deep blue jacket, cut to emphasize the strength of the physique beneath. The hands clasped behind his back boasted several gold and gemstone rings which glinted in the candlelight. The only things out of place amidst his highbred finery were the jagged patterns of ink covering his shaved head.

All of this I observed in an instant before my attention was drawn away by the Ferrier. In one fluid motion, he swept his robe aside and knelt before the newcomer, head bowed in deference.

"Behryn," he growled. "To what do I owe the pleasure of Your Majesty's company?" His sardonic tone belied the sight of the loyal subject still genuflecting before the demon.

"You disappoint me, Evander."

I gasped at the use of the Ferrier's given name, unwittingly catching Death's ear. As his head turned to track the sound, the shadows closed off my viewing window. Encased in darkness, I held my breath.

"Excellent," said the Ferrier—*Evander*.

I clung to his name, to the normalcy of it, as the shadows parted to allow me sight once more.

Without being given the order to rise, the Ferrier stood to his full height. "I would hate to have done something to make you proud." His eyes met mine over Behryn's head, conveying several things in one pointed look.

First, I needed to stay quiet. Second, he was as surprised by this visit as I. And finally, perhaps unbeknownst to him, Evander was just as terrified as I was.

I nodded, not knowing if he could see me through the darkness.

"You forget yourself." The King bristled, fists clenched at his sides. "I am the one who holds your indenture. I am your master. It is to *me* you've sworn fealty."

Evander winced, but his voice remained calm. "As you like to remind me."

Behryn growled, the sound as inhuman as that of a wild animal. It may as well have been a bear between Evander and I, though I'd have rather faced my chances with a bear. The hair on my arms rose at the perceived threat, and I retreated as far as I could into the wall behind me.

"There is the matter of this month's pay." Death prowled forward, tucking his hands into his pockets.

Evander rocked back, forehead creased as he looked anywhere but at Death.

"I'll save you the trouble of counting," said the King. "You're two days late on your last payment. I hate to add a penalty to your already staggering debt, but neither can I abide such blatant disrespect."

"Respect is earned."

The two men leaned into one another until less than a handbreadth remained between them. Muscles bulged on the side of Evander's neck, while Death appeared calm and relaxed, the easy victor in a rigged fight.

I didn't know how Evander managed to keep from tearing into the King, but there was more to their working relationship than I'd ever imagined. Perhaps his contract prevented him from harming Behryn. If so, I may have overestimated the protection he could offer me.

Death spun, and I had a split second to see dark eyes in a pale face before the shadows closed over me.

"Interesting."

My heart stuttered at the King's utterance.

Had he managed to see me before the shadows converged? I reassured myself if he had, he'd have stormed over to me or demanded answers.

"Have I not delivered my part of our bargain? Did I not resurrect your beloved after her untimely demise? It is you who desires to change the terms of our original agreement." Death's voice grew louder, closer.

"I desire nothing but to own my own soul again."

Was Evander always this combative or was he trying to distract Death from me? Unhurried footsteps moved away from me, and I exhaled slowly. The shadows did not open my viewing window again, so I strained to hear the rest of what was happening.

"Ah, but it is mine now." Death's words held a hint of a smile. "Until you pay the price that I have set, you answer to me. Do I make myself clear?"

A choking sound was the only answer. My hands clapped over my mouth to keep the despair from leaking out.

There was a heavy thud, followed by a *woosh* and the crackle of flames. "I'm adding fifty gold pieces to your debt. I expect you will not be late again."

The shadows disappeared, and I blinked at the sudden brightness. The King was gone, but the oppressive heat remained. I rushed to the Ferrier where he knelt with his hands on his knees, hoping Death had left him unharmed.

His head was bowed, dark hair spilling across his face. Up close, I could hear the breaths sawing out of him. He shuddered, and I placed my hand on his back, feeling the muscles tense beneath my touch.

"Evander?"

"Do not call me that."

My hand retracted at his harsh words. "Is that not your name?"

"Evander is dead."

I sighed. "No, he's just melodramatic."

This earned me a laugh. Though it was more a dark chuckle than a hearty guffaw, I considered it another point for me. He sat back on his heels and peered at me through thick lashes I'd envy at any other time. I noted the angry red marks around his neck but knew better than to bring them up. As though sensing the direction of my attention, he tugged his collar higher.

I sank to his level, hugging my knees to my chest as I balanced on the balls of my feet. "I'm sorry if I'm the reason you were late on your payment."

He waved a gloved hand. "It's nothing," he said. "I've been distracted of late."

"I can't imagine why." I smirked, and his eyes narrowed in challenge.

"A mystery, to be sure."

I stood, shaking out my skirts then held out a hand to Evander.

He glanced at my outstretched offering and rose through his own power. I dropped my arm, looking away while he rebuilt the invisible barricades around him.

"What is the cost of your soul?" I wondered if the price we bargained would see him freed, if that was the reason he'd agreed to help me.

"More than I care to think about." Donning his hood, he stalked over to the door and threw it open. "Come along then."

"What?" I asked, unsure if I'd heard him correctly.

"Come along." He enunciated each word with careful diction. "I can't very well leave you here with *him* popping in whenever he feels." He nodded toward the space Death had vacated moments before.

Before he could change his mind, I hurried through the door, all too eager to return to the land of the living.

Chapter 27
The Ferrier

I didn't take a full breath until the mists parted, and we passed into the living world. Behryn's appearance had unsettled me more than I cared to admit. Katrin, to her credit, was practically dancing by the time I prepared the carriage. If she had any lingering anxiety about what had transpired, I couldn't see it.

I, on the other hand, still struggled to control my trembling hands hours later. My thoughts vacillated between relief and rage. *Tyr Anigh* had been my safe haven, my sanctuary. It was the one thing I still possessed from my life, and Death had tainted it just as surely as he had the other aspects of my existence.

In a flash of firelight, he'd nearly undone my vow to Katrin. Her gold may not be enough to free me, but it would see me closer than I'd ever been. Once, I'd contemplated the worth of trading her outright, her life for mine, but Behryn had reminded me who the real monster was between the two of us. I would not stand to see her taken by such a demon even if it meant my freedom.

The weight of our bargain pressed down on me. Combined with the constant pull of my indenture, I felt like I was being torn in two.

"Evander." Katrin's voice floated to me through the small window into the carriage.

I sighed. The first time my name had spilled from her lips, I'd been too shaken to offer more than a clipped response. Now, the sound of the name I'd left behind scratched at something I kept buried deep inside. When Behryn used my name, it was a cruel reminder of the man I used to be. With Katrin, it was a call to the man I could be again. It grated on my cursed soul, and yet, I did not correct her again.

"Miss Fil'Owen?" I pitched my voice low, verging on menacing.

"Why are we here?" Her breathy words managed to reach me over the din of the horses and carriage wheels, my attention snagged by the wary shift in her tone.

With a start, I realized she might be fearing for someone she loved, a friend or relative.

"My territory covers only this kingdom. I've no jurisdiction beyond its borders. The souls beyond do not call to me." I trailed off as the rumbling hoofbeats grew louder, wishing I could see Katrin through the tiny grated opening. When only silence answered from within the carriage, I cleared my throat and pressed on. "You have nothing to fear, your town is not our destination for tonight."

Was she pulled home the same way I was toward the recently departed? Did her feet point the way without her realizing?

It occurred to me to tell her what I'd witnessed at her family home—that her parents mourned her as though she'd died. I'd held onto the information for selfish reasons, but now things were different—or were they? I shook my head. *Something* had shifted between us, brought on by the involuntary tell-all that I'd been unable to stop.

I pulled my hood lower over my face though there was no one around to see the heat that rose to my cheeks. My face contorted into a grimace, knowing she'd borne witness to my humiliation. She hadn't mentioned the incident, aside from using my name, but in her eyes I'd seen the difference. The concern. The understanding. The *pity*. Everything I'd shielded myself from, all those failures, now reflected in her deep brown eyes.

Felwyck came and went without another sound from the cabin. We followed the road as it wound through the countryside, the shifting winds carrying the scent of pine from the distant mountains. As the next village came into view, the small farms of the outskirts gave way to tightly packed hovels.

The horses stopped before one such home. Little more than stacked stone with a thatched straw roof, the structure leaned into its neighbor like old friends sharing a secret.

I leapt from the carriage, landing in a cloud of dust that coated me from head to foot. The door of the cab swung open, and Katrin peered out from the darkened interior.

"Stay," I ordered.

"But—"

"No."

Her chin drew forward, mouth puckering in an effort to contain the fire she wished to spew. Though my features were hidden beneath my hood, I returned her obstinate glare with one of my own.

One of the horses stamped his impatience, effectively ending our silent battle of wills.

With a *huff*, Katrin flopped back against the bench, crossing her arms over her chest. "Fine," she said. "But at least leave Storm and Inky with me."

I cocked a brow, freezing as her two sentinels broke away from my shadows without my command. They took up positions on either side of the door like actual guards. Recovering my wits, I closed my mouth and nodded once.

"Fine, then." I turned on my heel and strode for the hovel, squashing the seed of fear that sprouted at the thought of leaving Katrin. There was work to be done, and her distractions would see my task unfinished. Something about that niggled at the corner of my mind, but I turned my attention to the soul within.

The door to the ramshackle dwelling clattered as it swung on a single hinge. Parts of the frame had crumbled, and the remnants of a primitive lock lay scattered in the dirt before me. I hesitated before the narrow opening, waving back the shadows that had gathered around me. The interior was dark enough without their presence.

I ducked inside, and my stomach dropped when I beheld the scene within.

Funeral customs rarely varied among those in my territory. By the time I arrived to shepherd the soul, the empty vessel would be cleaned, dressed, and laid out for final farewells. Some nights, I arrived before those rites could take place. If it was a sudden death, or one that occurred late in the evening, most would wait until morning to begin those rituals. Even so, a level of care would be evident.

Then there were nights like this.

A single room lay beyond the busted door. Embers were all that remained in the small brazier, casting the scene in a warm glow that contradicted the harsh reality. Every piece of furniture was upended. Broken bits of pottery littered the ground around an overturned table. I traced strewn bits of straw to what remained of a crude pallet in the corner. The few cabinets were open and, upon further inspection, bare.

I picked my way through the debris to a slumped form half covered by the remains of a shattered chair. There were no visible wounds, but the unnatural angle spoke to what had happened.

In my many years, I'd seen plenty of violent deaths. The fact that there had been many did little to lessen the blow of each new one I faced. I turned from the empty vessel, knowing my quarry would not have wandered far. A soft sound caught my ear, and I whirled toward the source, black cloak billowing behind me.

Hundreds of years in the dark and my eyesight was no better for it. Squinting, I saw the vague shape of feet peeking out from beneath the open door of one of the cupboards.

I crept around to the side of it and saw a weathered crone huddled in a ball. With her hands holding either side of her head, I didn't think that she had seen me. Though it was possible she was hiding from me. I thought it more likely a result of her untimely death.

My heart ached for the woman as she trembled, holding on to the fears of the living even on the other side of death. Traumatic deaths often required more time and finesse. The shock of a violent end took time to wear off. Some never recovered.

I cleared my throat, and the old woman's eyes whipped to me. No sooner had she taken in my dark form overwhelming her tiny hovel, then she began to shriek.

Her wailing would go unnoticed by most of the living, but those sensitive to the other side would swear they heard a banshee on this night. Their rumors made no difference to me, but still I *shushed* her. Though I'd intended the sound to be gentle and raised my hands to indicate I meant no harm, I knew that I both sounded and looked like something not to be trusted.

Nights like this, I wished the reaper's uniform was something more gentlemanly.

The front door banged open behind me and Katrin burst in.

"What the—" she said, glancing around. Her eyes landed on the body, and she screamed.

Flinging out a hand, one of my shadows wrapped around her mouth, effectively silencing her. I still didn't know the extent to which Katrin's presence could affect the world of the living. She might be heard easier than the wailing specter.

"I told you to remain in the carriage."

Her answer was muffled by the shadow, and she glared at me until I waved it away. "I heard a scream and—"

"And you thought I was in trouble?" I asked. The quick aversion of her eyes told me otherwise. I pushed away the sting of her doubt. She wasn't wrong for it. I'd done little to earn her trust thus far. "Miss Fil'Owen, I cannot cause harm in this world."

Her gaze flicked from me to the spirit and back again, raising her brows in disbelief. "You may not be able to physically hurt her, but anyone can see you are frightening the poor dear."

"Do not involve yourself, Miss Fil'Owen," I warned, but Katrin paid me no heed, approaching the spirit with tentative steps.

She paused as though struck by a sudden thought. "Do you still ferry them if they can't pay?"

"Of course," I answered honestly. "My debt does not weigh against them. Everyone deserves the chance to enter the Afterworld."

She nodded and continued toward the frightened soul. As she neared, the spirit recoiled, milky white eyes darting around for an escape. Katrin eased to a crouch. "Please don't be afraid," she said, palms outstretched in a better approximation of harmlessness than I could muster. "My name is Katrin, and that is Evander."

I bristled at the use of my given name. The spirit flicked her eyes to me and emitted a small *squeak*.

"Lower your hood," Katrin hissed over her shoulder.

I raised a brow at the order, and though she couldn't have seen me beneath the shroud, Katrin raised one back. Sighing, I pulled the hood off my head, lowering the cowl until my entire face was visible.

Katrin smiled in triumph, turning back to the specter. "You see? He's really quite nice to look at under all that."

Though her words had been directed at the old woman, I felt the ground shift beneath my feet. I staggered a step and shook my head, righting myself before either woman could notice my distraction.

She thought I was nice to look at?

Despite my current predicament, I had to bite back a smile. I could count on one hand the number of times I'd smiled since becoming Ferrier. Every one of them had occurred since I met Katrin.

"My name is Eunice, and I'm waiting for Claude," said the spirit, drawing my attention back to her.

Katrin looked at me, her forehead crinkled, and I shrugged. With gentle hands she encouraged the spirit out of her hiding place. The old woman stood a full head shorter than Katrin, her back curved from what was likely a long, difficult life.

"Who is Claude?" asked Katrin.

The old woman's face lit up. "Claude is my husband. I'm waiting for him to return."

A glance around confirmed my suspicions, there was nothing to suggest anyone else lived here.

Katrin took hold of the crone's weathered hand. "Has Claude passed, ma'am?"

The light disappeared from the woman's face as deep creases formed between her brows. "I don't know. I can't remember."

"That's alright, Eunice. Don't fret." Katrin turned a beseeching gaze my way, but once again, all I could do was shrug.

Her eyes roamed the room, then snapped back to mine with a renewed gleam. "Actually, Claude sent us to retrieve you."

"He did?"

Katrin's head bobbed up and down. "He sure did. He's been waiting for you."

"Why didn't you say so?" Eunice bounded for the door, a new spring in her step. "Oh, but I must look affright!"

Katrin clasped the old woman's hand and pulled her in close. "You look beautiful."

Chapter 28

Katrin

All through the journey to The Between, Eunice regaled me with stories of her life. She told me of her life as a farmer's daughter, the day she met Claude, when they ran away to the city to be wed and start a life of their own.

Her tales enthralled me to the point of longing.

This was what I wanted. *This* was what I was fighting for—the chance to live a long and glorious life of my own making, unburdened by some gloomy fate that threatened to bottle me up at my peak ripeness.

The door to the carriage flew open, and I jumped, unaware that we had stopped. Evander had left his hood down, his windswept hair drawing my eye in a way that reminded me I'd called him nice to look at only minutes before.

My cheeks heated. Eunice smirked and gave me a knowing look. In return, I pursed my lips and widened my eyes, willing her to keep quiet. She smiled bigger and mimed buttoning her mouth shut.

Evander watched this all without a word. One look at his smug expression and I knew he was aware of everything that went unsaid.

"Eunice, this is your stop." He beckoned her forward with a gloved hand.

Eunice looked at me with watery eyes. "You're not coming, Kat?"

One look at Evander's stern expression told me his opinion on the matter. I shook my head and smiled at Eunice. "It's not my time."

"Just as well." Eunice shrugged. "Someone has to keep this fellow in line."

She ducked out the door, pulling Evander in tow. I smiled, clutching my hands in front of my chest as they disappeared into the mists.

When their forms blended into the trees, I fell back against the cushioned bench.

The journey to the living world had been much shorter than I remembered, or perhaps it was that I was filled with excitement rather than trepidation.

The manor had become a prison of my own making. Though I was accustomed to the confinement and solitude, accompanying the Ferrier soothed the part of me that yearned to experience everything. Finally, I was doing *something*. Though I never dreamed I'd be aiding the recently departed, I couldn't deny the overwhelming sense of rightness that warmed me from the inside out.

I wrapped my arms around my middle like I could contain the feeling and that was how Evander found me.

"What are you smiling about?"

His voice jolted me back to reality. I traced the shape of my lips with my fingers, surprised to find I was indeed smiling. "It was a good night, don't you think?"

He hummed a noncommittal noise and I rolled my eyes.

"I never noticed your teeth are black as well."

I clamped my hands over my mouth, eyes widening in horror before I caught the twinkle of mirth in his gaze. "Shut your mouth," I said, swatting his arm as heat rose to my cheeks.

He chuckled and my insides warmed for another reason. "Vain, Miss Fil'Owen?"

"You would care about your looks as well if they were holding you back from the life you desire."

"I thought it was the threat of Death holding you back." Leaning against the door to the carriage, he folded his arms across his chest, the gesture daring me to argue with him.

"No, not exactly. It's true I don't want to die. In some ways, I fear Death, but we're all dying, present company excluded." Evander's face betrayed no emotions, but he dipped his chin and I continued. "What I truly feared was dying without living. You might not remember, but people can be quite horrible when they don't understand something." I glanced down at the hand permanently wreathed in shadows. "They thought I was diseased or cursed. I was marked and suddenly, I was no longer human. I no longer mattered. Suddenly, everything I'd been looking forward to had become unattainable. It wasn't long before their prejudices began to sound like gospels. People thought me unworthy and I became so. Yes, I hid from Death, but I was also hiding from myself."

Silence stretched until the air between us was fragile with strain.

Evander cleared his throat and I glanced up as he shoved his hands in hidden pockets. "For the record, I think you are rather nice to look at."

It was an echo of the sentiment I'd confessed to Eunice earlier that night. Whether he meant it or was just trying to make me feel better, his words were a rainbow on a rainy day. I captured my bottom lip between my teeth, trying to contain the smile that threatened to betray my true feelings.

"Black teeth and all." He grinned.

I lunged, but Evander was faster. My hand passed through the shadows left in his wake, and I scrambled to keep from falling out of the carriage as his laughter filled the space around me. The door eased shut as by an invisible hand and we lurched into motion.

Though the forest beyond my window was dark as pitch, I felt lighter than I had in a long time. An unfamiliar feeling bubbled inside me, like being tickled, only deeper and less intense. If I had to put a name to it, I'd say I was giddy.

The scene beyond my window returned to the sparse trees and heavy fog of The Between. By comparison, I was radiant. My cheeks ached from being pulled up so long. I clamped my lips together to contain my smile, feeling like a fool as I grinned through the liminal space.

"This part of The Between is called The Corridor." Evander's voice was muffled by the layers of cloth and carriage between us.

It was as good a name as any for the road that stretched into eternity.

"You can't see them, but there are doorways branching off in every direction. Portals to other parts of The Between, the dwelllings of other reapers—"

"There are more of you?"

He laughed, and I wondered if he also felt the lightening effects of a job well done. "Thousands, all over the world."

My mouth opened on a silent *oh*.

Thousands of reapers. I didn't want to consider what would have happened if I'd met a different reaper on the crossroads that night. What were the chances that I lived in Evander's territory? I didn't know when I set out that night that luck was on my side in the form of a long-held grudge and a quest for freedom. I could just as easily have met a reaper who was loyal to Death and been delivered promptly to him.

The desolate forest blurred past us, each tree as unremarkable as the last. "How do you know which turn to take? I would never find my way home in this place."

"I am pulled toward *Tyr Anigh*, just as I am pulled toward the souls that I must ferry. Eventually, you'll notice the differences, little markers left by other reapers, signs of space beyond. It gets easier."

He spoke as if I'd be staying in The Between indefinitely or traveling it frequently on my own. "I think I'll leave that part to you," I said. "No need to fill my head with nonsense." They were my mother's words and they tasted foul on my tongue. I didn't think it was nonsense, but learning those things, seeking out the knowledge that would help me navigate this place on my own, it felt like too much commitment when I planned to leave some day soon.

My comment landed like a bucket of ice water, shocking us both into silence for the remainder of the ride.

CHAPTER 29
The Ferrier

When we'd returned to *Tyr Anigh*, Katrin had parted without a word. The shadows informed me she'd gone to her room and fallen asleep. I attempted to rest as well, all the while tormented by thoughts of her that bordered on obsessive. The way her soft, pliant body molded to my hands. How she leaned into me even when she didn't realize she was doing it. Her quick retorts and easy smile.

She saw me and did not balk from the creature I'd become. Though the occasional seed of doubt took root, they withered when exposed to the truth.

That evening, I was grateful not to feel the pull of another soul in need. For so long, I'd looked forward to ferrying as a chance to escape and reenter the world of the living. No matter how many times I went back, it never felt like home again. With Katrin here, I enjoyed the living world less and less. Ferrying was a wall between us that clearly defined us as monster and mortal. The only bright side to last night's visit had been the glow on her face after she'd helped Eunice. In that moment, I'd seen a future, an eternity with Katrin by my side, working together. It was a nice image, until she'd called me back to reality.

Just as well. Behyrn would have taken one look at our partnership and hauled her away—mark or no.

I dragged myself from the bed around an hour before sunset and went in search of Katrin. Even knowing I should put distance between us and spend some time reinforcing my inner walls, I couldn't stay away.

I'd been informed she was back in the library but stopped at the kitchen to grab some bread and cheese on my way there. Unlike the last time, Katrin was very much awake when I found her pouring over stacks of books.

"Found something you like?" I asked and set the food beside her.

She jumped at the sound of my voice, but she shot me a sheepish grin. "Research," she said, motioning to the stacks of books before her.

My library housed an eclectic collection of books, most accumulated when I was alive, but some I'd bartered and traded for in The Between. It was the latter that she had surrounded herself with.

They weren't all in demonic script, but very few were in languages that I understood.

I nudged her with my knee, and she moved aside for me to join her on the couch. "Any luck?"

Her hair fluttered with her heavy exhale. "Not at all. I don't even know what I'm looking for and the only books I've found that I can read are histories of the living world."

"Tell me what I can do."

She looked ready to reject my offer to help but seemed to think better of it as she surveyed the mess around her. "Can you tell me how you ended up enslaved by him?"

I flinched, unprepared for that line of questioning.

"It's fine if you don't want to talk about it, I only thought it may help—"

I held up my hand to silence her. "I don't mind. You're right, it might help. I am, after all, a prime example of what not to do when dealing with Behryn."

Katrin angled her body toward me, drawing her feet up and resting her head on her hands along the back of the couch.

"I made a lot of mistakes in my initial dealings with Death," I began, glancing away like I could see back to that first day. "Desperation does not make smart men. My fiancée had just died."

"The woman in the painting?"

Glancing down at my hands, I nodded solemnly. "I forget I still have it sometimes. I can't bear to look at it, but neither can

I destroy it." That room was the one piece of her I still had. Sometimes, when I felt particularly self-loathing, I would step into the perfectly preserved memory and remember why I had been willing to give so much. I drew in a deep breath and shook off the melancholy train of thought.

"After her passing, I could think of nothing beyond bringing her back. I met her reaper as you met me. There were methods of calling one that have since been lost to mortals. I tracked him down to a place he was bound to pass and demanded he bring me to Death. I had nothing to offer the reaper, but my request amused him. He called for Behryn and he appeared. I knew from the moment I laid eyes on that demon that I would do everything in my power to keep her from his clutches."

Katrin rested her hand atop my clenched fist. I forced my grip to relax and gave her a tight smile. Centuries had passed, but the memory of that night burned like an open wound.

"I was a wealthy man so, naturally, I offered him money first. Everything has a price in the mortal world, and I wasn't accustomed to being denied anything." I shook my head ruefully. "He laughed and told me to take my money elsewhere."

It should have ended there, but I was a man broken by the institution of love. My worth was reflected in her admiration for me. Without her, I had nothing. I *was* nothing—or so I'd thought.

I scrubbed my hands over my face, lapsing into silence. To her credit, Katrin didn't prod, though concern shone from her deep brown eyes. I knew if I didn't want to continue that she would let the subject drop, but I was determined to keep this woman from Death's clutches, too.

"I fell to my knees. It was the first time I knelt before him, and he's been forcing me to do it ever since. I asked him what it would take to bring her back. For whatever reason, he looked at me and saw something he wanted. The price, he'd said, was my soul in exchange for hers. It had seemed a fair trade, though I was reluctant to make it. In the end, I knew that she was more deserving of life than I."

"Why do you say that?" Katrin asked.

Her brow creased in bewilderment and I mirrored the expression. "I may not have had powers over darkness and shadows, but I have always been as I am. A black sheep, if you will."

"Being different does not make you less worthy," she insisted. "If anything, our differences should be celebrated, not punished."

"Most would disagree, but thank you. Unfortunately, Death does not deal in fair exchanges. Whereas my fiancée's soul would have been free to travel the bridge to the Afterworld and live in whatever peace can be found there, I became the Ferrier, enslaved to Death until my debt can be paid. The price of a soul, the price of my insolence."

"I'm sorry."

I huffed a laugh. "You owe me no apology. Together, perhaps we shall both be free of Death."

She hummed noncommittally. "I should like nothing better than to greet him when I am old and frail."

"I would like that for you, too."

Chapter 30
Katrin

No matter how long we lingered, the tapers in the candelabra never burned lower. The power of The Between held them in stasis just as it did Evander. And yet, it couldn't stop the shadows taking over more of my body.

"I've been thinking," I said, closing another ancient tome.

"Good," replied Evander.

I swatted his arm playfully and pushed my lips into pout. Secretly, I was glad for the return of his good humor after his somber tale. When he finished, he'd immediately retreated into himself, and I'd given him space under the guise of collecting more books. We'd gone through several stacks, but none contained mentions of Death or Behryn. The Afterworld was a popular topic, but mostly speculations and vague warnings.

"If we can't find a way to remove the marks, we should try to figure out why I've been marked in the first place. Maybe if we know why he wants me, we can work on making me less desirable."

Evander's gaze heated, and I blushed as I guessed the direction of his thoughts. "You know what I mean."

These small moments of flirtation were all we allowed to show of this thing developing between us. I hesitated to put a name to it. It was still too tenuous to be more than attraction, and I worried it was the result of proximity and loneliness and nothing more. We were two broken people testing how we fit together. Sometimes the way he looked at me made me wish it was more.

With the heat of his stare burning me alive, I struggled to grasp the thread of my previous thoughts. Finally, I turned away and began stacking books, the task helping to focus my mind. "We've been looking for accounts of Death, but if most of these are written by mortals, there would be very few factual accounts of encounters with him. We need to look for mysterious markings, shadow curses, *human* stories. I know you said you'd never heard of someone being marked like me, but if there was, it could at least give us some direction."

I glanced up at him, and he nodded.

"I'm with you."

I started returning books to the shelf and paused as I felt a gentle touch on my shoulder. Evander waved and a rush of darkness engulfed the books. When it cleared, all the books were lined up neatly on their proper shelves.

I smirked. "I keep forgetting about that little trick."

I pulled the next book off the shelf and carried it over to the couch. Evander joined me with a stack of his own. The cushion dipped as he sat, drawing me closer. I pulled my legs up and propped the book open on my lap, increasingly aware of the dwindling space between our bodies. Forcing my eyes to the pages, I tried to make sense of the strange pictographic writing. It looked as foreign to me as the demonic language, but I dutifully scanned each page for something to catch my eye.

The soft whisper of pages being turned did little to keep my mind from circling back to the man at my side. I grasped for something to fill the void and freeze my spiraling thoughts. "How does Death usually choose the souls he claims?"

"From what I can tell, there is no rhyme or reason to it. He is indiscriminate in his culling. Only those who pass his trials are deemed worthy of entering his demesne."

"Is he a god?"

Evander scoffed. "He certainly rules like he is, but no. He is of demonkind."

As a human, it was difficult to see the distinction between the two. He may not be all-powerful, but Behryn clearly possessed powers beyond that of mere mortals. "Are demons immortal?"

"No, merely long-lived and hard to kill."

"Are you immortal?"

"I don't know. I don't think so." His eyes glazed over as he stared unblinking at the page before him. "The rules are different in The Between. Some force is keeping me alive, preserving my youth and speeding my healing. I think that I could die, but I've never tested it. I don't think it would be the kind of death that grants me passage to the Afterworld."

"You would cease to exist."

He shrugged. "It is only a theory."

His nonchalance regarding his potential erasure from life as we knew it was concerning. As someone who'd only lived twenty-one years, I couldn't fathom accepting such an outcome. Maybe I would feel differently after hundreds of years.

Evander leaned forward suddenly.

"What is it?" I asked, eyes narrowing on his white-knuckled grip of the book.

He sat back just as quickly, face showing none of the excitement I'd expected from his spontaneous motion. "Nothing. Never mind."

"It is clearly something." Inching into his space, I attempted to read over his shoulder only to be met with more unfamiliar text. "What does it say?"

He pointed to an illustration of a young man half veiled in shadows. "It describes a man with markings like yours." He flipped the page and began to read. "'Dark shadows beneath the skin that were unable to be removed by soap or surgery.'"

I swallowed thickly as I considered what they could mean by surgery. "And? What happened to him?"

This could be the lead we needed.

"He...died before they could discover the source of the markings."

My stomach dropped. "Oh." The single syllable was all I could muster as I pushed away from Evander. I'd been so sure this was it, the clue we needed to solve this puzzle.

Evander lifted his hand. I thought he might reach for me, and I couldn't decide if I needed the comfort or the distance. In the end, it didn't matter. His hand came to rest on the back of his neck, wringing the tension out like water from a used wash rag.

"We'll keep looking," he said earnestly. "If we found one mention, there could be more."

I nodded but dropped my eyes. All the hope that had bolstered me was gone, leaving me a shell of a person. I was skin and bones, barely holding myself together as I rose to my feet. "I'm going to sleep now."

A look of concern flashed across Evander's face, quickly schooled into his usual stony expression. "Would you like me to accompany you to your room?"

"No, it's fine. *I'm* fine." I shook off my melancholy and flashed him one of my painted-on smiles, the kind that had satisfied my parents for years. He didn't return the smile, but neither did he follow me. I reached the threshold and glanced over my shoulder. "I'll see you tomorrow—later, I mean."

"Sleep well, Katrin."

I stumbled at the sound of my name from his lips. When I started walking again, I was smiling for real.

Chapter 31

The Ferrier

I stayed in the library all through the day, reading and researching until the text blurred. When Katrin woke, she joined me. And so, we continued combing through the massive library until the third night when a familiar, insistent tug altered our course. As I had the previous nights, I met Katrin in the library, this time handing her cloak over as soon as she entered.

She took one look at the cloak and another at my attire and lit up like the sun.

"We're leaving?" she asked, rocking forward on her toes as she awaited my reply.

I nodded. Her resultant squeal of delight set the window panes rattling. She danced as she donned her cloak, jumping and twirling to a song I couldn't hear.

"Are you always so excited to leave places?" I asked, chuckling. I didn't always know what I would walk into while ferrying. I'd had more bad experiences than good. So much so that I'd come to dread leaving the peace of *Tyr Anigh*, but Katrin's good mood was infectious.

"I wouldn't know," she said. "I so rarely get a chance to go anywhere even before coming here."

"You should know, the times you've accompanied me have been among the more pleasant souls that I have ferried. They are not often like that." Flashes of memories appeared inside my head, nights I wished forgotten and souls that continued to haunt me long after they'd crossed over.

Katrin sobered as she looked at me, her smile faltering at what she saw. "I have no expectations, Evander. The souls are not a reflection of you nor is my excitement reliant on their behavior. I wish only to experience what I may."

Days had passed since Katrin had learned my name and yet, the effects of hearing it from her lips had not diminished with time. Each repetition tore at my inner walls, threatening to tear them down entirely. I'd rarely conceded to calling her by her forename, enjoying the fire that sparked in her eyes whenever I called her Miss Fil'Owen. Her aversion to her family name was still a mystery even as I learned more about the woman behind the moniker.

Said woman danced her way down the hall and out the front door where she abruptly stopped. A small noise of surprise escaped her, and I lunged from my position close behind her, placing my body between Katrin and whatever had alarmed her. Shadows rose up around us, a barricade, but also a way out, should we need it. Looking around, I could see only the horses and carriage, my scythe gleaming at the driver's seat too far to be of use. Still, I did not let down my guard until her hand landed on my shoulder.

"I didn't realize you'd fetched the carriage already," she said, sweeping to my side.

Her hand did not immediately move from my shoulder, and the casual gesture pulled my focus more than it ought. Several breaths passed before I registered her comment. "I had the shadows ready the horses," I replied.

Placing my hand at the small of her back, I guided her toward the coach and opened the door. Every place we connected tingled with tiny sparks of electricity, but Katrin's gaze had fallen to the shadows drifting around us.

"Do they mind being ordered about?"

Her question caught me by surprise. My hands flinched away from her body, and I shoved them in my pockets. "I..." I was at a loss for words. Only since she'd come into my life had the shadows appeared anything more than extension of my power. I'd never considered their feelings because they'd hardly seemed alive, let alone sentient beings. I shrugged. "I don't know."

"They talk to you. Don't they?" She tilted her head at me from where she stood unmoving.

I blew out a breath and closed the coach door. "I'm not speaking through that tiny window the whole journey." Helping her into the driver's seat gave me another excuse to put my hands on her. The way my fingers sat perfectly in the dip of her waist had me biting my lip.

I watched as she settled herself onto the bench seat, fanning her skirts out before tucking them close. Her back was ramrod straight, her chin high as she turned and regarded me where I lingered on the step. For an instant, she was the picture of imperious grace, a dark queen staring down at me. Then her brows arched toward her hairline and her head jutted forward in an expression of impatience.

"Does the mighty Hand of Death require assistance?"

Laughing, I pulled myself up, taking hold of the reins and sitting beside her. If I sat closer than was necessary, she didn't remark upon it. I was intoxicated by her presence, by casual touches and small talk and looking up to find someone else looking back at me. It was addictive. I felt myself falling under her spell and did nothing to resist.

We set off and I explained how the shadow creatures communicated with me via images that appeared directly in my mind. "It's why I always thought they were an extension of me. I can see what they see."

"Then it's a good thing I send them out during my baths," she quipped.

"I will never observe shadow images of you in such a compromising position," I assured her.

She laughed nervously. "That's a relief."

"When I see you naked, I want to be able to run my hands over every inch of your body, followed by my tongue." I kept my tone casual, my expression neutral.

Katrin's gaze bore into the side of my face, but I kept my eyes trained on the road ahead, clicking my tongue to urge the horses on. I wanted to look, wanted to see if I affected her as much as she affected me, but I also feared what I would see. This playfulness developing between us could be nothing more. In less than a year, she would be gone, off to make a life for herself with some other man while I remained in The Between.

Always between.

The thought grounded me enough to quiet any further comments I had on the matter. We rode in silence for the remainder of the journey, though neither of us moved to create distance between our touching limbs.

When I finally brought the carriage to a stop, we were nowhere near any town. A great expanse of field stretched out around us, dotted with the occasional tree and shrub. We dismounted into tall grasses that brushed the tips of my fingers as I walked. The scythe in my hand seemed a mockery of its intended purpose.

Katrin followed closely at my heels. From her stumbling gait and the occasional muffled curse, I knew she was having a difficult time navigating the terrain. I didn't waste my breath asking her to remain at the carriage. She wouldn't.

A whisper of sound carried on the gentle breeze and I halted, forcing Katrin to do the same. Lifting one hand to prevent the expected barrage of questions, I turned my ear to the wind and listened. At first, the only sound was the susurrus of swaying grasses. Then came the unmistakable sound of human anguish.

I twisted, but Katrin moved first, hiking up her skirts and sprinting into the night. Her crashing footfalls were a beacon in the darkness. Calling forth my shadows, I stepped into their embrace and flew after her, exiting several paces in front of her. I thrust out my hand holding the scythe, and she skidded to a stop. Her eyes were saucers, but she wasn't looking at me or the scythe. She was looking past me.

Turning, I switched my grip on the scythe to a defensive one and took in the scene before us. We had found our recently departed soul, and he wasn't alone.

CHAPTER 32
Katrin

In the times that I'd accompanied Evander, we had never come across any mourners. Presumably, Lord Rencourt's family had retired to bed after a day of funeral rites and Eunice had been alone.

Tonight, the soul in question stood beside his own body. Another man—a *living* man—knelt between the divided parts of the first, hiccupping sobs rending the otherwise silent night.

"What do we do?" I whispered, unwilling to intrude on the scene.

Evander hesitated. He hadn't yet donned his hood and indecision flickered across his face as he glanced at the sky. "It is early in the night. We could wait."

I glanced at him sharply. "Is that what you'd usually do?"

By his answering glare, I knew it was not. I likely didn't wish to know what he'd do without my presence there to temper him. He lifted his hood, face vanishing as he became the fearsome Ferrier. I took one look at his gleaming scythe and knew what I had to do. For the second time that night, I scrambled to overtake Evander, stepping into the small clearing before the spirit could notice the shadows roiling around him.

"Good evening," I shouted, my voice a thunderclap compared to the gentle rain of the living man's tears. I lifted my hand in a wave and pushed down the feeling that I was barging in on something private.

The soul glanced at me, startled. He was younger than I would have guessed, barely into manhood, with unkempt blond hair and a wiry frame he'd never get the chance to grow into.

"Who are you?" he asked, eyes darting around nervously. "What are you doing here?"

"My name is Katrin. I've come with a friend, and we're here to help." I couldn't see Evander, but I didn't want his presence to come as a surprise for the soul. Risking a tentative step forward, I glanced down at the empty body and immediately regretted it. I snapped my gaze back to the soul and attempted to school my features into their practiced neutrality. "What's your name?"

The soul looked back down at the grieving man then back at me. "Theodore."

I smiled. "It's nice to meet you, Theodore." As I stepped closer, I hoped the moonlight masked the mark on my face. Just in case, I angled my head away from spirit. It was not my intention to scare the poor soul. "Can you tell me what happened?"

There was nothing in the immediate vicinity to suggest a fight or struggle and yet, the body on the ground was drenched in dark blood.

Theodore shook his head and looked back at the man kneeling in his spilt blood. "He won't leave."

I looked down again, eyes darting past the blood to take in the other details. The living man was just as young as Theodore, likely a year or two younger than I. His face still held onto the roundness of youth, though there was definite strength in the width of his shoulders and the corded forearms revealed by rolled-up sleeves. He was missing a jacket, but I soon found it balled up into a pillow beneath the body.

"Who is he?" I asked. Their love was a palpable thing. From their dissimilar looks, I figured they weren't brothers. Friends? Lovers?

"He was my world," Theodore whispered, voice cracking. He reached for the other man. When his hand passed right through, he looked at it as if something valuable had just slipped through his fingers. His face crumpled, and he dropped to his knees beside his lover, both mourning the same tragedy.

I watched the sundering of two bonded souls with tears pooling at the corners of my eyes. My thoughts strayed to Evander and he stepped to my side as though summoned. I felt his attention glide over me. The brush of his hand against mine was a silent question, one I didn't know how to answer. When his fingers twined in mine, I gave them a grateful squeeze.

"We can wait a while," Evander said.

I leaned my head against his shoulder and let my tears fall.

***

Hours later, when the sobs had quieted and the moon had traveled to the other end of the sky, the living man pressed a kiss to his lover's forehead. Slipping his arms beneath the body, he pulled it to his chest and heaved out a great breath. With a jerk, he planted one foot on the ground, brow contorted in concentration as he lurched forward. He staggered to his feet in the inelegant manner of someone who bore too great a burden but remained vertical. His steps were labored but unfaltering as he carried away Theodore's body.

Theodore's spirit floated over to us as though suddenly untethered. He didn't remark upon Evander's presence. Judging by his unfocused gaze, it was possible he didn't notice the Ferrier.

"What now?" he asked no one in particular.

"You go on," Evander replied. "And so does he. It won't be easy for either of you, but you'll make it and maybe, someday, you'll find each other again."

Theodore looked unconvinced. His gaze swept from shadows to scythe, finally taking a good long look at Evander. "Did you do this?"

My heart skipped a beat at the question, but Evander's shoulders drooped as if he'd fought this battle too many times.

"I am not Death. I am merely here to guide your spirit to the Afterworld."

"I assure you he is not your enemy, Theodore." My voice hitched despite my attempt to remain calm.

Theodore's eyes took in our still-conjoined hands and his expression morphed. I had only an instant to recognize the rage directed at me before he was swallowed by shadows.

I yanked my hand from Evander's, whipping an accusatory glare his way. Yanking his hood off, he returned my glare and lifted a gloved finger between us.

"Before you go accusing me of cruelty or voicing any of the other hateful things reflecting in your eyes, remember that your safety is my primary concern, Miss Fil'Owen. We still do not know to what capacity you can be harmed, but I am not willing to risk it for the sake of some poor soul whose feelings are completely warranted."

I blinked at him, at the finger still quivering between us. Whatever indignation I'd felt for the soul had melted away in the face of his honesty. "Alright."

Evander lowered his finger, though the frown didn't leave his face. "He can hate me if he wants. So can you, I suppose."

"I don't hate you, Evander." My comment struck his back as he turned and set off toward the carriage. I followed closely behind but didn't reach for his hand again.

The shadows had loaded Theodore into the cabin, an endless stream of curses and shouts echoing from within. Without speaking, Evander helped me into the driver's seat. The whisper of fabric was the only sound as he pulled himself up behind me.

This time, as the horses lurched into motion, I didn't get the sense of purpose I had with Eunice, nor the tickle of curiosity I'd felt with Lord Rencourt. Rather, I just wanted the night to be done. I was weary in a way I'd never experienced. Was this how Evander felt all the time? I couldn't imagine an eternity of souls ripping away at pieces of me until I became immune to the bite of their words, the burn of their anger, and the pain of their despair.

I regretted that I could not spend this time with Theodore's spirit. Though young, I was certain he had stories to tell. You didn't find a love such as he'd had without great tales to accompany it. I hated to think of those memories disappearing with him but comforted myself in the knowledge that, for now, his lover held a part of them.

When Evander left to escort Theodore to the bridge, I bid farewell to the troubled spirit and slipped into the safety of the coach. Even without the ability to see my surroundings, the four walls felt more secure than being out in the open.

Geese honked from far above. I craned my neck to look for their silhouettes against the light of the moon but was thrown back against the cushions as the carriage suddenly surged forward. What little was illuminated by the lanterns and the moon outside the window became a blur of darkest gray as we sped on.

After a moment to right myself, I pushed off the bench and collapsed gracelessly onto the other side. I managed to open the small window to Evander but could see very little past the jet steeds running at breakneck pace.

"What's happened?" I called over the frantic beating of the horse's hooves, or perhaps it was my own heart.

"Nothing yet." Every trace of emotion was gone from his voice. This was the Ferrier I'd met that first night. Cold. Commanding. "Stay inside. Close the windows. Draw the curtains and keep quiet."

"But—"

"Now, Miss Fil'Owen!"

Then the howls began.

CHAPTER 33
The Ferrier

Theodore had been loathe to enter The Beyond, and by the time I'd convinced him, there were sounds in the forest around us. The shadows saw me swiftly back to the coach. I was glad Katrin had chosen to wait inside as the sounds grew nearer. The horses had sensed the lurking danger and eagerly took off at my command. Katrin did not share the enthusiasm. The slamming of the window was the only confirmation that my order was followed. I could only hope she would heed the rest of my warning as well.

The hounds brayed, and I urged the horses on. If they were remotely similar to the mortal beasts they resembled, they'd have collapsed long ago. But my wicked steeds pushed on, swift and unyielding.

I released the reins, trusting the horses to carry us onward. Taking up my scythe, I stood on the bench and peered over the coach's roof.

Like bone-white arrows they pierced the night. Their sleek fur glowed in the moonlight except their eyes that I knew would be blood red.

Death's Fangs. Demonic dogs bred to find lost souls and deliver them to Death. They were hunters, and now, they were hunting us. The question was, were they hunting me or her? Had Behryn discovered her presence in The Between? Or was this what happened when Death came to collect his due?

A wave of protectiveness surged within me, an effect of the vow, no doubt. Shadows rose up on either side of the coach, mine to control, but their power was not limitless. They couldn't transport the two of us very far, but they could give Katrin a chance to get away if things went south. Best to conserve their energy.

The wind roared and tore at my cloak. Despite the blur of trees passing by, the Fangs continued to gain on us.

There were three in total that I could see. If there were any more lurking within the trees, we might not manage to escape.

Again, I considered sending Katrin away by shadow, but what good would it do her to be alone if I fell victim to these beasts? Without my protection, she would still be lost to Death. The only option was to fight.

The hounds ran in perfect formation, one in the center, leading the pack and two flanking the leader on either side. They were close enough now that I could see the spittle flying from their open maws. Hunger radiated from their blood red eyes.

The leader hung back as the two flanking it surged forward. They gained on the carriage, taking up positions on either side. A scream from within let me know that Katrin had not followed all my orders.

I slammed my hand twice against the roof. "Close the curtains, Miss Fil'Owen."

Holding my scythe in one hand, I gripped the edge of the roof and swung over the side. My foot landed solidly on the small step beneath the door. The beast lunged, and I swiped with my blade, the motion awkward as I struggled to hold onto the carriage. It danced back, easily evading the blow.

When it rushed me again, I lifted my weapon. It opened its dripping jaws, revealing razor sharp teeth. I swung wide and it jumped. Blocking its bite with the handle of the scythe, I wrenched it sideways, throwing the hound beneath the wheel. The carriage bounced as it careened over the demon, but I knew it wouldn't be out for long.

Katrin screamed again. I glanced over my shoulder but the curtains were drawn over the window. Backing up to the edge of the step, I flung open the door and plunged inside. The second Fang hurled itself against the opposite door. Huddled to my left, Katrin looked at me in alarm.

"What are those things?" she asked, breathless.

I pulled my scythe in. If I'd thought it unruly outside the door, it was completely useless inside the cabin. "They are Death's Fangs."

The weapon clattered to the floor. I left it there as I lifted up the cushion of the unoccupied seat, revealing a small box carved into the bench itself. I opened the lid and pulled out two mismatched daggers.

Onyx claws punched through the door, wood splintering as they tore. There was a flash of the Fang's red eyes before it fell. I waited for it to pounce again, but it never came. A glance out the window confirmed the demon had either dropped back or moved elsewhere.

Snarling sounded behind me, and Katrin screamed. I whirled, catching a flash of white before it knocked me down. Claws raked at my chest. Instinctively, I thrust my daggers up, narrowly avoiding the namesake fangs as I split open the beast's abdomen. Black blood poured from the gaping wound and the Fang grew still.

My chest barked in pain as I rolled the demon off me.

"Help me." I panted as I heaved the great beast toward the door. I needed it out of the cabin before it healed.

"You're bleeding."

Katrin looked pale as the Fang at my feet. I leveled her with an unimpressed stare. "That is not helpful."

This seemed to shake her from her shock. She stood with one hand braced on the wall and the other on her chest. Blowing out a deep breath, she bent and helped me push the great beast out the door. The forest still blurred past. I had no idea how far we'd gone, or what area of The Between we were in, but I knew there was still one more Fang to contend with.

I plucked the daggers from the pool of black blood, wiping the hilts with my cloak. Katrin watched me with a mixture of concern and curiosity.

"I'm going to draw out the last of the hounds," I told her calmly. Panic would be deadly for both of us. "No matter what happens, I want you to keep going. Stay with the carriage if you can. If it's compromised, the shadows will protect you." Her head bobbed up and down. "Say it, Katrin."

Her eyes whipped to mine as expected at the sound of her name. "If anything happens to you, I'll keep going."

I held her gaze and exhaled heavily. "You are a terrible liar."

She shrugged sheepishly.

It came out of nowhere. One second she was there smiling cautiously at me from across the cabin. The next, she was dragged from the coach by the great white beast.

"Kat!" I bellowed.

I didn't think. I leapt from the speeding carriage, rolling as I hit the ground in a wave of agony. Sliding to stop, I sprang to my feet. I'd lost my daggers in my tumble from the coach, but I could only think of Katrin as I ran weaponless toward the white beast.

They hadn't gone far. I could see Katrin resisting the foul creature, fighting with all the fire I knew she possessed. Her shadow guards had joined in the fray, but they could only do so much as long as the Fang still had a hold of her. I needed to get her free.

I called the shadows to me, closing the distance in a blink of an eye. I fell onto the demon's back, wrapping my arms around its neck and squeezing tightly. The beast released Katrin almost immediately. I shouted for the shadows to take her, breathing a sigh of relief at the fading sound of her protests.

Without Katrin to distract the Fang, it bucked and jumped, trying to dislodge me. My chest throbbed in pain. As though sensing my weakness, the creature redoubled its efforts. I flew from its back, crying out as I struck a tree and collapsed to the ground.

The beast prowled toward me, its red eyes little more than pinpricks on its bone-white face. Everything hurt, but I sagged knowing the demon's attention was focused on me. Katrin would escape. I ordered the rest of my shadows to aid her and pushed myself up to sitting. Death would not find me on my back.

But it was not Behryn who came on the heels of his demon. Like an avenging queen, Katrin stepped from a billowing cloud of darkness, my scythe raised above her head. She brought it down with a battle cry and a mighty swing, slicing clean through the demon. Black blood sprayed and the beast crumpled in a cloud of dirt.

Her eyes found mine, sparkling in the hazy dawn. The scythe fell from her grasp, hitting the ground with a dull thud. She took one step toward me and collapsed beside it.

CHAPTER 34

Katrin

Pain blinded me. My leg was on fire. It radiated through my body until it felt like I was being burned from the inside out.

I screamed, and Evander was there, little more than a dark smudge against the lightening sky. If he spoke, the words were lost to me, drowned out by the steady beat of my heart hammering in my ears.

He'd called me Kat. That thought alone kept me from the darkness that beckoned when I closed my eyes. I almost laughed at the absurdity of it. After weeks of hoping for that level of familiarity between us, it had finally come on the heels of disaster.

Gentle hands flitted over me. Unable to make out his features, I imagined him assessing my condition in that cool, detached way of his. He reached my leg and recoiled.

How bad did a wound have to be to make a reaper hesitate?

His feather-light touch returned and glided over my wound. I screamed again, back arching to escape the pain. The ground was blessedly chill beneath me. I turned, pressing my forehead to the dirt as Evander tugged my injured leg back to him.

I took a deep breath in through my nose, shaking as I forced it through gritted teeth. The rushing in my ears disappeared so suddenly, I worried my heart had stopped. Only the enduring pain reminded me that I was still alive.

Cold slithered over my neck, and I turned my head to see one of my shadows—Inky or Storm, I couldn't tell which. It sprawled across my back, a cooling blanket to bank the fire burning within me.

Fabric tore, and I glanced over to see Evander clutching a ragged piece of his cloak. Capturing my lip between my teeth, I bit back my cry as he bound my leg. The metallic taste of blood coated my tongue, but his movements were quick and efficient, practiced even. Where had the Ferrier of Souls learned medicine?

He leaned in close, and I failed to suppress a whimper as he scooped me off the ground. My body folded into his, seeking comfort in his strength. I expected him to put me on my feet. I braced for it, certain he'd distance himself the first chance he got, but he only pulled me closer and carried me toward the horses.

Laying my head on his shoulder, I breathed in the scent of him. He smelled of the forest and rain and something I couldn't quite place, but it was heady and intoxicating all the same.

"You have a heartbeat," I remarked, surprised at the steady beat that sounded beneath my ear.

"Yes, Miss Fil'Owen. I am unfortunately still alive." His dry tone held a hint of strain, but I couldn't tell if his continued mortality or my injury was the cause.

I closed my eyes and when I opened them, we were atop the carriage. I didn't know if I'd fallen asleep or if we'd been transported by shadows, though I suspected the latter. Supporting me with one arm, he sat in the driver's seat and took up the reins. With a quick command to the horses, we were moving.

"Why didn't we..." I trailed off. My voice was weak and hoarse, so I gestured at the shadows swirling around us.

Evander seemed to understand what I was saying. "They tire too quickly to transport both of us over long distances, more so the closer we get to dawn."

I glanced at the sky that had lightened to a deep azure. I wasn't sure how far we'd traveled in our attempt to outrun the Fangs, but I doubted we'd make it back to the manor before dawn.

He must have seen the concern on my face. "We'll find other lodgings for the day."

I figured that meant we'd take shelter in some cave but didn't have the energy to care. Though my shadows kept the fire at bay, my leg was throbbing. Slumping back against the Ferrier, I thought to close my eyes for a moment and quickly succumbed to the dark.

When I awoke, I had no idea how much time had passed.

The sky had brightened though it was barely visible through the canopy of cypress trees and hanging moss. A quick glance around confirmed we were still in The Between, but we were nowhere near what I'd come to know of the liminal space. Like the world beyond *Tyr Anigh*, there was a sense of otherness, a wrongness that bordered on the impossible, as if the land itself were in stasis. It was unchanging, unalive but not dead.

Unlike the familiar part of The Between, the air here was thicker like wading through a swamp. Every bit of my exposed skin was damp, which I hoped was due to the climate and not fever.

Evander shifted and I made a weak attempt to disentangle my limbs from his. I tensed and his arms tightened around me, effectively halting my efforts. In one fluid motion he rose, lifting me with him like I weighed nothing at all. He pivoted and repositioned me in a prone position along the bench seat. I squirmed as whatever venom the beasts had infected me with made comfort a long lost luxury.

"I shall return momentarily." His eyes held mine. In them, I saw his sincerity, but creasing the edges were the first signs of worry.

I stretched my mouth into the semblance of a smile. "Not going anywhere." Whatever he saw on my face overrode any attempt at humor.

With a tilt of his head, my shadow guardians came rushing in. I sighed at the cooling pressure their presence provided.

Evander disappeared into the dark, as was his way. This time when he left me, I felt no fear. Though his hounds were temporarily incapacitated, Behryn hunted us. I was injured and we were far from home—the manor, that is—but I trusted Evander. Perhaps even beyond the confines of our agreement, I trusted him.

I'd never known many people I could rely on aside from my parents, and even their affection had been complicated, tainted by grief and a desire to *fix* me.

Maybe I was being foolish. After all, I knew Evander acted out of his own interests. I was his means to an end. Or was I? Sometimes, it felt like there was something more between us. Or was that just my bruised heart eagerly latching onto the first person to show me kindness?

I was disgusted by how much I craved a connection to him. Our time together was finite. A little less than a year from now, he would be a memory.

I blew out a breath and watched the shadows swirl above me.

Hushed voices jolted me back to the present. I froze until I recognized Evander's deep baritone. But who was the other?

Footsteps approached, and I lifted my head, turning pleading eyes in their direction. In that moment, I knew nothing of pride. There was only pain and the foolish hope that somehow, Evander and this stranger could ease it. I pushed myself upright, unwilling to meet anyone on my back. Pain lanced up my leg, and I immediately regretted the action. Clapping a hand over my mouth, I let loose a belated howl.

The shadows parted as the two men neared the carriage. I squinted to make out the figure next to the reaper I knew so well.

"This is her?" The newcomer's voice was like whiskey, smooth and deep. He stepped forward, moonlight illuminating a tall, leanly muscled form.

I had only a brief moment to appreciate his dark skin and depthless eyes before another wave of pain struck me. Doubling over, I squeezed my eyes shut, mouth open on a silent scream.

"The venom is moving swiftly."

Something touched my wounded leg, and I flinched away, gasping for breath as the pain receded.

"Then we'll need to be faster," said Evander.

"You'll bring the Devil to my door."

My head rolled back and forth in a silent 'no', but it was true. Behryn was seeking us, and we were putting this man in danger by coming here.

"Will you help us or not?" Evander's tone left little room for argument, and the second man sighed.

"You know I can't resist a pretty face."

Arms encircled me, and then, I was being lifted. I knew it was Evander before his familiar scent reached me.

"I've got you," he whispered into my hair.

My bones were heavy, but he held me tightly. I tipped my head onto his shoulder and fell into the waiting darkness.

Chapter 35
The Ferrier

Katrin lay limp in my arms as I carried her into the small cottage. When Behryn's beast had captured her, a familiar rage had taken hold of me. It had been too reminiscent of another time—another woman—but I would not allow Death to steal from me again.

Sam walked ahead of me and quickly cleared off the small dining table. A fellow reaper, Sam was the closest thing I had to a friend in The Between, and even that was a stretch. Decades had passed since I'd last seen him, but I was counting on his hatred of Behryn to overcome any deficiencies in our personal relationship. True to form, he hadn't taken much convincing.

I cradled Katrin's head as I set her down on the table, brushing loose strands of hair out of her face. Her mark had spread. Where once the shadows had stopped at her temple, they now stretched from brow to hairline, plunging almost the entire left side of her face into darkness. Only her eye remained unmarked.

Pain contorted her features even in rest, small lines visible at the corners of her eyes and mouth.

I stepped next to Sam as he inspected her wound. Blood had soaked through my hasty bandage. Though it seemed to have clotted, vivid red lines streaked away from the punctures. The Fang's venom needed to be counteracted before we could set about healing the injury.

"At least the bite was clean," Sam murmured. "There's no tearing and the bones appear to be intact. It could have bitten clean through her leg if it had wanted."

"They were likely under orders not to maim or kill," I speculated.

"Lucky for you."

I grunted in response. Nothing about this felt lucky.

Behryn shouldn't have known I was harboring Katrin unless I'd let something slip during his visit. But then, why wouldn't he have pounced on it then? It didn't add up.

My power over shadows felt woefully inferior compared to Death's arsenal. The misty forms hung back as though shamed by their failure to protect Katrin—or maybe I was projecting. I motioned to the deeper pockets of black within the room. "Whatever you need, they can fetch it." The shadows surrounding us perked up at my suggestion, eager to aid.

Sam rattled off several herbs, and they scattered to the wind—all but Katrin's two personal shadows who hovered nearby.

Before me, he placed a rag and a ewer of water. "You look like you need something to do."

I grabbed the rag and set to work cleaning the wound. Any time she flinched, I gentled my ministrations. The task took longer than it should have, but it kept my mind and hands occupied long enough for my shadows to return with the requested herbs.

Sam mixed a tonic and a poultice. Half the tonic he poured over the open bite marks. "The rest she should drink when she wakes," he said.

As I watched, the lines on Katrin's face smoothed, her body relaxing from its contracted state. By the time her leg was rebandaged, she was snoring softly.

Sam crossed to the other side of the room. With a snap of his fingers, a fire blazed to life in the hearth. It would be some time before the heat fended off the chill in the air. Regardless, I tore off my cloak, sickened by all that it symbolized. I debated throwing it into the flames but thought better about sending literal smoke signals of our location to Death. Bunching it into a tight ball, I threw the garment at the corner. It hit the floor with a less-than-satisfying *hiss*, but I was happy to be rid of it.

Two arm chairs occupied the area in front of the fireplace. I chose the one facing toward Katrin and collapsed into it, my limbs weighing more than they had in years.

"She'll live," Sam said, eying me curiously from where he leaned against the mantel.

My hands fisted despite the good news. I dragged them through my hair under the guise of tying it back, but Sam's keen eyes missed nothing.

"The venom was concerning, but after a couple days of excruciating pain, she would have been fine. Her wound was not life-threatening."

"But Behryn is," I growled.

"Ah ha." His dark eyes lit with interest. "And you care because..."

I cursed my mental exhaustion for making me loose-lipped. "We have an arrangement."

"Right." Sam's tone suggested he knew there was more to this story.

"She's my ticket to freedom, nothing more," I snapped, my temper on a short leash. Even if I'd thought about her being more to me, our relationship would be doomed from the start. She had a whole life to live. Her big plans did not include abandoning her dreams for a self-imposed sentence in The Between.

Sam raised his hands in submission. "Whatever you say, Van." He picked a bottle off the mantel and began pouring, appearing to let the subject drop.

He'd been roped into reaping the same way I had, by losing a bad bargain. Unfortunately for him, his territory was far less populated than mine, which meant he relied on less savory means of acquiring coin to pay his debt. Still, he'd taken to his afterlife easier than I had.

Sam handed me a glass of amber liquid that I took gratefully, swallowing it back in one swig.

"You still think she's waiting for you on the other side?"

The question hit me like a blow, and I choked as the burning liquor threatened to make a reappearance. My gaze flicked to Katrin before narrowing on Sam.

"Of course I do." That hope was the pillar of my desire for freedom.

Sam tilted his head, brows raising toward his hair line. "All I'm saying is Livia lived an entire life after you saved her. What makes you think she's still pining for you in the Afterworld?"

"She lived a full and happy life exactly as I wanted, and now, she awaits our reunion in The Beyond," I seethed. "If the way were not barred to me, I would be there with her already."

"And where does the girl factor in?" He gestured to Katrin's prone form behind him.

"She's a means to an end." The words tasted sour, but they were true. They had to be. Livia waited for me and Katrin would get me there.

Sam tossed back his drink like water to a dying man. "Then she's available? I already told you, Van, I can't say no to a pretty face like that."

"She is absolutely not available!" I exploded out of my chair, knocking it onto the floor with a crash. In two strides, I was in his face, one hand pressing into his chest. "You'll keep your tricky fingers to yourself, you hear me?"

From across the room, Katrin stirred, whimpering softly. I winced and lowered my voice. "She deserves better than either of us."

It wasn't what I meant to say, but I couldn't deny the truth of it.

Sam grinned and lifted his glass. "I'll drink to that."

CHAPTER 36
Katrin

I woke to the sound of clinking glasses and boisterous laughter. The pain in my leg had lightened to a dull throb, but my head was pounding. I debated sinking back into oblivion before anyone could notice I was awake, but whatever surface I was lying on left something to be desired.

My limbs were stiff, and I failed to suppress a moan as I roused.

Chair legs scraped the floor, followed by the pounding of quick footsteps, and then Evander was before me. The unguarded emotions flickering across his face rendered me speechless. Curiosity. Anger. Concern. Each one made me more certain I'd crossed into some alternative reality. This version of Evander was nothing like mine—like the one I knew.

Perhaps the bite had killed me and this was the Afterworld. It seemed unlikely, but nothing in my life was ever as it appeared to be.

I opened my mouth, debating which question needed answering first but hesitated as Evander's eyes flicked to something beyond my shoulder. When he looked back at me, his features had returned to their usual position of bored indifference.

"How are you feeling, Miss Fil'Owen?" he asked, tip-toeing around all that lay unspoken between us.

I would not be so evasive. "Back to formalities now, are we?"

His head tilted to one side. "I have no idea what you're talking about."

Again, his gaze flicked beyond me. I turned and caught a glimpse of the man I'd seen from the carriage. He held a cigar in one hand and a glass of amber liquid in the other. Lounging casually against the fireplace mantel, he did not attempt to hide his blatant observation of us.

I leaned closer to Evander, lowering my voice to that of a whisper. "You called me Kat."

"That never happened," Evander's voice matched mine for quietness, but I didn't miss the note of teasing.

"Liar." A smile tugged at the corner of my mouth.

"You were gravely injured. It's obvious you were hallucinating."

His mention of my wound drew my attention to my bandage-wrapped leg. His gaze followed mine, and he frowned.

"Does it hurt?" he asked earnestly.

I nodded. "Less now but walking should prove an interesting task."

Shimmying to the edge of the table, I slid onto the packed dirt floor. I was careful to keep most of my weight on my uninjured leg. Evander's arms appeared on either side of me. He didn't touch me but offered support should I need it.

I shifted my weight to my other leg, bracing myself against the table. My ankle twinged in pain but nothing I couldn't handle. Bolstered, I lifted my good foot to step again and tumbled into Evander's waiting arms.

My hands splayed over his muscled chest, and I looked up to find our faces entirely too close together. Our eyes locked, breath intermingling. I bit my lip and his gaze dropped to my mouth.

A throat cleared from across the room and we sprang apart. Well, *he* sprang. I shuffled. Somehow, he managed to keep a hold of me while putting distance between us. My cheeks heated, and for once, I was glad for the shadows that hid the reaction from the two men. With Evander's help, I half hopped, half walked to one of the arm chairs before the hearth.

As soon as I was safely seated, Evander released me and took a decorous step back. I eyed the space between us with distaste. Next time, I'd just ask my shadows to help me walk.

The dark stranger watched our interactions with a look of mild amusement. As the silence began to stretch toward uncomfortable territory, he approached me, offering his hand with a flourish.

"My dear, please forgive him," he said, tossing his head toward Evander. "Our mutual friend seems to have forgotten how to exist among polite society." The twinkle in his eye suggested he himself had never belonged in polite society. He took my hand in his and pressed a chaste kiss along my knuckles. "You may call me Sam."

I giggled despite myself. There was something about him that put me at ease. "It's a pleasure to meet you, Sam. You may call me Kat."

"The pleasure is mine, dear Kitty Kat. I assure you." His lips found my hand again, lingering intimately.

Evander scoffed from his place against the wall, arms crossed and a scowl on his face.

"The two of you are friends?" I asked, though it seemed unlikely. Evander wasn't exactly friendly.

Sam laughed and Evander brows pinched at the outburst.

"Evander and I are two sides of the same coin," said Sam. "Both of us gamblers who bet on the wrong hand and paid the ultimate price."

"It wasn't the wrong hand, it was a fixed game," Evander corrected.

I considered what I knew of Evander and put the pieces together. "You traded your soul to Death as well?"

All traces of humor left Sam's face. He leaned forward, dark eyes staring into mine, demanding my focus. "There is no winning when it comes to Death. There is only avoidance. Even the luckiest of men succumb eventually."

That didn't bode well for my predicament.

Evander watched me with a guarded expression. Did his thoughts align with mine?

I wondered if they'd discussed my situation as I slept. I shook my head. "I'm not trying to live forever. I just want a fair chance at a normal lifespan."

Sam's brows rose in interest. "Ah, but what is fair in life and death, Kitty Kat? Is it fair for the babe born too sick to survive its first winter? Is it fair that the rich live long while the poor die young? Is it fair that a man will trade his very soul to be with the one he loves, only to be torn away by Death without so much as a farewell?" His eyes flicked to Evander, who appeared to be ignoring both of us. "Not all deaths are so plainly marked upon one's skin. Most people live not knowing when their end will come and have no choice but to accept it when it does." Sam took a long drag from his cigar. "Perhaps you are the unfair one here."

The fire crackled in the hearth, the only sound within the small cabin. Sam's words sent my thoughts spiraling into the darker corners of my mind. I'd heard what had gone unsaid.

My plan was selfish. *I* was selfish.

Whether he'd held his tongue out of consideration for me or respect for Evander, I didn't know, but my chest ached like he'd cleaved me in two and taken out my self-serving heart for all to see.

I blinked rapidly to dispel the tears filling my eyes. I would not cry.

"You always were an ass." Evander's voice speared through the dark room, a hint of humor dulling the edge. "She did what either of us would have done—what we *did* do."

"That was different."

"How?"

"Because neither of us were trying to save our own asses." Sam threw back the contents of his glass in a single swallow. "Because our sacrifices were gladly made in the name of love."

"So you would fault her for desiring a chance to find a love like that?"

"Is that why you're helping her?"

"You know why I'm helping her."

"But does she?"

"*She* is right here," I interjected. "And I don't appreciate being spoken about as if I wasn't."

Evander appeared chastened as he looked down, clearing his throat. "We should go."

"Nonsense." Sam's smile returned, and the space brightened. "There is room enough here for two more."

It was then I noticed Inky and Storm hovering nearby. Had it been my imagination or had they closed in when the conversation had taken a turn? Though they now bobbed innocuously near the rafters, Sam watched them with undisguised curiosity, his gaze sliding down to take in Evander and myself as well.

"I appreciate what you've done for us, but our presence here jeopardizes your safety. It would be foolish to harbor us." Evander stepped to my side, offering his hand to help me stand.

Sam slammed his glass upon the mantel. "Behryn can suck my bollocks. Begging your pardon, my lady." He didn't look sorry at all as he dipped his head in my direction. "His Fangs will need longer than the day to recover and you're safer here away from prying eyes."

Evander's eyes met mine, indecision written across his face. I shifted and winced as a sharp pain lanced up my leg. His gaze dropped to my bandaged ankle, and I got the feeling he was weighing our options. When his face lifted again, his features had hardened with resolve.

"Fine," he said. "We'll stay, but only until it is safe for Miss Fil'Owen to travel again. And she gets the bedroom."

Sam tipped his head. "Agreed."

Chapter 37
The Ferrier

I didn't wait for Sam to show us to the bedroom. It was easy enough to find. There was only one other doorway off the main room besides the front door. A beaded curtain partitioned it from the rest of the cabin, swaying in a phantom breeze.

Katrin's weight at my side was a welcome distraction as I helped her into the adjoining room. I gripped her tightly, knowing it wasn't just her injury dragging her down.

What Sam had said...my hands clenched in memory of the hurtful words—words that had hit their target if the expression on her face was any indication. They'd struck a chord with me as well, but if Sam had hoped to sway me to his side, he'd failed. If anything, the urge to protect her had intensified.

Katrin may not be fighting for something as foolishly noble as love, but maybe if I'd had the sense to fight for my own life, I wouldn't be stuck in perpetual purgatory. I wouldn't let the same fate befall Katrin.

The beads jingled as I pulled the curtain aside. Katrin tensed at the sound but didn't hesitate to enter the room beyond. Together, we hobbled toward the only piece of furniture in the room.

The bed was modest with a simple wooden frame and a mattress barely large enough for two people. Worn but tidy linens lay haphazardly overtop.

I slipped the cloak from Katrin's shoulders, marking the blood and dirt upon it. For a moment, I'd forgotten she was mortal. Forgotten how vulnerable she was in this place of ghosts and monsters. The bright red of her blood had been a harsh reminder.

My fingers lingered on her shoulders, seeking reassurance she'd survived.

She sighed beneath my touch, and I yanked my hands away as though I'd been burned. Worried she'd felt my sudden recoil, I reached out to help her into the bed. Her delicate fingers were dwarfed by my own, but the strength of her grip was true to the stubborn woman I'd come to know.

Her eyes remained downcast as I pulled the covers over her legs.

"Kat." I kept my voice low, but I knew she heard me from the flicker of movement at the corner of her mouth.

"I knew you called me Kat."

The knot that had formed in my chest eased at the sound of her voice, though she still refused to meet my gaze. My hands itched to touch her, to hold her hand and run my fingers over her soft skin.

I fisted my hands and sat at the foot of the bed a safe distance away.

"Are you alright?" I asked quietly.

She looked at me then. Silver lined her eyes. Her bottom lip trembled until she captured it between her teeth.

My hand reached for her, settling upon the small mound of her foot beneath the blanket.

She blew out a breath and a single tear traced a line down her shadowed cheek. "Do you think I'm a fool?"

"Not at all," I answered honestly.

"But I'm selfish."

"You are not selfish for wanting to live."

She stayed silent for a long time. "Was it all for naught?"

"What do you mean?" My brow furrowed as I leaned closer.

"It is the nature of living things, is it not? That we should die. Who am I to prolong the inevitable? Who am I to alter fate's design?"

My thumb stroked small circles atop her foot. "It is human nature to desire control over your destiny. Do not let Sam or anyone else tell you otherwise."

"You did the same when you bargained with Death."

I nodded slowly. "Livia and I had been engaged since we were children. Our parents arranged it when I was eleven." Katrin shot me a look, and I shrugged. "I didn't mind. We grew up together, and I loved her. *Everyone* loved her, and I thought I was *in love* with her." I shook my head to clear the memory. "She was bright and joyful, kind and beautiful. She was everything I wasn't. But then she fell ill."

When Katrin's hand landed on mine, I didn't pull away.

"The doctors had done all they could for her, but it wasn't enough. You know the rest. I made a fool's bargain, but it did the job. It saved her, and I never saw her again."

"Would you do it again?"

"What?"

"Knowing what you know now, would you sacrifice your life for hers again?"

I considered my answer carefully. "I don't regret what I did, though I'll always wish there could have been a way for us to be together. I wouldn't choose differently."

"I would."

Katrin and I startled apart at the sound of Sam's voice through the doorway. His dark form passed through the beads a moment later.

He'd donned his top hat and cloak, looking more aristocrat than reaper.

"Duty calls," he explained. "You heading out tonight, Van?"

I shook my head, glancing at Katrin fast enough to catch the relief that flickered across her face. I'd felt the call of a soul since the sun had set, but I wasn't keen to leave her without protection. The soul could wait.

Sam raised a brow knowingly but didn't comment. Strolling from the room, he called over his shoulder "I'll be back before sunrise."

I stood to follow. "I should let you rest."

"Evander."

The note of panic in Katrin's voice halted my feet.

"Will you stay with me? Just until I fall asleep. Please? I don't want to be alone right now."

I scrubbed a hand over the rough stubble on my chin, a refusal poised at the tip of my tongue. The blanket draped over her form accentuated the curve of her hip, the dip of her waist. Her cheeks flamed at my open perusal, but she didn't rescind her request, didn't apologize for her boldness.

My arguments died before I could voice them. I loosed a breath and motioned for her to move over. "Make room, then. I'll not perch at the foot of the bed for hours like an animal."

She pushed back on the bed unable to hide her smile of triumph.

"Do not expect this to be a regular occurrence."

"Of course not."

I slid onto the bed, the space she'd occupied still warm beneath me. The mattress sagged in the middle, and I fought against the force that threatened to pull me to her side. With a thought, the shadows expanded, blocking out the firelight from the room beyond.

My sight adjusted quickly in the dark, once again honing in on the peaks and valleys of her body. Though her eyes were closed, her breathing had not yet slowed to the easy rhythm of sleep.

She rolled toward me and winced, tension forming lines around her eyes and mouth.

For once, I didn't stop my hand from reaching out to soothe those lines. She jerked at my touch, eyes darting open. I pulled back, but she captured my hand in hers before I could mutter an apology.

"I'm sorry," she said. "People don't—" She bit her lip, hesitating. "People don't touch me. Not of their own volition and *not* skin to skin. And certainly not with gentleness." As she spoke her fingers traced the scars and calluses marking my hand.

I slipped free of her touch. The edges of her mouth turned down at the loss of contact. Again, I reached for her face, but this time, she didn't retreat.

"It has been some time since I've touched anyone this way as well," I said, gliding over her shadowed skin. "Your mark has grown since I met you."

Katrin nodded. "I'd hoped it would disappear completely in The Between, but it seems my clever scheme is not enough to save me from Death."

Guilt twisted in my gut. I'd promised to protect her, but I'd done nothing to help her out of this predicament, too enamored by the idea of someone to share in my misery. It wasn't fair to her. She deserved the life she desired. A real life, free from the shadow of Death.

"Tell me about your mark."

Her eyelids fluttered shut. The bed creaked as she rolled onto her back. She was quiet for so long, I thought she would refuse, but then her voice floated to me through the dark, detached and unfeeling.

"I had just turned thirteen when we noticed a dusky tinge to my fingertips. I thought it was dirt at first, but it didn't wash away. The surgeon called it gangrene and threatened to cut off my hand. My father refused. When the shadows spread, he got a second opinion then a third. We saw countless doctors before he expanded the search. It wasn't until we met an oracle in a nearby town that anyone came close to the truth. She'd called it 'the Devil's stain', a mark from Death himself. Still, my father refused to believe it. I've been poked, prodded, cut, bled, submerged in freezing water, all in the name of fixing me."

I heard what she'd left unsaid: the pain, the loneliness, the fear. "It just appeared?"

"Yes. One day it wasn't there, the next day it was. There was no injury or incident, not that I can recall."

I felt more than saw her gaze return to my face. "It doesn't make sense with the pieces we have, but Behryn must have some reason for wanting you. Something he knew about eight years ago but decided he needed to wait to claim."

"That's the strangest part. If he wants me so bad, why not take me at thirteen?"

"Indeed."

The conversation left me unsettled. I could only imagine how Katrin felt after so many years without answers, and I'd done nothing to help her.

No more.

As her breaths deepened, I vowed that I would see her returned to the world of the living. And when her body, heavy in sleep, curled into mine, I pulled her closer and offered what comfort I could, taking no small amount of satisfaction in the sigh I drew from her.

CHAPTER 38
Katrin

When I woke, Evander was gone. I hadn't expected him to stay, but after an all-too-real dream where he'd held me in his arms, his absence hurt more than it should. I'd confessed so much to him last night ensconced in his shadows. I'd felt safe in a way I never had before. The cold light of morning had me reconsidering where we stood. Despite his actions yesterday, I couldn't shake the feeling that I was still a means to an end—a literal ticket to his freedom.

Sitting up in bed, I jolted as my two shadows detached from the wall, one flying through the beaded curtain to the other room. The second—Inky, I thought—turned down the linens so I might swing my legs over the side. I froze as a bolt of pain shot up my leg and reconsidered going back to sleep.

The beads parted and Evander slipped through, no doubt alerted by my shadow guard. I glared at Storm who followed in behind him. At least he had the good sense to appear chagrined. When the shadow sidled up to my side, I gave it a sidelong glance before nodding subtly. It was my fault for forgetting that they answered to Evander first. I couldn't fault their loyalty.

Evander watched our exchange with mirth sparkling in his eyes.

"How are you feeling?" he asked. He knelt to inspect my leg, and I flinched away with a wince, suddenly self-conscious.

"Fine," I answered quickly.

"Does it hurt?"

Faster than I could avoid, he caught my foot in his sure hands. I hissed as he probed it with gentle fingers.

"A bit," I admitted.

Releasing my foot with a nod of understanding, he rose to his full height, towering over my position on the bed. For once, his intimidating presence was tempered by an easy smile.

Perhaps I hadn't dreamed our late night entanglement.

"Sam has made a salve for your wound and procured fresh bandages. When you're ready, we can clean and redress it."

I nodded, at a loss for words. When he reached out his hands, I took them without hesitation. Lightning sparked through my body at the contact. The pain in my ankle became a distant memory as he helped me to my feet.

Chest to chest, my breath caught. I lifted my face to his and found it a mere handbreadth away. This close, I could make out the color of his eyes, not black as I'd originally thought, but darkest brown, warm and deep. He hadn't shaved, and I itched to run my fingers over the stubble. I probably would have had my hands not still been clasped in his.

My attention snagged on his full lips. I marveled at the way they turned up at the corners.

What a strange time to be happy.

But even as I thought it, I felt my own mouth curving. It occurred to me that I would very much like to kiss him.

That thought was like a bucket of cold water. I jumped away and was instantly reminded of my injury as my leg buckled with the sudden movement. Evander's arms were around me before I had the chance to fall.

"I've got you," he whispered, sweeping me off my feet like a hero in one of my books.

With those words, I melted, unable to resist pressing a kiss to his cheek. He looked at me sharply, surprised but not angry. Heat crept up my neck, and I turned my face away, embarrassment following swiftly on the heels of my brazenness.

I caught my reflection in the window and gasped. Evander's arms tightened around me, and I shook my head to ease his mind.

He'd mentioned my mark spreading last night, but I'd thought little of it at the time. It had been slowly taking over my body for almost a decade, so some growth was not unexpected. I did *not* expect to see more than half my face lost to darkness.

"It's not that bad," he muttered into my hair, guessing the direction of my thoughts.

"It doesn't matter." It didn't. It never had. Secretly, I had a fondness for the way the shadows transformed my skin. The way they sharpened the planes of my face and acted like camouflage in the night. They made me feel dangerous, beautiful, powerful. But how I felt was irrelevant when society refused to accept, or even acknowledge, a woman marked by Death.

"You're still beautiful."

His declaration startled me, as out of character as the now-constant smile upon his face. I whipped my head back to his, expecting to find some hint of mockery in his features, but his eyes shone with sincerity and something else I wasn't ready to acknowledge.

"I know." I'd meant to say I was surprised someone had noticed, but my mouth had another idea. Of course, if anyone was capable of seeing beyond the shadow of death, it would be the Master of Shadows himself.

Evander's attention dipped to my lips, and I knew no one had ever looked at me with such heat in their eyes. For a moment, I considered how it would feel to close the short distance between us and press my lips to his.

My kissing experience was limited to the quick, stolen peck with James Haywynn in my father's garden before I'd been marked. The giddiness of an adolescent infatuation was nothing compared to the heat now pulsing through my veins.

His gaze found mine, an unspoken question in the angle of his brows. I parted my lips, prepared to answer, when the beaded curtain clattered behind us.

"She lives."

Sam's timely entrance shattered the spell that had woven between Evander and me.

I shot him a wry look over my shoulder. "Your concern is noted."

He smirked, taking in our cozy position. When his mouth opened to comment, I silenced him with a glare.

"Ooh! Kitty has claws!" Sam mimed a cat scratch and hissed.

"And a sharp tongue," Evander added.

"I'd like to see what else she can do with that tongue."

Several things happened in the span of a breath, but I watched the scene unfold as if in slow motion.

Evander turned, placing his body between Sam and me. With efficient gentleness, he placed my feet on the floor then whirled to face Sam. At the same time, two shadows flew at Sam, pinning him to the wall and holding him spread-eagle.

"The next time you want to disrespect her, I'll cut out *your* tongue and feed it to Behryn's hounds," Evander said, his voice lethally calm.

I shivered at that tone, the reminder of just who I'd been flirting with so casually.

Silence stretched, and I held my breath as I waited for Sam to kick us out, or worse, fight back. I didn't know the extent of his power, but I had no doubt a battle between two reapers would be catastrophic.

But Sam didn't fight back. He laughed.

"There you are, Van," Sam chuckled.

I blinked at his good humor, stepping around Evander to get a better view.

"My apologies, Miss Kitty." Sam winked at me, and the shadows around him tightened. "I was just testing a theory. You can call off your dogs, Van. I'll leave her alone."

"Don't make me regret this," Evander growled. The shadows shrank, releasing Sam. He held his hands up in surrender, his smile a slash of white against his dark skin.

Evander, seemingly satisfied by this reaction, turned and lifted me back into his arms. He carried me to the main room where he and Sam cleaned and redressed my wound. True to his word,

Sam remained a silent participant until the angry, red flesh was completely covered.

"You're off then?" Sam asked.

My head whipped to Evander, shock warring with relief. "We're leaving?"

"*I'm* leaving," he clarified.

"What?" My voice came out as a squeak.

"You need food." The way he said it reminded me that I was the only human among us. They were both *other* with none of the same needs as me. Though Sam clearly enjoyed both smoking and drinking.

"And you're just going to, what? Leave me here?" He wouldn't, surely. There's no way he planned to leave me here with a veritable stranger who didn't even like me half the time.

"You're safer here," he insisted.

I dropped my voice and leaned in close, giving Sam a sidelong glance. "I'm safer with you."

"I'll be back before you know it." Evander retrieved his cloak from where it hung near the door. As he draped it over his broad shoulders, he instantly transformed to the Ferrier.

Easing to my feet, I hobbled after him. I'd jump in the carriage if I needed to. He wouldn't leave me here.

"You'll only slow him down." The voice of reason had never been more annoying. I glared at Sam, the gesture becoming something of a habit between us.

Sam grabbed his chest, face contorted in mock pain. "If looks could kill, Kitty Kat."

Evander opened the door. Beyond him there was no carriage, not even a solitary horse.

"Where is the coach?" I asked, alarm pitching my voice higher.

Evander turned, hands tucked casually into his pockets. Only the muscle feathering along his jaw revealed any hint of the same distress I felt in being separated. "It was too conspicuous. I sent it back to the manor shortly after we arrived. No reason to alert Behryn to our location. I can travel faster without it."

As if proving his point, the shadows deepened around him.

"My deal is with you, not Sam."

"Your shadows will remain to protect you in my stead."

Inky and Storm floated to my sides, flanking me like the guards Evander claimed them to be.

"It is day," I said, stating the obvious. "Where will you go?"

"There is food still at the manor." He had an answer for everything.

"It can wait. I'm not even hungry." I wasn't. In fact, I became nauseated at the thought of food.

"You've just been through a major ordeal. Your body is running on stress. You must eat. Starving will not keep you from Death."

I opened my mouth to protest, but Sam spoke first.

"You may want to remember, Kitty, neither Van nor myself are strangers to starving bodies. I think I can speak for both of us when I say we have no interest in seeing you suffer in that way."

"So you'd prefer I suffer in other ways?" I was being dramatic, but I didn't care. The thought of being separated from Evander made my skin feel too tight.

"In this instance," said Sam, "I do believe I'm the one who is suffering."

Evander stared at us both incredulously then focused his gaze on me. "Your shadows will remain in communication with those traveling with me. Should anything go wrong—for you or me—they will alert the other."

The knot in my stomach eased at that knowledge. Evander's eyes met mine, unflinching. He had weighed both options and decided leaving was worth the risk. Somehow I knew, if I asked him to stay, he would, but I had placed my life in his hands. I needed to trust him.

My stomach rumbled an untimely growl, and I relented. "Fine, but I don't like this."

"Your opinion has been noted," said Sam, stepping close and draping an arm over my shoulders. "We'll be just fine."

Though he addressed the latter part to Evander, his attention slithered along the marked side of my face.

Evander flicked a wary glance from my face to where Sam touched me. I kept my expression neutral, biting back the urge to jam my elbow into Sam's ribs. With a curt nod, Evander turned, the sweep of his billowing cloak like a wave goodbye. The shadows engulfed him, and he was gone.

CHAPTER 39
Katrin

Shrugging out of Sam's hold, I hobbled to the door, ignoring the shooting pain in every other step. I halted at the threshold, immediately struck by the scent of moss and rotting wood. Evander was well and truly gone. The familiar heaviness of being left behind settled on my shoulders, only this time, I was alone with a veritable stranger. I dared a behind me at the man in question.

Sensing my eyes on him, Sam looked up from where he'd been pouring himself a drink. "Don't look at me like that. I mean you no harm."

"You didn't seem too keen on me yesterday," I snapped.

Sam straightened, a glass in each hand. "I don't dislike you, Kitty Kat." The distance between us shrank, eaten up by his easy, long-legged stride. He extended one of the glasses my way, brows raised in question.

My etiquette training had me accepting the drink before I could think better of it.

"You could have fooled me," I said, sniffing the amber liquid.

Sam barked a laugh as my nose wrinkled.

"It is hard to watch someone make the same mistakes I did."

"But it's not the same. Wasn't that your point? That you and Evander bartered your souls to save others while I was merely protecting myself." My ankle throbbed in pain. Unwilling to make the trek back to the seating area before the fire, I slumped to the ground.

Sam squatted, setting his forearms on his thighs and gesturing at the drink in my hand. "That will help."

I eyed it. In the search for a cure, I'd downed innumerable concoctions, received countless doses of different drugs. I was no stranger to alcohol, but I'd never developed a taste for it. Pinching my nose, I tossed back the entire glass, sputtering as the liquid fire burned its way down my throat.

Sam laughed again.

"If you tell me it will put hair on my chest, I may just kick you," I rasped.

"You're alright, Kat." Sam held out a hand, and I placed the glass in it. Setting it aside, he reached out again, this time taking my hand and hauling me into a standing position. I expected him to let me go once I was again upright, but he gripped me with surprising strength. "If I spoke unkindly, it is only because I envy your potential."

"What do you mean?"

"There are doors still open to you despite the choices you've made." He motioned to my darkened skin. "These shadows, your bargain with Van, neither have sealed your fate. Death may take you tonight. He may take you in a year, but there is still a chance that you will win. There's still a chance for you both to be free. In the end, both options are ones that have been denied to me for centuries."

I stood in stunned silence, noting open expression and watery gaze. He was telling the truth. I'd never thought of death as a gift, but after centuries of lonely existence trapped between life and death, would I yearn for the latter as much as the former?

Still reeling from the revelation, I allowed Sam to guide me to a chair. I stared into the flickering flames, contemplating all that he'd said. Twisting the words around in my mind until I started to question my sanity. At some point, he'd refilled my drink, the glass once again clenched between my hands. This time, I didn't hesitate to gulp it all down. It warmed my belly and eased some of the tension in my limbs. I blew out a breath, glancing at Sam in the chair beside me.

"Do you think I'm on a fool's errand?" I voiced the fear that had nagged at me these last few days. Though I hadn't intended to befriend Evander, our hot-and-cold relationship made me unwilling to share my deeper doubts with him. I didn't have the same reservations about Sam. I didn't care what *he* thought of me. "Should I accept my fate and be done with it?"

Sam tilted his head, considering. "You cannot go wrong on this path. Either you will thwart Death or you will meet him as you were always meant to."

I pulled at the torn threads of my skirt. "I think if I were dying—and only that—that I could come to terms with that. I don't know what awaits in the Afterworld, but I'm no longer afraid to find out. Don't get me wrong," I added at his knowing glance, "I want to live, but dying doesn't seem so bad anymore."

"See. Nothing to worry about." He sat back, propping his hands behind his head.

"But that's not what's happening," I said, rubbing my shadowed skin. "Death has claimed me—Behryn has claimed me—to whatever end. More than anything, *that* is what terrifies me. I am merely a pawn in some game, and I don't even know the rules."

Sam nodded in understanding and took a quick sip from his glass. Leaning forward, he propped his elbows on his thighs, eyes never leaving the drink as it dangled between his knees. "I didn't trade my life for my wife's. I would have, but our son—" His voice broke on the word, and he swallowed thickly before continuing. "He was all we had. When he came down with the fever, he was too young, too small to fight it. I gave my life for his. I will never regret that, but I missed everything. I missed him growing up and becoming a man. I missed growing old with my woman, and I missed their deaths. Now they wait for me in the Afterworld, and I may never join them."

"I'm so sorry, Sam."

"I'm not telling you for pity. When you're sitting pretty in that manor, sharing a bed with Van—"

"We've never—"

"I don't care." He cut me off. "When you think you've found the easy way out, that you can just exist in The Between forever, I want you to remember that anything is better than this. This is not living. It's hiding. Don't throw away your possibilities for the safe choice. More often than not, it's not a choice at all."

With one conversation, Sam had turned my world upside-down. He'd known my inner turmoil without me having to voice it, and now, I had to figure out how to accept his wisdom. There was no future for Evander and me. I'd already known, but Sam's confirmation solidified the idea into an impenetrable wall around my deepest desires. The truth was, I'd begun to see myself here, assistant to the Hand of Death. I'd found a part of myself I hadn't known existed, and Evander had completed that version of myself.

I swallowed back the contents of my glass and tipped the empty vessel toward Sam. "I think I could go for another."

Chapter 40

The Ferrier

My journey to the manor was quick and uneventful. The mists were calm and quiet as usual, no sign of Behryn's beasts to be seen. Without the horses and carriage, the distance was quickly covered within the dark embrace of my shadows.

I checked on the beasts upon my arrival, ensuring they had been unhitched and cared for by my shadows when they'd returned. I detected no other presence within the confines of my property, but I sent my shadows ahead to sweep the manor just in case. I would need to perform a thorough search before returning with Katrin.

A sharp tug deep in my core gave me pause. Somewhere in my territory, a soul waited to be ferried. I couldn't ignore the summons forever, but it could wait another night or two. I would not be so quick to leave Katrin again once I returned to Sam's. Even if anxiety hadn't sunk its claws in me, she'd nearly bit my head off when I left. I had no desire to upset her again.

My shadows returned signaling all was clear, and I hurried inside, heading for the kitchen to gather what food I could. Little remained of what we'd pilfered from her family home. Soon, we would need to find more, but what was left should be enough to last through our stay at Sam's.

I placed the food in a rucksack and handed it off to my shadows. My body moved with an unfamiliar urgency as I strode from the room. The sun was still high in the sky, but I was eager to return to Sam's—to Katrin.

I turned the corner to the foyer and bounced off a shadow blocking my path. Glaring, I stepped to the side and flew backwards as the shadow again obstructed the way through.

"What now?" I asked, holding my arms out in an exaggerated shrug.

Darkness swept toward me, plucking at my shirt and pulling on my trousers. In my mind I saw Katrin, lovely but filthy.

"Fine," I acquiesced. "I will change. You fetch Katrin something to wear."

The shadow disappeared with haste. I didn't want to waste any more time by bathing, so I grabbed some clothes to change into and handed them to the shadow when we met up again in the foyer.

"Satisfied?"

The darkness moved aside, allowing me to pass unhindered. A sign I took for agreement. I rolled my eyes as I passed the shadow, wondering when they had gotten so bold. I knew the answer. She'd had a similar effect on me as well. I wasn't surprised to find myself eager to return to her side.

I smiled as I reached for the doorknob, cursing when it burned my skin. I yanked my hand away and stared down at the mottled flesh as it healed. My instincts told me to run, to gather my shadows and disappear into their darkness, but I knew that he would hunt me. Running was futile, and it wouldn't keep Katrin safe.

Squaring my shoulders, I winced as I opened the door and found Death waiting at my doorstep.

His hands were tucked into the pockets of his deep red suit, a bold color against the backdrop of The Between. Though his posture was casual, his body radiated power, a coiled serpent prepared to strike. Upon seeing me, he cocked an eyebrow. "Going somewhere?"

"Behryn," I growled, ignoring his question. "Why are you here?"

He had the nerve to look affronted by my words. "Can a king not visit his people? Can a master not check in on his servants?"

"You did receive my last payment, did you not?"

The king's eyes swept the space behind me, assessing, searching. "And then some," he replied distantly.

I'd sent some of Katrin's money with my last payment, enough to ease the sting of my tardiness, but not so much as to draw attention—or so I thought. Was that how he knew of Katrin staying with me?

He stepped to the side, and I mirrored the movement, blocking his view as I invaded his space. "What do you want, Behryn?"

"I have reason to believe there is someone else residing here."

Crossing my arms over my chest, I plaster a look of boredom across my features. "What gave you that impression?"

"Come now, Evander," Behyrn hissed. "Do not play me for a fool. Who is she?"

It took all of my strength not to react to those words—not to deflate in relief that he did not know her. He had no idea I harbored the girl he'd marked for himself all those years ago. Somehow, he knew *of* her but not who she was.

My mouth twitched with the effort of holding back my smile. Behryn tracked the motion, his dark eyes squinting as he filed the information away.

"She was nothing." I shrugged, adopting the cocky grin I'd seen on demons after they engaged in carnal activities. "A bit of fun."

Let him think what he wanted as long as it kept Katrin safe.

"And where is she now?"

I huffed out a laugh. "Gone. She wandered into the mists yesterday afternoon. I spent the night searching for her but came up empty handed."

"Your duties didn't call to you last night?"

As if in answer, the tug in my chest amplified. I didn't have to fake the wince of pain as I rubbed at my chest. "Of course it did, but I know my limits. I'll get to it."

"See that you do."

"Is there anything else I can help you with?" I hoped for a miracle. I didn't want to leave Katrin in Sam's care, but at least I knew she'd be safe. She'd been right, of course. It had been foolish to risk coming here, especially if his eyes were not yet focused on Sam's place. Now, I had to decide if it was worth returning and potentially leading Death right to Katrin.

Behryn looked me up and down. I didn't blink as he took my measure, forcing myself to breathe normally. The air reeked of smoke and brimstone, but I choked it down. He turned without comment, striding away as though he'd walked here and not appeared in a flash of fire like he always did. He made it ten steps before he lifted one hand and snapped his fingers.

I fell to my knees, head bowed, unable to move even to blink. Pain lanced up my legs, but I was glad. I'd played this game before. The spell would release me when Behryn was out of range, leaving me free to return to Katrin without fear of being followed. I just hoped he didn't linger in the area long.

***

Night had fallen before I could finally move, though movement was an overstatement. By the time the spell wore off, I couldn't feel my feet. If it weren't for my shadows, I'd have crawled from the manor. As it was, I raced to Sam's under cover of darkness heedless of the incessant tug that urged me toward the mortal world.

When I burst through the door, I stumbled to the floor, the shadows unloading all I'd packed along with me as they, too, battled exhaustion.

"Are you moving in?"

Sam's sarcasm was a welcome sound after fearing I'd never return again. My answering laugh was equally sardonic. I sat up, dusted off my shoulders, and looked around curiously. Concern swept through me when Katrin did not immediately greet me, but my eyes quickly found her asleep on one of the chairs before the fireplace. "What happened?"

Sam showed me his palms, cigar grasped between his right thumb and forefinger. "Nothing happened. She was having a good time."

I shot him a look to rival Katrin's.

"I kept her mind off you." He sucked on his cigar and blew out a line of perfect *Os*. "Well, I tried to."

"What is that supposed to mean?" I snapped, pushing up to standing.

"Not what you're thinking." Sam smiled like he'd told a joke, but I wasn't laughing. "I thought she was doing all right. We talked and made nice, but she cannot hold her liquor."

I growled.

"Nothing happened. She had a few drinks and passed out." He glanced to where she lay sprawled over the armchair. "You learn a lot about a person when they're in their cups. Did you know she's an only child? Or that she was promised in marriage, but the deal fell through when she was marked?"

I shook my head, feeling the slimy worm of jealousy take hold in my gut.

"She called out for you while she was sleeping." Sam's voice was quiet as his brows pulled together in concern. "What are you doing, Van?"

"I'm earning my freedom." It wasn't a lie, but it wasn't the whole truth, and the words tasted wrong as I spoke them.

Sam raised his brows like he saw the lie for what it was. "Is that all?"

"Of course it is," I bit out.

"Oh, really? Because I see the way you look at her like she's more than just a means to an end. You know this can't end well."

I nodded, though part of me disagreed with him. A larger, more rational part of me knew he spoke true. The Between was not a place for happy endings. It was not a place for endings at all. It was a world of eternities, never ending and never changing.

I perched on the arm of the chair Katrin occupied, needing to be near her, to know that she was safe. My encounter with Behryn had left me shaken. I exhaled shakily. Even if he'd only guessed at Katrin's involvement with me, it was enough to paint a target on her back. The second he realized she was the girl he'd marked—the woman he'd likely been hunting since she disappeared all those weeks ago—he would stop at nothing to capture her. And I would likely see another hefty fee added to my indenture.

Katrin was my one shot at freedom. I was all in.

Sam observed me with an inhuman tilt of his head, his keen eyes missing nothing. "What has happened?"

Scrubbing a hand down my face, I blew out another breath. "I ran into Death."

Sam lurched forward. "Where? When?"

"At the manor as I was leaving." I stared at my hands. If only I possessed a modicum of power beyond the shadows granted to me by Death himself. "He was looking for her. Not *her*, specifically, but he knew there'd been a woman staying with me. Whether he'd gleaned some hint of her existence at his last visit or learned of her from one of his beasts or subjects, I don't know."

Sam chewed on his lip. "And he just... let you go?"

I nodded.

"Shit."

"We should leave now," I said, making no move to act on the statement.

"And go where? If Behryn doesn't already suspect my involvement, this is the safest place for you. If he does—" He shrugged. "Then, I'm already doomed."

I took in Katrin's sleeping form, the injured leg, the dark smudges beneath her eyes that refused to abate even in sleep. "I suppose you're right."

Sam scoffed. "Of course, I'm right. Now, take your woman to bed before I do."

I glanced sharply at him.

"Take her to *the* bed. Come now, Van." He chuckled, but the words had their intended effect. Images of Katrin sprawled beneath me replaced the dark thoughts about Behryn.

Ignoring Sam's knowing wink, I scooped Katrin into my arms and carried her into the bedroom. She stirred only once, her eyes fluttering open as I set her down on the mattress. Her smile nearly undid me. No one had ever looked at me that way, like I was her rock, her hero, her true north. As she slipped off to sleep again, I pressed a kiss to her cheek, one I'd longed to give since I'd felt the feather-light brush of her lips against my skin. My lips still tingled as I walked away, content to let her rest and heal while I worried over darker problems.

CHAPTER 41

Katrin

I awoke in a bed with no recollection of how I'd gotten there. My stomach roiled, and I groaned, draping an arm across my face. I opened and closed my mouth, trying to rid it of the taste of stale paper. My head pounded, but the throbbing in my ankle had receded. Slowly, the events of the day before returned to me.

I remembered Evander leaving, drinking with Sam, the words we'd shared. I felt better staying here knowing he harbored no ill will toward me.

Weak sunlight filtered in through the single window, and I wondered if it was later that day or if I'd slept through the night. I rolled over and blinked to clear my vision. Beside me, the bed was empty. Not surprising even if Evander had returned, but it didn't answer the question of if he had. Pushing myself into a sitting position, I rubbed the remaining sleep from my eyes. Blinking them again, I tried to look around and froze.

"Evander!" I cried.

There was commotion in the next room then a wild frenzy of beads exploding as Evander ran in, closely followed by Sam.

Sam gasped, but Evander's solemn face told me everything I needed to know.

"I can't see out of my left eye." The mark had been spreading. Over the last several weeks, it had overtaken more of my face. I never dreamed this would be the result.

Evander rushed to my side. My body tipped as he sat on the edge of the bed, taking my face in his hands.

"You can't see anything out of it?"

I closed my good eye and shook my head, Evander's hands sliding to my shoulders. "It's just black." When I opened again, his face blurred through my tears. I tipped my head down as they fell, leaving tiny dots across the blanket.

With sure fingers, Evander tilted my chin up, dragging his knuckles over my tear-stained cheeks. I willed my gaze up to his and inhaled sharply at the strength radiating from his eyes. There was no condemnation in the grim set of his features, only concern and an edge of what I dared to call protectiveness.

Sam approached with the same casual air he always projected. "You look half demon now, Kitty Kat."

Catching Evander's hands in mine, I searched his face as though I would find Death's plan written upon it. "Is that what he's doing?" I asked, voice so high it squeaked. "Is he turning me into one of them?"

Evander's mouth formed a hard line. "There's no way of knowing what his plan is or what is within his power to do. We can only keep searching for a solution and hope that our luck does not run out."

"Is this the luck you are referring to?" I gestured to my mark.

"I'm referring to the luck that brought you to perhaps the one reaper who has as much to gain from opposing Death as you do. I'm referring to the fact that up until now, you've managed to evade Death, a feat very few people have ever done."

Sam nodded, and I bit my cheeks to keep from making a face.

Evander's thumb absently stroked the back of my hand. "There are fresh clothes and food for you when you're ready."

At the mention of food my nausea returned. I pushed the blankets away, seized by a desperate urge to visit the outhouse. The reapers wisely moved out of my way as I half ran, half hobbled into the main room. I made it out the front door before the afternoon's festivities caught up to me,

Kneeling at the bank of the swamp, I heaved into the dark waters until there was nothing more. With a final spit, I sat back on the mossy ground, wiping my sleeve roughly across my face.

"How charming," hissed a voice from behind me.

I screamed, every nerve screaming at me to run.

Evander burst through the door before the echo of the sound fully faded, Sam on his heels. I rolled to face whatever demon had spoken and froze, mouth agape as I took in the creature before me.

"Ani." Sam's usually jovial voice was laced with confusion. "I don't recall ever seeing you in my neck of the woods."

The Ani in question may have stood on two legs like a person, but that was where the similarities ended. Standing a full head and shoulders over Evander, the demon towered over me where I remained on the ground. Black skin gleamed over a lean but muscular form with matching claws that looked like they could rip me open with a moment's notice. To top it all, a face that was more canine than human. Not quite the dogs that Death's Fangs were, but something clearly *other*.

"It has been an age since I've deigned to stoop so low." She—and it was female upon closer inspection—spoke with a mouth unaccustomed to speaking our language, her enunciation clumsy and full of teeth.

"And to what do we owe the pleasure now?" Sam asked. A black cane appeared in his hand, seemingly from nowhere. He twirled it absently as he took a casual step forward, placing himself in the center of the triangle created by Evander, myself, and the newcomer.

It was an effort to keep her within the sightline of my good eye. I scrambled to my feet, still dwarfed by her sheer size. Her focus found me over Sam's head, and she bared her teeth. Even between the two reapers, I was prey before a predator.

"There's a lot of talk around The Between. Rumors claim a reaper brought over a human, but this—" Those inhuman eyes saw everything. "This is really something, Evander."

Evander stood taller as the shadows gathered around us. "Can we assume you are here to validate those rumors?"

"His Highness is curious," she hedged.

"Is that how he knows about her? Who started these rumors?"

"It is said the whispers began in his court." Ani inspected her claws, a picture of lethal calm. "I wouldn't be surprised if he sent the words on the wind himself just to stir things up. It seems you have managed to slip through his fingers thus far."

The sharpness in her tone was the only warning before she lunged.

Sam met her blow head on, raising his cane in time to deflect the worst of it. Evander yanked me behind him, reaching into a nearby shadow and removing his scythe. The wicked edge gleamed as it sliced through the air, forcing Ani to jump back. The reprieve was short lived as she sprang between them. I watched in horror as she effortlessly exchanged blows with both men, somehow avoiding the whistling steel and quick jabs.

I was suddenly very aware that I was a human among demons. The three beings formed a maelstrom of claws and onyx. Evander was a sight to see, when I could see him. With only one eye, I struggled to track him amongst his shadows. One moment he was there, the next he was swallowed by darkness, reappearing steps away in a blink.

In the chaos, I'd somehow ended up on the wrong side of the fight, unable to cross the melee to sneak back inside. Two of the shadows broke off from the group to stand sentry beside me. I welcomed Inky's and Storm's cool embrace as they ushered me back from the fray. Together, we inched away, the three demons too engrossed in their battle to notice.

I stumbled over the unfamiliar terrain, unwilling to turn my back on the terrifying creature in our midst. My next step reached the space where the ground should have been and kept going. Water soaked my skirts as I tripped into ankle-deep water. Though the splash barely sounded over the ruckus of the three demons, Ani halted mid-strike, canine ears swiveling to locate the source of the noise.

I froze, holding my breath against the scream that wanted to crawl up my throat.

Evander and Sam swung at once, a powerful strike that Ani parried effortlessly. With a swift kick, Ani sent Sam sprawling. Evander stepped into his shadows, disappearing once again.

Thinking she was distracted, I hoisted myself out of the putrid water. Ani's head whipped toward me, but Inky and Storm formed a wall of darkness before me.

Somehow, I could still make out her form through the gloom, though it seemed I was fully hidden from her view.

Evander reappeared behind Ani, scythe held high. She turned, exposing her back to him as though he were no real threat.

In a gesture more canine than human, she sniffed the air. Her head snapped in my direction, gaze narrowed on the space I occupied, still camouflaged by my shadows. I tensed as her eyes slid over me, unseeing, and yet, I had the distinct impression of being found.

Evander's scythe arced down, but she was already moving.

Toward me.

I spared no thought for her superior strength or longer limbs. I ran.

Inky and Storm kept pace with me, covering my retreat as best they could in spite of the noise I was making. I ran until Ani's panting breaths sounded from far too near. Two sets of footsteps joined with mine, and I wondered if Evander was keeping pace with her, or if she sprinted on all fours like a hound.

The air shifted, and I veered sideways, narrowly escaping a swipe of her deadly claws. Black surged around me, and for a moment, I was weightless. Heartbeats later, the darkness broke. My feet stuttered as I found myself in a different area of the swamp.

A howl of frustration went up from somewhere nearby, too close for comfort. I ran away from the sound, vaulting over mossy rocks and fallen trees. The sounds of pursuit followed me as I splashed into another shallow pool. I risked a glance behind me and bit back a sob at the fearsome image of the demon crashing through the brush.

I knew the moment she saw me, knee-deep in the acrid water. She stalked toward me with a smile that looked all wrong on her canine face. That smile transformed into a snarl as Inky and Storm picked me up again.

This time, I started running the moment I touched back down. I had to trust that my protectors would not face me toward danger.

Ani bellowed her fury, and farther off, I heard Evander calling for me.

I didn't dare giveaway my location in case Ani hadn't yet picked up on my scent.

A wall of shadows erupted in front of me, but I didn't slow. I knew those shadows.

The path cleared, and I flung myself into Evander's waiting arms. One hand cupped the back of my head as I panted into his chest.

"Kat, I want you to run." His voice was a rumble against my skin.

I shook my head, unable to form words. I'd been running, didn't he know? My leg throbbed at the mere thought of going any farther.

"Do you remember what I told you about the Corridor?"

I nodded.

"Ani is night-bound as we are. My shadows can take you to the Corridor, then I want you to run until you're back in the world of the living."

I jerked back. "You want me to leave?"

"Just for today." Evander brought his hands to either side of my face, eyes beseeching. "After nightfall, I will come for you. I'll find you."

"But—"

Ani howled again, the sound nearly upon us.

Everything I was about to say was pushed aside by Evander's lips on mine. The kiss left me breathless. A quick, passionate caress that left every inch of me burning.

I grasped for words, but before I could find them, darkness engulfed me.

CHAPTER 42

Katrin

The shadows dispersed, all but two fleeing back to their master. I looked around at the misty Corridor, the skeletal trees as foreboding as they were my first time through. There was no way of knowing how far the shadows had taken me from Sam's. My leg pulsed with pain, and I hoped Evander and Sam could keep Ani distracted long enough for me to get through, though part of me wanted to return and fight beside them. I knew that line of thought was foolish. They were demons and I was mortal. It wasn't a fair fight.

I didn't think to ask if I should expect to see other demons along this path. Like Evander, they would be unable to cross into the land of the living until sundown, but that didn't mean they couldn't travel throughout The Between as we had.

My steps faltered as I shuffled along. I had no idea how far I needed to travel, nor what direction. There were several paths that branched off from the one I traveled, but it all looked the same. Again, I trusted the shadows to steer me to the right choice.

Inky and Storm remained by my side, flowing in and out of various shapes as they moved. When they paused, I paused, wondering if they heard someone approaching or if I'd somehow taken a wrong turn.

Then I heard it. The sound I was sure would haunt my dreams for the rest of my life. The baying of a half-dog demon.

And there she was, sprinting down the Corridor directly for me.

My leg buckled as I tried to run, but the silky, cool grip of the shadows wrapped around me. I held my breath as they carried me, setting me back on my feet all too soon. Without sparing a glance for my pursuer, I hobbled as fast as I could down the tree-lined Corridor, knowing it would not be enough.

No sooner had the thought struck me than my shadow guards swooped in again. They held me for even less time, and I knew they were flagging. Still, if they could fight through the dregs of their strength, I could do the same. I bit back a cry as I launched into a full-on sprint, gliding in and out of the shadows like little bursts of speed.

Ani's growls grew louder, her footfalls closer, but I knew we stood a chance when I spied the beams of sunlight piercing the forest ahead.

Warmth seeped down my leg, and I knew without looking that I'd reopened my wound. The metallic scent of blood filled my nostrils. My chest burned and pain blossomed below my ribs, but I pushed on, imagining the feel of that sunlight on my face.

My shadows fell back, and I bid them a silent farewell as I tumbled to the ground and landed in a pool of sunlight.

I looked back at where I'd come from, but there was no trace of Ani, no trace of the Corridor or my shadow guards. I hoped they would tell Evander I'd made it. I wouldn't be able to find my way back without him.

The sun warmed my face just as I'd imagined. I couldn't believe I made it. I tipped my head back and closed my eyes, waiting for my heart to return to its normal rhythm.

Some time later, I startled awake, surprised to find the sun lower in the sky. I'd had no intention of drifting off, especially in the middle of a forest road. I sat up, feeling slightly dazed and more than a little disappointed to find I could still see out of only my right eye.

"All right, Miss?"

Lightning zipped through my body, and I repressed the instant urge to flee as I turned to find a modest coach and concerned footman.

"Yes," I said, pushing to my feet. With growing horror, I realized how much of my shadows were visible in my current ensemble.

I brought my hand up to my forehead, not needing to feign the headache as I covered my face. "I must have fallen from my horse."

The young man looked relieved at my response until the door to the coach opened and a statuesque woman stepped out.

"Don't be a fool, Harold. Anyone can see the poor dear is in need of help." Though she spoke my language, her accent marked her as being from another territory. Perhaps I wasn't so far from home after all. "Please join me inside the carriage. I'll see that you're taken care of."

The woman's face was kind, but I couldn't shake the feeling that there was something off about her. Neither could I continue to await Evander in the middle of the forest while injured.

I curtsied graciously and the footman offered his arm to help me into the coach.

Once inside, I felt immediate shame at my appearance compared to the woman helping me. From afar, she'd been beautiful, but up close, she was beauty personified. Her unmarked skin was radiant in the sunlight. Rosy cheeks, full lips, and bright eyes played in perfect harmony upon her face. Her sunny, blonde hair was styled into an elegant coiffure, and her form fitting dress revealed she had all the desired curves as well. She seemed older than me but not old. Mature yet youthful. Ageless and timeless. An enigma made flesh.

I'd taken the rear-facing seat opposite her and regretted not sitting beside her as she leaned forward and fixed me with an all-seeing stare.

"It *is* you," she said, slapping her thigh. "I should have known." Twisting, she propped one leg on the seat beside her, and leaned back into the corner of the coach. She knocked against the carriage wall two times. There was a sharp command from the driver and we eased into motion.

I didn't know if I was more caught off guard by her informal posture or her words, but after several seconds of gawking, I found my tongue. "Do I know you?"

The woman scoffed. "I know it has been some time since I last visited you, Katrin, but I thought our first meeting was rather memorable."

"I'm sorry," I started, unsure why I was apologizing.

"I guess it has been over eight years now. I thought my parting gift would have made an impression," she said, running a pointed nail over the darkened side of my face.

I flinched away from her touch, brows creased as what she said sank in. "*You* marked me?" I gasped, taking in the woman before me with new eyes.

"Indeed, I did."

"But I thought Death—Behryn—marked me?"

"I know you did, silly girl, but that's all right." She waved me off with a flick of her bejeweled hand. "I'm blamed for everything. I don't mind him taking credit for this one thing."

My brow crinkled in confusion. "I don't understand. Who are you?"

She leaned forward as if sharing a secret, lowering her voice so that I was forced to sit forward as well to hear her. "Some people call me Fate, but you may call me Moira."

"Fate?" I sat back stunned, and she hummed her affirmation. "Why did you mark me?"

"Well, if you must know, Behryn insisted I do it when I revealed that you are destined to become Queen of the Afterworld."

"Excuse me?"

"An amazing destiny, if I do say so myself."

"But I don't want to be Queen of the Afterworld. I could never marry that monster." The thought alone had my stomach roiling.

Moira shrugged. "It is not for me to decide such things. Nor you, I'm afraid."

"So you've come here to warn me?"

Her answering laugh was a bubbling brook. "Not at all. There's no sense in warning you of something that can't be changed. I merely wanted to see what all the fuss was about."

"What fuss?"

"Don't you know?" Moira smiled conspiratorially. "Your presence at *Tyr Anigh* has caused quite a stir."

I shook my head. "What do you mean? My presence in The Between is known only by Evander and myself..." I trailed off. Clearly, if she was bringing it up, my stay there had not been the secret I thought it to be. Something I ought to have figured out between Death's Fangs and Ani. I dropped my head into my hands as the realization struck me.

"You do amuse, little Katrin."

It had been many years since anyone had called me little, but she seemed to say it with affection rather than condescension.

"How?"

"Behryn, of course. He came running to my door the moment he saw you with Evander."

"But he didn't see me. I was hidden." I thought back to that day and distinctly remembered Inky and Storm blocking me from view.

"Behind some shadows, I know. You have much to learn about demons, my dear." She leaned back, inspecting her nails as her words landed like physical blows.

"Death knows where I am."

"Not exactly."

"Explain," I snapped. Fate didn't balk at my tone, which was good because I was through apologizing for it.

"While it was foolish to think the shadows could hide you from Death, it seems they managed to help camouflage your mark. When His Highness came to me, he asked only about the mysterious woman staying with Evander. He sent me to investigate, not knowing you were the very girl I'd marked all those years ago."

I deflated as all the air whooshed out of my lungs. Abandoning decorum, I slumped in my seat, tipping my head back and closing my eyes. "He doesn't know it's me," I whispered the words that moments before had seemed impossible.

"He doesn't know *yet*."

My head shot up, and I glared at the woman across from me. Her quicksilver eyes met mine, cold and assessing. Considering what I knew about Fate, I would need to proceed carefully.

"What is it that you want from me?" I asked slowly.

Moira inspected her nails. "There is nothing you could offer me that I don't already have. As it stands, I have no plans to alert the King to your true identity. It is not in the stars for me to do so. But do not think that means you are safe. Behryn has many in his employ, and it is only a matter of time before he learns the truth."

"That sounds like a warning."

"I suppose it is."

Cocking her head to the side, she regarded me thoughtfully. Her nose crinkled in distaste as her eyes flicked over my ruined dress and bandaged ankle. I ran a hand through my hair, fingers catching on the tangled mess. She lifted a hand and a sudden wind tore through the cabin. It pulled at my dress, making ribbons of satin. My hair whipped around me, and I lifted both of my arms to shield my face. Just as fast, it was gone.

"That's better," said Moira.

Tentatively, I lowered my arms, expecting to see her as wind-whipped as I felt. She rose, still the picture of grace and beauty, and shuffled toward the exit.

It was then I noticed the pain in my leg was gone. I looked down and gasped at the modest yet clean linen dress where there had just been rags. It was nowhere near as fine as Moira's garments, but it was free of dirt and grime. I didn't need the attention she surely commanded.

My fingers danced over the pewter fabric as if it would disappear beneath my touch. I lifted the skirt to confirm what I already knew. Gone was the filthy bandage and torn flesh. She had healed me.

"Wait!" I yelled after her. She turned, and I hurried to say what I could before I thought better of it. "If you marked me, can you take it away?"

Moira's brows pinched together as she tilted her head, regarding me like a cat sizing up its prey. "It is within my power to do so."

"Then will you? Please, I want no part of this."

"You cannot lie to me. Besides, the removal of your mark would do little to improve your situation, dear Katrin. Behryn will find you with or without it, and I think you'll find that bearing the mark has its advantages." I could only stare as she reached for the handle and opened the door. "This is your stop."

There was nothing remarkable about the place, but it was as good as any to disembark from this hell ride.

"Remember, Death is not bound by the constraints of night. You would do well to remain inside until your reaper can come for you."

With that advice, the carriage pulled away, leaving me stranded once again.

CHAPTER 43

The Ferrier

Ani disappeared as soon as I sent Katrin away. Sam and I followed as best we could. With my shadows otherwise engaged, we had no choice but to run as mortals, quickly losing her to the maze of the Corridor.

We stopped when the trail went cold, both of us panting for breath. Sam slid to the ground at the base of a tree, arms resting on his knees.

I paced the area in front of him. My fists clenched and un-clenched.

"Do you suppose," Sam said, his voice unnervingly calm, "that this game of prey and hunter has only made him desire her more?"

I remained silent, though the thought had crossed my mind.

He tipped his head back, eyes glazed as he looked toward the skeletal branches. "What could he want with her?"

My shrug was lost on his still distant gaze. "Whatever it is, he wanted her enough to mark her but not enough to take her then."

The mystery had driven me mad these last few weeks. I suspected the answer to her curse lay in that reason. If we knew what drove him to hunt her, perhaps we could change his mind. "I guess I could ask him."

"Ask Behryn? Are you mad?" Sam looked at me now, brow crinkled in concern. "Asking Death to explain his actions is like asking fire why it burns."

I nodded, half lost in thought.

The back of my neck tingled, and I pivoted, sighing at the surge of energy that accompanied my returning shadows. Even drained as they were, their presence buoyed my strength.

"She made it," I translated the shadow's whispers for Sam. His body slumped in relief, and the gratitude I felt in that moment gave me pause. We'd never been close, Sam and I. We were more acquaintances than friends, but somehow among the thousands of reapers, we'd connected over our similar stories. His willingness to help had been a welcome surprise when I'd had nowhere else to turn.

Sam pushed to his feet, eyeing the darkening sky. "You've got an hour, maybe two, before sundown, depending on what territory she ended up in."

The shadows continued to relay information. "Ani is there. Waiting."

Sam dusted off his clothes. "Then I guess we better get there before sundown."

Sending one shadow to fetch the carriage, the rest worked in tandem to transport Sam and me as close to Katrin—and Ani—as possible. It was slow going, especially with two of us, but I didn't dare leave Sam behind and risk taking on Ani alone. She'd already proved to be a formidable opponent, and I got the sense she had only been playing with us thus far.

We blinked in and out of darkness, the forest growing darker with each step closer to our destination. As we neared the place where Ani waited, I instructed the shadows to veer off the path. They deposited us in the thick of the forest, utterly spent, their shrunken forms nearly transparent. It was another mystery that these creatures served me so thoroughly.

I placed my hand over my heart and bowed my head in thanks.

One shadow shifted, appearing to point behind us. I nodded in understanding and pulled Sam into a jog. Leaves and branches crunched underfoot, but I didn't dare slow enough to tread carefully.

Sam spotted Ani before I did. She was a smudge of black against the gray trees. Her focus narrowed to a single spot along the path. The way Katrin had left?

My chest eased as I beheld no signs of a struggle. The tension radiating off Ani suggested Katrin had gotten away just in time.

I signaled for Sam to circle behind her, slowing my pace to give him a chance to get into position. Ani gave no indication she knew we were there. I hoped the element of surprise would give us the edge we needed.

Daring a step closer, I crept behind a thick, oak trunk. Still, Ani's focus did not waiver. I caught movement on her other side. Sam met my eye and gave a slight nod.

With a deep breath in, I stepped out from around the tree and froze as someone else appeared on the road right where Ani had been staring. My heartbeat quickened as my first thought was of Katrin, even knowing that she could not cross over on her own.

Sure enough, the woman that appeared was fair in both skin and hair with not a mark to be seen upon her skin.

Ani snarled, and I ducked, gesturing for Sam to hide as well. From his facial expression, I gathered that he knew the newcomer. Knew her and was not pleased to see her.

The two women exchanged words, but none of them reached my ears. When Ani bared her teeth, the other woman reacted with lightning speed, reaching up to capture her with one hand on her neck. I'd seen few creatures move with such speed, fewer still who could walk between worlds at will. If this woman wasn't in Behryn's employ, she was at least as powerful as him.

The question remained. Was she friend or foe?

More words were spoken. Against my better judgment, I inched closer, trying to capture the whispers on the wind. The newcomer frowned at something Ani said and sent her flying backwards. Ani yelped as she sprawled on the ground several paces away. She glared across the clearing but made no move to retaliate. The other woman took one step toward her, and Ani scrambled to her feet, turned tail, and ran in the opposite direction.

On the far side of the scene, Sam slowly shook his head. In disbelief? Horror? I didn't get the chance to find out before the remaining woman called out.

"I know you are there." Though she didn't shout, her words carried through the forest. "You need not fear me."

I stepped clear from the tree I'd hidden behind, drawing her eye. Over her shoulder, Sam's eyes widened. I gave him a subtle head tilt in return and hoped he understood my meaning.

Hide, my eyes beseeched him.

For all I knew, she'd guessed at there being someone nearby. By making myself known, I hoped to keep Sam's presence a secret. Raising my palms for good measure, I stalked toward the unknown woman.

Every step closer revealed more about her. The finery of her clothes, the lack of lines upon her skin, the haughty tilt of her chin. It wasn't until I neared that I realized how much shorter she stood. The top of her head sat just below my chin, but she stared down her nose at me nonetheless.

"May I ask whose acquaintance I have the pleasure of making?" I asked, inclining my head.

"There's no need to stand on ceremony, Evander."

I tensed at her use of my name.

"Nor does Samedi need to remain hidden." She glanced over her shoulder to where Sam hid, now reappearing to join us on the path.

He passed me a look that conveyed all the confusion I felt.

Facing the stranger, Sam turned on his full charm, transforming into the gentleman he'd once been. "You have us at a disadvantage, my lady, for you clearly know our names, but we do not know yours."

The woman looked him up and down, unimpressed. "I am Moira, though it will do you little good. I've come to let you know that Miss Fil'Owen is safe for now."

A weight lifted from my shoulders as Sam flashed me a dazzling smile. I had so many questions. Sensing the need to tread carefully where this woman was concerned, I asked the most pressing. "Where is she?"

"She is beyond." Moira gestured to the road behind her, suggesting Katrin had made it to the world of the living. "I left her at an inn. When you cross, my footman will be waiting to take you to her. He is blessed with the Sight and knows for whom he waits."

The sun had nearly set. A small band of light illuminated the horizon. "Thank you, Lady Moira," I said, placing my palm over my heart.

"Do not thank me yet, reaper."

My blood iced. Instinctively, the shadows gathered closer to me. "What do you mean?"

Moira looked from me to Sam and back again. "Her mark is a mark of Fate. It cannot be undone. Her stars cannot be unwritten. Fetch her if you will, but it is the Afterworld that calls and to the Afterworld she will go. Her days are numbered."

"How long?" I growled, unwilling to accept the word of some stranger in the woods. "If you know so much, how long does she have left?"

Moira considered me. She opened her mouth and closed it as though debating her answer. "Do you really wish to know?"

Yes.

No.

I didn't want to know, but would Kat? Was it worth it to put a timestamp on our time together?

My silence was answer enough. Moira pressed her lips together and nodded once.

"Why her?" I asked.

She shrugged, and I balled my hands into fists to keep from shaking her.

"Why anyone? That is what they all want to know, isn't it? Why was he poor and she rich? Why did she die young? Why did victory favor one kingdom over another? Why were you both made reapers and denied entrance to the Afterworld?" She shrugged again. "I cannot say."

"Cannot or will not?" Sam asked.

"Knowledge is not the gift you think it is. There is beauty in ignorance. Happiness in naiveté. Enjoy what you have today, Evander, for tomorrow is never guaranteed."

Without another word, she strode away, a specter floating through the forest. Sam and I watched until she faded from view, the last of the sunlight fading with her.

Sam turned to me, brows raised in silent question. Shaking off the strange encounter, I nodded once and slipped through the door to the mortal world.

CHAPTER 44

Katrin

I'd never patronized an establishment such as this. Either I'd been too young or too firmly distanced from society to ever find myself in this sort of place.

The noise struck me first. After so many weeks being one of only two—or now, three—souls in a given place, the boisterous crowd hit me like a physical blow. I staggered back upon opening the door, clamping my hands over my ears until I could adjust to the clamor.

A lively band played from the far corner. Several people danced, clapped, and stomped their feet along to the bawdy tune. Everywhere I turned different conversations vied for attention over the music. The crowded bar overflowed with drinks and still, people shouting for more.

No one paid me any heed as I tried to blend into the stone walls. Moira had done well in selecting a dress that wouldn't draw attention. I was unremarkable but clean. The setting sun cast enough shadows around the space that I hoped my own would not stand out as unnatural. Luckily, I'd had the forethought to draw my hair over the left side of my face.

I crept through the room, avoiding stares and errant elbows, and finally found a table in a secluded room off the main dining area. The patrons in this area appeared to be more of the travel-weary sort, content to make small talk and enjoy a hot meal in relative peace.

Not long after I slid into the small corner booth, a curvy woman with a stained apron sidled over to take my order. At least, that's what I assumed she said, but her flowy, lilting words meant nothing to me.

I shook my head and pointed to my mouth. "I'm sorry. I don't speak your language."

I spoke slowly in case she knew any of my native tongue, but she only smiled and bobbed a curtsy, returning moments later with a lukewarm ale and a bowl of stew. The ale was sour, but the stew was filling. After I finished, I contemplated licking the bowl clean, only my desire to stay unnoticed stilled my tongue.

Sipping my ale, my thoughts strayed to the new direction my life had taken. I supposed this had always been the trajectory of my life, but now I was in on the plans. Aware of them but unable to alter them to my will—a fact which grated on me.

Queen of the Afterworld.

What an insane notion.

It had been mere weeks since I'd wrapped my mind around the idea that Death was coming for me. Now, I had to believe he wanted me as his wife? I shivered despite the warmth of the inn.

"Miss Fil'Owen."

I looked up to see Fate's footman—Harold, that was his name—standing beside my table. "Yes?" What more did Fate have in store for me that she must send her manservant to fetch me from where she'd unceremoniously abandoned me?

"The Ferrier is here for you, Miss."

I jumped to my feet. Sure enough, the sun had fully set in the time I'd been contemplating my entire existence. The footman dropped a handful of coppers on the table for my tab, and I nodded in thanks. Without waiting for him to lead, I rushed from the room, weaving through the crowded main dining room and exploding out the front door.

I ran into Evander's waiting arms, overcome by the feeling that I was coming home. It was a preposterous notion, but breathing in his familiar scent, I could understand why my body reacted that way. Fate had been wrong. Behryn wasn't my destiny, Evander was.

Shadows erupted around us, cocooning us in their cool embrace. He pulled away first, and I made a sound of impatience as his eyes scanned me from head to toe. His fingers followed, confirming what his eyes refused to believe, that I was well and whole and here.

Taking his hand in mine, I pressed a kiss to each of his fingertips. His eyes darkened, and I bit my lip as he leaned in. My eyelids fluttered closed, waiting for the press of his lips to mine.

A pointed cough had us springing apart like young lovers caught in a compromising position. The irony wasn't lost on me as the shadows around us cleared to reveal Sam leaning casually against the side of a carriage. Heat rose to my cheeks as he exchanged a knowing glance with Evander.

"I'm sure we all have much to catch up on." Sam winked at me. "But we still have an angry demon out for our blood—several, in fact. It may be prudent to keep moving."

I nodded and allowed Evander to pull me into the carriage as Sam held open the door. He entered behind me, and I was struck by the amount of space the two reapers occupied. Once the door closed, there was hardly room to breathe between the three of us, let alone move.

Evander and I sat on the same bench I'd occupied less than an hour earlier while Sam took Moira's seat. I'd expected to see her within and searched the cabin for evidence of her existence.

When Evander caught my eye, I asked him the question that had niggled at the back of my mind since the footman came to fetch me. "Are you working with Fate now?"

At Evander's genuine expression of surprise, I looked to Sam. "We are in her carriage, are we not? That is her footman driving us."

Sam glanced behind him like he could see the man in question, but Evander answered. "You mean the fair-haired woman, Moira?"

I nodded slowly, marking the wide-eyed look that passed between the men.

"She only told us her name and where to find you," said Sam. "We did not know that she was the Lady of Fate."

So I told them of my encounter with Fate and all that she had revealed. When I finished, Evander cursed. I echoed the sentiment.

"Now, what?" Sam asked, the corners of his mouth pulled down.

"I think we must return to the manor." Evander worried the edge of his cloak between his fingers. "It was your original plan, Katrin, to search the libraries for anything that might contain a clue to freeing you."

I shook my head. "A fool's plan. Besides, we've already done that."

"Yes, but now we have a lead."

"And what if we still find nothing?"

"Then we seek out other libraries, hunt down forgotten scrolls of wisdom or whatever is necessary to see it undone."

"There are other reapers who would oppose Behryn." Sam's voice was soft, a contrast to his usually boisterous self. "I'll put out feelers for aid. Surely, there are some who would answer the call, if only for a little excitement from the monotony of reaping."

I buried my face in my hands as if I could hide from this destiny laid out before me. Suddenly, this selfish quest to free myself from an early grave had become something that felt insurmountable. "Why does this feel like we are declaring war?"

Silence answered, and I knew the two men were exchanging more glances, holding private conversations through looks alone. "Out with it," I said. I didn't want to be kept in the dark anymore.

"If Behryn learns that you are the wife he so desperately seeks and knows that we have been actively keeping you from him..." Evander hesitated. "He will see it as an act of war already, regardless of what we do from here."

A new fear blossomed in my chest, and I looked up sharply. "What will he do to you for aiding me?"

Sam opened his mouth to answer, but Evander silenced him with a sharp look, capturing my hand between his. "It doesn't matter. We knew the risk when we agreed to help."

"You couldn't have known why he wanted me."

"It doesn't matter," Sam echoed. "Going against Death in any capacity would result in the same consequences."

His expression told me I didn't want to know, but my imagination had no trouble filling in the gaps between their words. If I'd known trying to save myself would put others at risk, would I have done it?

I couldn't answer for the woman I'd been at the crossroads that night. I no longer knew her. The woman I was now couldn't stomach the thought of any harm coming to the reapers.

I had barely enough time to lift the window covering before my stew and ale made an unpleasant return.

"Lovely." Sam's tone was dry as I spat, but I refrained from glaring at him as the carriage bounced over the uneven road.

Swiping my sleeve across my lips, I closed my eyes and sank to the floor. There I knelt in a puddle of gray and laid my head upon the seat cushion until the carriage slowed to a stop.

The mortal footman, unable—or perhaps unwilling—to pass into the Corridor, had promised to take us to yet another entry point. Though I could discern nothing of the hidden Corridor beyond, I wondered at his knowledge of their locations. Perhaps his Sight, which allowed him to see departed souls and those of other worlds, also gave him the ability to sense what lay beyond. Or maybe he had Fate to thank for that information.

Evander stepped from the carriage first, scanning the area for any threats before reaching back to help me down. I felt immediate relief at having the firm ground beneath my feet. Though the ride had been short, I couldn't stomach another minute within the cramped space.

Evander kept a firm hold of my hand as we walked. His touch radiated comfort and safety. Part of me balked at the surety I felt at his side, knowing it was only temporary, only fulfilling his end of the bargain. The rest of me reveled in the confidence of standing with someone as powerful as he. I was strong by proxy. How would I have expected to return to life as I'd known it? How could the life I'd known be anything but mundane by comparison?

Sam followed close behind as he stewed. The three of us stepped off the road to make room for the carriage to depart. After a farewell dip of his chin, the footman urged the horses into motion.

I watched in silence as they continued down the mortal road, half expecting them to disappear into The Between as we would. Eventually, the coach's lanterns faded from view, and I turned to face Evander and Sam, twin expressions of determination upon their faces.

"We should have borrowed a lantern," Sam said.

Evander nodded in agreement.

"I can see just fine," I said, and I could. Though full darkness had descended and the moon was absent from the night's sky, I saw everything with perfect clarity.

"You don't have to prove anything," said Evander. "I can guide you until we reach my carriage."

"But I can see." Pulling my hand from Evander's, I marched toward the road with all the confidence of someone walking in full daylight.

I laughed as Sam and Evander stumbled after me, waiting for them to catch up.

Evander did not share my humor. Upon reaching me, he captured my chin with his hand, tilting it up until my gaze met his. His eyes roved over my face, brows drawn and mouth a harsh line. His other hand came up to cover my eye. My good eye, or so I thought.

I stared up at Evander, unblinking.

"What do you see?" he asked, his voice a low rumble.

It wasn't possible. "It is as if someone has lit a thousand candles across the land. I can see you as plain as day. Both of you."

Grasping his wrist, I moved his hand from one eye to the other.

Darkness.

"And now?" he asked.

I shook my head, unwilling to believe what my own eyes showed me. "Only the barest hint of shapes."

"Remarkable." Sam stepped up beside Evander, little more than a shadow against the night.

Evander's hands fell away from my face and once again, I could see everything.

"What does it mean?" I asked.

"It means you just got a lot more interesting, Kitty Kat," said Sam, waving a hand in front of my face.

Batting his hand away, I huffed in annoyance. Evander continued to watch me with a mixture of surprise and suspicion.

"It's obviously a side-effect of your mark," Sam supplied. "Perhaps a gift from Fate."

"I asked her to remove it," I admitted.

Evander's head tilted as his eyes squinted in question. "Your eye?"

"My mark! She refused, obviously. Something about how Death would come for me anyway. Pointless to give me false hope, I guess. She did mention something about there being advantages to keeping the mark. Do you think this is what she meant?"

Sam shrugged. "Could be."

"Come, then." Evander held out his hand. "We shall explore the full benefits of this power. From my perspective, it can only be an advantage."

Though I felt none of the hope I'd had the first time I entered The Between, I took his outstretched hand and allowed him to lead me through the doorway.

Evander's familiar black carriage and horses waited on the other side, silent and gleaming. I was glad they were the only ones that greeted us on the other side. I'd accrued far too many enemies for my liking. We made it one step past the barrier between worlds before Evander cried out in pain.

CHAPTER 45
The Ferrier

I erupted in pain.

Invisible blades stabbed through my gut. Fire seared through every limb. My skin ached. My clothes chafed. Even breathing became too much. I fell to the ground, hardly registering the damp earth as it soaked through my trousers. Wave after wave of pain crested and broke against me. I heaved and trembled, awaiting an end that was too long in coming.

Finally, the torture receded, and I sat back on my heels. My muscles spasmed in the aftermath, my body still trying to fend off the invisible attacker.

"What was that?" Katrin's voice held more anger than concern, but when I looked up her eyes shone with unshed tears, with fear.

Fear *for* me, not of me.

The thought was enough to throw me off balance. I stumbled as I stood and Sam saved me the trouble of answering as I dusted off my rumpled pants. "He's been resisting his duties."

"Why would you do that?"

Katrin's glare burned white hot, but I didn't balk from it. I faced her head on, taking in her light and dark halves. Two sides of the same coin, one that pulled her toward death and the other life but nothing tethering her to this world. Like all, she would pass from The Between into whichever world would claim her, and here I would remain.

"Because you needed me," I answered honestly.

She jabbed a finger toward the portal we'd passed through. "Those souls need you."

"They can wait." I held up a hand before she could interject. She scowled but remained quiet. "You are my priority. I am made to ferry the dead, but I promised to protect you, and so I shall."

"To free yourself?" There was a question in her eyes, a vulnerability that she hadn't allowed me to see before.

Stepping into her space, I gave her time to retreat before placing my hands on either side of her face. I willed her to see the truth in my eyes, to hear the conviction in my voice. "To save us both, Kat."

Her eyes flicked to Sam who shrugged as if to say "what can you do". When her gaze returned to mine, she nodded. The movement was subtle, unsure, but it was there.

"Shall we?" A phantom pain tugged below my chest, but I ignored it as I gestured to my carriage. Katrin looked as though she wanted to say more but turned and entered the coach.

"Good luck with that one," Sam said as we clasped hands.

"You're sure you don't want a ride?" I offered as distance was a curious thing in The Between.

"Van, you couldn't pay me to enter that carriage right now." He laughed, but I sensed it for the act that it was. His expression quickly sobered, his other hand coming up to grip my shoulder. "This will be an uphill battle."

I nodded. "It already is. Thank you for all you've done for her, for us. It means a lot."

"She deserves better."

"We all do," I said, clapping him on the back. "Next time I see you, bring allies."

"I hope this is not farewell, my friend." With a dip of his chin, Sam released my hand and strode into the mists.

I felt it then, not the pull of the soul, but something greater, like game pieces being set into motion. But if Behryn was king, and Katrin queen, did that make me a knight or a pawn?

***

Halfway through the journey to the manor, I heard a rustle of fabric as the curtain of the small front window was drawn aside. For several long moments, the galloping hooves were the only sound. As the silence stretched, I worried she was expecting me to speak first. I opened my mouth, but no words came out.

What was there to say?

I wouldn't apologize for my actions. I'd vowed to protect her, and if that meant shirking my duties as Ferrier, so be it.

"Does it hurt when the souls call to you?" Katrin's voice floated to me in the dark like an apparition, tentative and fragile.

My comfort had always been the furthest thing from my mind, and it took me a moment to answer. "Not usually. It can be unpleasant like a persistent tug, but over time, the tug grows stronger."

"What happens if you ignore it completely?"

I lifted my eyes from the trail, considering. "When I was first enslaved, I fought it. I refused to answer the summons for days. At first, it was distracting. Then, it became painful. By the fifth day, the physical compulsion overpowered any will I had. It dragged me like a man possessed through the Corridor and back to the world of the living. That first night, I ferried three souls. To this day, I do not know if it was the length of time or the number of souls that finally beat me."

"That sounds awful."

I shrugged though she couldn't see me. "It is the price I paid."

"And what price shall I pay?" Her voice was little more than a whisper. I wasn't sure if she'd meant for me to hear her, so I remained quiet, hoping she'd never have to pay a price and at the same time, suspecting that she already had.

We reached the manor and I pulled to a stop inside the gate. Dropping to a crouch, I spun to face the window and sought out her mismatched eyes within. "Your bargain is with me. If we fail, I'll not hold you to any repercussions."

"But Fate will."

"Somehow, I got the sense that Fate was on your side." Slipping from the driver's seat, I made quick work of closing and locking the gate behind us—the first time I'd done so since Katrin had come. She looked at me curiously as I returned to the carriage and opened her door.

"It won't stop Behryn," I explained. "But it should help keep out anyone else that comes around or, at least, slow them down." I made a show of commanding two shadows to stand guard at the gate as well, messengers who would alert me if anyone or anything came near. There was still Death's Fangs to consider.

I sent two more shadows to sweep the manor while I untacked the horses. My fingers slipped into the familiar rhythm as Katrin waited for them to return.

"Sometimes, I think I made a mistake. That I was foolish to chase life instead of making the most of what I had. What if I've traded away the last days of my life for nothing?"

My hands stilled. She didn't intend the words to be hurtful, but they struck me like a fist to the gut. "You have always been free to return home if that is what you desire."

I didn't look at her as I spoke, but I sensed her ire anyway.

"That is not what I meant." Impatience sharpened her tone, and she exhaled a slow, steady breath. "It is only that I left my family without saying goodbye, hoping that I would see them again. Now, I'm not so sure. I did not expect Death to learn of my presence in The Between. That I've been compromised puts everything else into perspective. He could find me, take me away, and my parents would be none the wiser."

"The choice you made was one of desperation. No one can fault you for the path you chose when you thought there was nowhere else to go."

I paused my task long enough to seek out her form in the darkness. She nodded, but her eyes remained distant, her mind likely forging a dozen other possible scenarios.

I knew the taste of regret. It was not something that could be easily washed away.

The shadows returned, and I waved her forth. "Go on, take your Midnight and Thunder or whatever you call them and take a bath."

"Inky and Storm." Her tone was serious, but a slip of a smile ghosted across her lips.

"Of course. How could I forget?"

"Be sure it doesn't happen again," she said, sauntering toward the entrance.

I took my time freeing the horses and returning everything to the stable. In the manor, I looked for anything amiss, furniture out of place, doors open that should be closed.

When I could avoid it no longer, I passed by the bathing chamber Katrin occupied. The door was shut, as expected. Though my mind conjured a million excuses to open it, I settled for pressing my ear to the wood.

The faint sound of lapping water could be heard within. Unbidden, my mind conjured an image of Katrin shoulder deep, every part of her yet unknown to me hidden beneath frothy suds.

I pushed the thought aside.

Even before our last conversation, I knew there was no future for us. The Between was a temporary escape for her, but it was my prison. If we were not cleaved apart by Death, we would be separated by life.

The doorknob gleamed in the candlelight, so close and yet utterly out of reach.

I shoved away, needing to put distance between myself and my dark thoughts.

Katrin's voice echoed in my mind. For a moment, I thought I'd imagined her calling my name until I heard it again, clearer.

"I can hear you brooding out there."

She couldn't know I was there, unless...my eyes strayed to the shadows around me, and I cursed. Betrayed by my own creatures.

Still, I could leave. Leave and ignore every instinct, every ounce of my blood urging me forward. *Walk away*, my mind commanded, but each step only brought me closer to the bathroom door. My hand found the knob, though somehow I had enough sense to leave it only partially ajar.

Steam billowed out, scented with jasmine and rose. I breathed in the heady aroma and closed my eyes.

"You can't possibly," I replied dryly.

Her throaty chuckle caught me off guard. I went as taut as a bow string, hand clutching the door to keep from flinging it open.

"Was I wrong?" she asked. I could hear the smile in her voice.

"I didn't mean to intrude."

"And so you haven't. I was just finishing anyway."

Did I imagine the disappointment in her voice?

Water sloshed, and I pictured her rising from the bath like a siren, water dripping from every glorious curve. Were I a weaker man, I'd have pushed open the door and seen for myself. Her mark tormented me. I longed to see what parts of her were covered, longed to follow the dark trail with my hands, my tongue.

My own shadows shifted, sensing my restlessness.

The door swung wide. I released the handle in time to avoid stumbling after it, but my knees buckled anyway at the sight of Katrin wrapped in only a dressing gown, her hair tied back in a hasty chignon.

My eyes dipped to the swell of her breasts beneath the thin, dark fabric. Her nipples were peaked despite the heat billowing out from the bathing chamber.

"Say something," she breathed.

My mouth opened and closed as I willed my tongue to form words. I pulled my gaze back to her face, to her eyes, so wide and vulnerable in that moment.

"You never wear your hair up."

It was the wrong thing to say. Her face fell. It was a blink of pain, of hurt, so quick I might have missed it if my focus hadn't been wholly intent on her. She smiled, but it didn't reach her eyes.

"I don't have to hide here." She glanced down, fingers playing with the lace that edged her robe. "It's nice. Refreshing, actually. I don't have to care what anyone thinks of me."

I dared a step closer, close enough to mark her trembling hands as she feigned composure. "And what about what I think?"

Her head snapped up, teeth capturing her bottom lip.

I licked my own lips, remembering their pillowy softness.

"What do you think, Evander?" She looked up at me through half-lidded eyes.

"I think that you have driven me mad since the moment you halted me at that crossroads." I closed the distance between us, snaking a hand around her waist as I pulled her body flush against mine. "You are the most captivating creature I've ever met, and I would like nothing more than to—"

Shadows danced around us, a frenzied rush of darkness that demanded attention. I cursed. Katrin's brow furrowed with confusion, and I pulled away with a growl.

"It's Behryn," I tried to explain. "He's—"

"Here."

Chapter 46

Katrin

The shadows scattered, and Behryn came into view, pale skin glowing in the candlelight. The dark marks across his head and neck stood out in stark contrast to his white and gold suit. He almost looked the part of the white knight, aside from the dark eyes that marked him as a demon.

"Hello, Katrin," Death growled. "It is a pleasure to finally meet you."

Evander shifted, placing himself between Behryn and me.

"The pleasure is yours alone." My voice shook despite the steel I'd intended.

Death had come. Death was here. He'd found me.

He smiled, revealing elongated canines. "I'd heard you had spirit. It would be a shame if someone broke it."

"Is that a threat?" I bit out, finding strength in my anger.

"Not at all." Behryn stalked closer, hands in his pockets, his gait deceptively casual.

Shadows swarmed to my side, Evander and I islands in a sea of darkness. Why didn't he reach for me? With his shadows, we could be swept away in the blink of an eye.

"I don't know what lies Evander has been telling you, but I am not your enemy," Death crooned.

"Bullshit," Evander spat.

Behryn's head whipped to him as though noticing him for the first time. He tsked, bringing one hand to his chest as though pained. "You wound me, Evander. After all I've done for you. I think you've interfered enough."

With a downward slash of Death's hand, Evander fell to his knees.

"No!" I lurched forward, halted by shadows that rose to block my path. Their translucent bodies hardened to resist where I pushed. Evander trembled where he knelt but made no move to rise. "What did you do to him?"

"I merely reminded him of his place."

"If you take her," Evander bit out, "it will be your undoing."

"Silence." Death flicked his wrist, and Evander fell quiet.

With growing horror, I watched as those same shadows that kept me from Evander yielded to an ever-approaching Behryn.

My surprise must have shown on my face. The king of the Afterworld chuckled, flicking a stray shadow from his shoulder like a piece of lint. "These shadows are a gift from me to my servant. It would be foolish to grant him anything that would give him power over me. They do not impede me, not even my sight."

His eyes danced with mirth, and I knew he'd seen me the first time he'd visited Evander. I'd thought his comment was mere coincidence, but he had known I was there. Known and done nothing.

"You're a monster," I spat.

I stepped back, needing space from the stalking beast. Two shadows diverted from the pool, lazily creeping in my direction. Inky and Storm. They eased closer, a step ahead of Death.

"I am nothing more than what I was born to be."

"You are cruel." My shadow guardians wrapped around my legs.

"Some would call me tough but fair." Though his steps were unhurried, Behryn was nearly upon me.

"You enslave people. You take their souls." A familiar tug urged me to step into the shadow and disappear. I shook my head. I would not leave Evander.

"I do not take what is not willingly given."

"You wish me dead."

Death paused a step away, head tilted as he regarded me.

"You needn't die to join me in the Afterworld. In fact, I find your vitality quite alluring." Behryn's gaze traveled the length of my body, reminding me that I wore only a dressing gown. "I could show you such wonders—"

I held up my hand, silencing whatever pretty promises he was about to make me. "I have no interest in coming with you. I want only to live out my life as I had before I was marked."

His eyes left mine, regarding that mark with open curiosity. "Was it so interesting, this life of yours? Was it so satisfying that you yearn to return to it even now? The Between is a mere glimpse of what awaits in the next world." He leaned in close until his words were a soft caress against my cheek. "I would give you everything."

He lifted a hand toward my face but did not touch me.

"Why?" I asked, squirming to create distance between us. "To convince me to be your bride? I have no interest in ruling the Afterworld with you." My eyes flicked to Evander, a small movement that Behryn noticed immediately.

His answering smile was all teeth. "What if I make you a deal?"

"What kind of deal?" I'd made one bargain already, was I so ready to enter into another?

"I'll free Evander of his indenture, return him to the world of the living." Behryn's hand dropped from my face, extending between us as an offering.

I eyed his hand dubiously, taking in the thick black lines that wove over it like veins. "What do you ask in return?"

"Come with me to the Afterworld and remain there for the remainder of your bargain to the Ferrier."

I didn't ask how he knew of our bargain, nor did I confirm how much time remained of our deal. "And after that time is up?"

He shrugged. "The choice is yours. You may return to the world of the living and live out the life you dreamed of as a child, or you will remain in the Afterworld as my queen."

Moira had said being queen was my destiny, that I was only prolonging the inevitable.

My focus shifted over Death's shoulder to the reaper still held in a position of submission. It should have been an easy choice. Here was Death, offering me everything I thought I wanted. The only cost was spending the rest of my twenty-first year in the Afterworld rather than The Between, with Death instead of Evander.

In less than a year, Evander and I could both be free, both be *alive.*

"I tire of these games, Katrin. Do we have a deal or not?"

A sour taste filled my mouth. All I knew of Death were his deceptions, and there, I had my answer.

The shadows tugged again, and this time, I submitted to the pull. As they gathered me into their cool embrace, Behryn's expression morphed into one of pure fury, brows furrowed and lips pulled back in a snarl. The world began to fade, and I conveyed the order to collect Evander as well. Darkness engulfed me, and a pale hand punched through.

I screamed as Death clawed his way into my shadows, tearing through them like bits of paper. His fingers grazed my bare skin, and he flew back as if pushed away by invisible hands. He grunted as he collided with the wall.

Redoubling their efforts, the shadows swirled around me. They plucked me from where I stood rooted to the floor and launched me into motion. Again, Death grabbed me from midair, and again, he was blasted by some unknown force.

I dropped to the floor, and strong hands lifted me back up. I whirled to find Evander, upright and furious, Death's control having slipped in the fray. He urged me behind him, turning to face Behryn where he dusted fallen plaster from his clothes.

The king straightened, heat rippling from him in waves. "You have twenty-four hours to consider my offer."

I debated telling him where he could shove his offer, but with a burst of flame, he was gone.

Evander faced me, mouth set in a grim line. I didn't give him the chance to speak before I fell into his arms and wept.

CHAPTER 47
The Ferrier

At the sight of her tears, I wished I were a different man—a better man—someone who knew all the right answers, someone who could take away the hurt.

There was something to be said for enduring so much so young. When all was said and done, you'd be left somehow older than your years, as though you'd lived more lives than one in the same span of time.

She'd been so brave, so strong for so long, but no more.

I had failed. Death had found her. And now, her greatest fear was coming with the next dawn. Of course, he would come for her when I was weakest. Of course, he would tempt and tease her with false hope. I should have prepared her for this, for *him*.

Katrin inhaled a shuddering breath, exhaling slowly. She repeated this several times as though willing herself to calm, but I could still feel the thundering beat of her heart in her chest.

All the while, I held her, not knowing if it would be my last chance to do so.

She lifted her head, not quite pulling away, but making enough space between us that I could meet her red-rimmed eyes. Salt tracks lined her cheeks, more visible against her shadowed skin.

"Tell me not to accept his deal." Her voice, pitched high with emotion, floundered over the words.

Taking her by the shoulders, I willed her to see the truth in my eyes. "Never accept any kind of bargain proposed by Death. He serves only himself."

She nodded like she'd already guessed as much. Her shoulders curled inward. "Then if neither of us are to be free, I think we should consider extending our current agreement."

I tensed. "For how long?"

Seeming to gird herself, she took another deep breath in and lifted her chin. "Indefinitely."

My hands dropped from her shoulders. Taking first one step back, then another, I pushed my fingers through my hair, tugging gently like it could wake me from this dream—this nightmare where Katrin asked to stay with me, and I had to refuse.

"No." The single syllable sounded cruel even to my own ears.

"Evander—" She stepped toward me, and I lifted my hands to ward her off. The hurt that flashed across her face nearly crumbled my resolve. "You saw what happened. My touch repelled him. *Our vow* repelled him."

"No!" I said more forcefully. "This is not a life." I waved my arms at the evidence around us. The crumbling manor, the hazy daylight, the demonic shadow creatures that cowered in corners.

Katrin's gaze swept the space, her expression thoughtful. "Death is not life either, Evander."

"You don't know that. The Afterworld is—"

"A complete mystery to both of us," she interjected. "But Behryn isn't. He's a monster. And in case you might have forgotten, he wants to take me as his bride. I will not be some mere inhabitant of the Afterworld. I will be its queen with all the duties that entails."

My mind conjured a list of duties a demon queen might have, each more terrible than the last. Not the least of which would be sharing the king's bed.

"Then I will find somewhere else for you to hide. Somewhere Behryn will never find you." Desperation clawed up my throat, making pretty promises as bad as Death.

Katrin's mouth hardened into a slim line, her jaw set. "For how long? Until our year is up and he regains the ability to touch me? I am marked for a reason. He's ensured that I will be recognized wherever I go, even by those who know me by rumor only."

"We'll find somewhere secluded. Somewhere we can be alone." I couldn't stop the empty words from spilling from my mouth.

"And when you leave to ferry souls each night? What then?" She shook her head, decided. "I have lived in a prison of my own making. I will not do it again."

"It's the same plan you always had. We keep searching for a loophole, a solution, anything to make you undesirable to him. We're just changing the location."

Katrin opened her mouth to say more, but agony lanced through me. I doubled over as my insides twisted, gritting my teeth against the wave of nausea. My knees buckled, and I squeezed my eyes shut as I slammed to the ground. I arched as phantom knives plunged into my back, the pain so much worse than any call had ever been.

I risked a glance toward the window, panting at the effort it took. The sun had dropped significantly since we'd arrived. Dusk was near.

The distance to the stairs had grown, and I groaned. Wincing, I put one hand in front of the other and slid my knee forward. Pain shot up my chest, but I forced myself to move another inch. I halted as two delicate hands wrapped around my arm.

"Oh, no, you don't," Katrin said, crouching beside me. "The only way I'm watching you crawl is if it's toward me."

She ducked beneath my arm, one of hers circling behind my back. I almost laughed at the audacity, but then she heaved upward. She strained against my mass, and I grunted, feeling like I was being torn in two. When she stopped, labored breaths mingling with mine, the desperation in her eyes fractured something deep inside me.

"Shadows." My voice was little more than a whisper, but she nodded.

As though the word alone summoned them, dark forms peeled from the walls, swarming us within seconds. I cried out as they yanked me upright, but Katrin remained at my side, her quiet support a rock in my raging storm. The shadows eased away, and I stumbled, but she didn't balk at my weight as I struggled for footing.

Together, we walked down the hall, our pace slow but steady, even as I trembled in pain. Somehow, we made it outside where dark forms were already darting around the horses, readying the carriage for yet another journey.

I knew then what she meant. There could never be peace between us. We would never have the luxury of idle time together. There would always be another soul to ferry, another threat keeping us alert and on edge. My vision of a life together for the two of us had been a pretty dream, but a dream nonetheless.

When the carriage was ready, I braced my arm against its side, freeing Katrin of my weight. I opened the door and offered my hand to help her up. She took a step away and crossed her arms, eyebrows raised in confusion.

"You're in no condition to ride alone," she said, eyeing my white-knuckled grip on the carriage. "I'm sitting up front with you."

I glared but didn't argue, secretly grateful for her company.

She mounted first, then the shadows swept in to lift me. I sagged onto the driver's seat, keenly aware of every point of contact between us. I reached for the reins, but she grabbed them first.

"Tell me where to go," she said, steel infusing her words and her spine.

I pointed, and we set off through the gate. The sun set as we entered the Corridor, and a doorway quickly appeared to take us to the world of the living. I continued to point out directions as best I could. The pain eased with every second we approached my quarry. Soon, I was well enough to sit straight on the bench. I wiped the sweat from my brow and offered to take the reins from Katrin.

"How do you know where to go?" she asked, handing them over.

"It is a feeling, a tug deep in here." I placed my fist over my chest. "I simply allow it to guide me."

She sat back, appearing to contemplate this as I steered the carriage onto a wide, tree-lined road. It was a well-traveled path that wound straight through the town. Katrin perked up, noticing our location.

"We are in Felwyck."

"Yes," I agreed, though she hadn't asked.

"Why are we here?"

The urgency in her question caught me off guard. "This is where I've been called."

Though my confusion must have been clear on my face, she didn't elaborate. Sure, we were in her hometown, but we hadn't yet arrived at our final destination. The persistent tug still pulled us onward.

She bit her lip, eyes darting over the familiar landscape.

We passed through the town, and my heart sank as we turned onto a long, winding road. At the top of the hill sat the Duke's estate.

Katrin expelled a breath like she'd been holding onto the same one all this time. "Who, Evander?"

There was no way for me to know, not until I met the soul. I urged the horses faster.

As we crested the hill, she leapt from the coach in a flutter of fabric, her shadow sentinels darting out to slow her fall. Her feet touched down, and she took off. I sprang to my feet, swaying slightly as I followed her path to the front door. She hesitated at the threshold, and I offered my hand in silent support. As the shadows ushered us through, I prayed that Death would not be as cruel as I feared.

CHAPTER 48

Katrin

I stepped into the foyer, my footsteps silent on the marble floor. Where I'd expected to be greeted by a lost soul, there was nothing. I was grateful for Evander's stoic presence at my side. The urge to lean into him nearly toppled me. Though he was no longer doubled over in pain, I managed to keep myself upright without his aid.

"Where?" I breathed.

Evander's shadows melded with those cast by the flickering candlelight. The air was heavy with tension as he interlaced his fingers in mine. I could feel his eyes upon me even as I refused to look. If there was any hint of sadness or pity in his gaze, I thought I would crumble to pieces. He gestured to the left, to my father's study.

I ran, already knowing what I'd find, but unwilling to accept the truth until I saw it with my own eyes.

The door was open, the first sign that something was amiss. In all my years, my father had never left it ajar. Its gaping maw threatened to swallow me whole as I barreled toward it. I froze at the scene inside.

Like something from a dream, the room I entered belonged to another world. There was the desk and the bookshelves, but nothing else aligned with my memory of the room. Gone were the haphazard stacks of research. Gone were the relics of a life gone by. The hardwood floor shone as if from a fresh mop. The shelves were neat and orderly, no book out of place. And seated at the great desk, not a scrap of paper upon its surface, was my father.

Well, my father's soul.

"Katrin?" My father's brows shot to his hairline. "What are you doing here? Where have you been? What's happened to you?"

His questions slid off me like raindrops in a storm. I felt them land but paid them no heed as I stalked across the room.

"Father," I started then paused, unable to find words for every emotion spilling from my heart. "How?"

It was the only question that mattered. Had I done this? Had I angered Death into taking my father prematurely? Or was it a coincidence that he should meet his end as I became entangled with Death?

His eyes grew distant, forehead creased in concentration. "I was sleeping, and then, I wasn't." He frowned. "I was more asleep than I'd ever been, and yet somehow, more awake, too. There was no pain. It didn't feel like what I thought dying ought to feel like. It was like waking up to a different life."

"And Mother?" The sour taste of fear coated my tongue, but I needed to know.

My father shook his head. "She's fine—alive," he amended.

His focus shifted over my shoulder, and I knew Evander had joined us.

"Can I see her?" I asked Evander. "Can she see *me*?" I heard the desperation in my own voice. I started to step around him, prepared to search the entire house if need be.

"She's not here." It was my father who answered.

My head whipped to him. "What? Where is she?"

The floor tilted, or maybe it was me. It only stopped when Evander's hands gripped my arm, holding me steady against the raging current of emotions.

My father's eyes dipped to that point of contact. When they lifted back to mine, there was no judgment, no reproach, though something like understanding flickered across his features. "She left to stay with her sister for a few days. She's supposed to return tomorrow."

"We can come back tomorrow night." Evander's words were a gentle murmur, too quiet for my father to hear. He meant to comfort but nothing chipped away at the wall of dread building in my chest.

I nodded—more for his benefit than my own.

"Your Grace," Evander said, addressing my father.

"There's no need for fancy titles. We're all equal in death, are we not?"

Evander dipped his head, a small smile on his lips. "As you say. We have come to guide you to the next world."

I didn't miss the way he included me in that statement. Whether Death knew it or not, this time with my father was a gift—a chance for us to have a proper goodbye.

***

We left as we'd entered, this time with my father in tow. I joined him in the carriage, Evander fully capable of driving now that the source of his pain had disappeared.

For several long minutes, the only sound was the crunch of gravel beneath the wheels and hooves. From the unhurried pace, I knew Evander was granting us what time he could. The hours until sunrise were too few, the things left to say too great.

I chewed my lip and twisted my skirt between my fingers. My leg bounced incessantly, but my father remained the picture of serenity. Peace had settled over him like it never had in life.

"I'm sorry," he said, folding his hands in his lap.

My eyes widened at the statement. "What do you have to be sorry for? *I* am sorry. For leaving the way I did, for not saying goodbye, for doubting your care when you wanted only what was best for me."

"I did, but possibly at the expense of what was actually best for you." His gaze dropped. "You were a duke's daughter, but you were so much more. You could have been so much more if I hadn't failed you. Even before you left, you were trying to tell me, and I wouldn't listen."

I shook my head, blinking back tears. "It was unbelievable."

"It was true. Even if it hadn't been, you believed it to be true, and a father should always trust his daughter above all else, even reason."

A laugh bubbled out of me, half sob. "You were the only one that fought for me. I could never fault you for that."

He smiled, but I couldn't find it in me to return the expression. Nothing could erase the very real possibility that I was to blame for my father's death.

As if sensing the direction of my thoughts, my father cleared his throat. "Tell me about this reaper fellow. You and he seem to have grown close in your time away."

My cheeks heated at his insinuation, but I was grateful for the change in subject. "His name is Evander, and he is the Ferrier of Souls."

I told him everything. From my plan to leave to its execution, to my bargain with Evander and the threat that Death posed. I told him of Moira and Sam, of Death's demon beasts and Ani. All the while, my father listened. Occasionally, he'd nod or ask for clarification. By the end of my tale, his serene expression had morphed into one of concern.

"And what do you plan to do now?" he asked, reaching across the carriage to capture my hands in his.

I shrugged, unable to speak around the knot in my throat.

The carriage slowed and halted.

"We're here." Evander's voice filtered into the cabin clearly enough that I suspected he'd heard our entire conversation.

My grip on my father's hands tightened as my heart beat faster. Too soon. It was too soon. The door opened, and I couldn't let go. I wouldn't. Not yet.

"I will be accompanying my father." My tone left no room for argument. "As far as I can."

Evander nodded like he'd expected as much.

We trekked through the forest, following no discernible path. I kept hold of my father's hand the entire way for fear he would slip away to The Beyond before we said our goodbyes. Evander led the way, speaking quietly about what my father could expect moving forward, the trials and the demons he may face to gain entry to the Afterworld. Though he'd likely recited the same information hundreds of times, his voice was soft, compassionate.

I did not think we had crossed into The Between, but the world around us was just as eerily quiet. There were no sounds of life beyond our footsteps and the calm, even cadence of Evander's voice. No animals sounded. Even the leaves did not rustle in the breeze.

Eventually, trees gave way to shrubs and the view opened to reveal a large body of water. The glassy surface glistened in the moonlight, giving the appearance that you could walk right onto it. Whatever existed on the other side was hidden by a thick layer of fog.

A weathered dock jutted out from the shore with a small vessel tied at the end. Evander took my other hand, helping me into the boat. My father and I took a seat on one of the built-in benches and Evander the other. He faced towards us and picked up a set of oars, placing them into the oarlocks on either side of the boat. With strong, steady strokes we moved across the water, ripples left in our wake.

We entered the fog, so dense I could make out nothing past the ends of the oars. I gripped my father's hand in both of mine, placing a kiss on his knuckles as tears rolled freely down my cheeks.

"I love you," I whispered, certain I hadn't said it enough during his life.

"I know," he said, patting my hand. "You were my everything, Katrin." Leaning forward, he pressed a kiss to my brow.

The small boat ran ashore, throwing me forward. My father's hand ripped from mine as I careened into Evander. I looked around, but still the fog remained too dense to see beyond.

"It will clear for him alone," Evander explained.

A splash sounded, and I twisted around to see my father standing knee-deep in the water.

I screamed. "Father!"

Evander's hands wrapped around my middle as I reached for the man who had devoted the last years of his life to helping me.

He looked at me, took in Evander's arms around me, and smiled. "I always told myself I would not rest until you were taken care of. It seems I may rest easy now."

I leaned into Evander's strength, giving my father this final gift, even if it wasn't real. As he faded from view, I was overcome by the sense of being unmoored—only in part due to the boat in which we stood. In the space of a single night, I'd lost one of the few tethers I had to the mortal world. Only my mother remained there. With my father beyond and Evander at my side, I was stretched thin by the desire to be in three places at once. I knew then that wherever I ended up, I would abandon parts of myself with those I did not choose. The woman I'd been on the eve of my birthday had been irrevocably severed, but I needed to decide who I wanted to become when I was forged anew.

Chapter 49

The Ferrier

From the moment I met her, Katrin had burned with the fury of a wildfire. Life—or Fate, it would seem—had beaten her down, but still, she had fought. She had raged.

That fire was gone now, snuffed out by grief and her own impending doom. I couldn't stand to see her light dimmed, to watch the vibrant woman be reduced to ashes.

We journeyed to the manor in somber silence. Everything I thought to say failed to articulate the despair I felt for Katrin. Nothing would ease the hurt that weighed down her shoulders and hollowed her chest. And so, the quiet stretched until it was all that lay between us, a chasm I longed to bridge.

Keeping the reins in one hand, I reached between us to intertwine our fingers. Her hand remained limp in mine, but she didn't pull away.

It was near dawn when we returned to *Tyr Anigh*, and still, she had not spoken. I kept hold of her hand as we reached the foyer, reluctant to let go even as she made to head upstairs. The resistance gave her pause, and she glanced down at our conjoined hands. Finally, she lifted red-rimmed eyes to me and voiced the question that had likely plagued her from the moment she saw her father's spirit.

"Do you think I did it?"

"No." The word was quick and sure. I would be confident if she could not.

She turned away as tears fell anew. I pulled her back toward me, wrapping her in my arms. Though she did not resist, her body did not immediately melt into mine as it usually did. She pressed her face into my shoulder, trembling from the tension that held her rigid. I willed my strength to her. If only I had the ability to take away pain, I would fix the broken parts of us.

"No," I said again, more firmly this time. "Fate is a tangled web of possibilities. One can get lost following the threads of human will. Your father died because he'd reached the end of his own thread, something that would have happened regardless of your actions."

"Fuck, Fate," she growled. "I've half a mind to cut *her* thread."

"Bold words." Though they lost the heat of their fire to my shirtsleeve.

She pulled back, not out of reach, but far enough to lift her face to mine. "I'm just so angry and so tired" Her fists clenched at her sides.

"I know, Kat."

Like a marionette whose strings had been cut, she collapsed. I gathered her to me, willing to take on whatever burdens she would share. "What do you want to do?"

She shook her head. "I don't know what to do."

"Then pack your things. We'll leave. We'll join Sam and recruit allies to our cause. There are others who would stand against him. We can fight this. I'm prepared to fight, to flee, to stay. Anything for you." My heart raced as I gave voice to my plan. I showed my cards and held my breath that she would do the same.

"To what end? What are we fighting for anymore? I look in the mirror, and I don't even recognize myself. The life I thought I wanted is..." She trailed off, eyes uncertain as she fought the truth that was in her soul.

"Is what?" I asked.

"Inconsequential."

The word was the whisper of flint on steel, igniting the flame of hope in my chest. She turned her face. With a gentleness that belied the fire raging within me, I brushed away her falling tears.

"Why?" I asked, drawing her eyes back to mine. "Why, Kat?"

She shuddered as she inhaled. "Because I have lived more in The Between with you than I ever did in the world of the living. I'm certain I will never fit in again if I go back home, and I don't think I want to." She swallowed. "Go home, that is."

The fire in my chest blazed hotter than a thousand suns. "Then stay." I gripped her hands in mine, all but choking on the hope that burned inside me.

As though blinded by that fire, she ducked her chin. "What about Behryn?"

"We'll figure something out. There's time. He can't touch you, remember?"

"But my mother—"

"We can fetch her tonight, bring her back with us."

Slowly, she lifted her eyes to mine. Something flickered in their dark depths, but I forgot it in an instant as she whispered one word. "Alright."

"Yes?" I asked.

She laughed, and it was the most magical sound in all the worlds. "Yes."

I brought my forehead to hers, closing my eyes as our breaths mingled. "Say you'll stay with me."

Her lips grazed mine, and I went taut as a bowstring. "I'll stay with you."

She'd spoken the words against my mouth. I felt the upward tilt of her lips as she smiled, and it broke down every one of my walls. My answering kiss was punishing. I pressed her to me and moaned as her fingers threaded through my hair. When she tugged me closer, I slid my arms over the swell of her hips and hauled her against me. I swallowed her gasp, plunging my tongue between her parted lips as her legs wrapped around me.

Darkness surrounded us. The shadows felt like ice to my fevered skin. They tempered my heat enough that I pulled my head from Katrin's as they cleared. Whether acting of their own accord or anticipating some unspoken order, they'd brought us to my bed chamber. My body throbbed with need, but I looked at Katrin's flushed skin and swollen eyes and knew this was not what she needed today.

I carried her to the bed, laying her reverently atop the blankets. She watched me, capturing one swollen lip between her teeth. It would be so easy to climb on top of her, to press my hardness to her softness and watch her writhe in pleasure, to be the reason her breath hitched.

My hands traced the length of her legs, removing her shoes and tossing them aside. Finally, I stepped from my own boots and crawled into the bed beside her. She rolled into me, fitting her curves against my side. My arm snaked beneath her, and I held her tightly, overwhelmed by the sudden fear that she would disappear in the coming day, banished by the sun like a shadow that had only appeared to be a woman to a lonely, unstable mind.

Dread coiled in my stomach, but I pushed it aside. If our time was limited as Fate had said, I would not sully it with dark thoughts. I closed my eyes and surrendered to the welcome respite of sleep.

CHAPTER 50

Katrin

I waited for a sunrise that did not come—not in the dramatic sense anyway. Slowly, the overcast sky lightened from blue to melancholy gray, the clouds heavy with rain that refused to fall.

Evander's chest rose and fell in the deep, even rhythm of sleep. Laying in his arms, I could almost forget the world crumbling around me.

Almost.

My thoughts strayed to my mother. I hoped she was safe. I hoped that Death would not find her before I could. It was the only plan I had. With Evander unable to leave The Between and my mother an unknowing pawn in Death's games, it only made sense to bring her here. Only once she was secured could we explore the other options Evander had mentioned. *Tyr Anigh* was compromised, but there had to be somewhere in this cursed land that was safe from Behryn.

Slipping from the bed, I padded across the room and picked up my shoes from where Evander had discarded them earlier. A glance back confirmed he still slept. He'd told me once that he rarely required sleep, but when he did, he slept like the dead. I could only hope that was true.

I said I'd stay, and I had. I'd stayed when everything in me had screamed to find my mother. I'd stayed though it hurt my heart to learn how perfectly our bodies fit together. I'd stayed through the dawn, knowing Behryn would return at any moment.

And now, it was time to leave.

Time raced on, and I felt my heart beat like a ticking clock counting down the seconds to my doom. I wished I had the time to write Evander a note. He deserved an explanation, but every second I delayed put us all in danger.

I made a stop at my room to grab my old glove, the match to the one I'd left at my family estate. It was time they be reunited. The woman that had worn these gloves was gone, but I could pretend to be her for one more day.

A shadow stretched across the floor. I jumped and whirled, but there was no one behind me. Confused, I turned back to the shadow. It stretched far longer than my own, longer than was natural with the direction of the sunlight through the window. Now that I examined it, I could make out other differences as well. The edges were too sharp, the color too dark, and as I watched, it shifted as though caught in a current.

I crossed my arms over my chest and glared down at the shadow. "What are you doing here?"

The shadow morphed, mimicking my stance in a way that I took to mean "what are *you* doing here?"

I snorted in recognition of Inky's impudence and glanced around for his companion guard. "I'm leaving," I said.

As soon as the words left my lips, Storm slithered out from beneath the bed. Together, the shadows rose to my height—taller—their forms coalescing into an uncanny likeness of Evander. My eyes darted away from the dark copy, remembering the way his stubble scratched my cheek. "It is safer for us both."

Shadow Evander made a show of placing his hands on his hips and sticking out one foot, a gesture the real Evander would never make.

"Fine." I threw my arms in exasperation. "My leaving does nothing to diminish the risk to myself, but it is safer for both Evander and my mother if I can find her in time. You heard Behryn. I'll not see Evander punished for trying to keep me safe." I rose and tilted my chin up. "It is time for me to take control of my own destiny."

Inky and Storm shrank to their usual amorphous selves, swaying uncertainly.

"You can do something for me, though," I said.

They straightened, soldiers reporting for duty. Even shadow creatures needed purpose it seemed.

"When Evander wakes, tell him—" My voice broke, and I inhaled deeply before I could begin again. "Tell him that I left of my own free will, and that I couldn't stand by and watch others fight my battles. Tell him that I hope our paths cross again someday." I blinked at the ceiling to keep the tears from falling. "And tell him thank you for seeing me beneath the shadows when no one else did."

The words tumbled out of me without thought. I planned to return. I would bring my mother in tow, and we would live forever sustained by the magic of The Between. But something in me knew the truth. I could be walking right into Behryn's trap and the likelihood of me making it back was slim. No matter what I wanted the outcome to be, I wouldn't leave without a proper goodbye. I'd made that mistake once and paid for it dearly.

My lips trembled as I offered my guardians a half-hearted smile.

A path opened between them, an exit large enough for me to pass through to the doorway beyond. I stepped between them and was immediately wrapped in their cool embrace. They smelled of The Between, of mist and loam. I closed my eyes and committed the scent to memory. Too soon, the light beyond my eyelids lightened. The air around me warmed as they separated again. I opened my eyes and gasped as I stepped into the Corridor.

Tyr Anigh was gone. Evander was gone. Though my surroundings looked just the same as every other stretch along the endless winding road, I trusted my shadows had led me to the right place. They'd given me this chance, and I would not squander it.

Inky and Storm faded from view, blending into a darker patch of shade beneath the trees. I whispered my thanks and turned toward the land of the living, toward home.

As a mortal not bound by the magic of The Between, the doorway would always be open for me to return to the mortal world. Once there, I would be trapped until Evander or Death came for me. Perhaps I would beat Death in his own games and be reunited with Evander come nightfall. More likely, this was the last I would step foot in this world.

A faint shimmer marked the passageway, and I halted with my feet mere inches from it. Lifting my unmarked hand, I slid my fingers over the seam between worlds. There was no resistance, only a drop in temperature to let me know I'd reached into another world. A breeze slipped through, blowing my hair back from my face.

Another Evander-shaped shadow stretched along the ground to my right. I laughed even as a deep ache settled in my chest. "Come to say goodbye again?"

"Katrin." The whisper was a benediction.

My heart stuttered as goosebumps rose along my arm. I turned, mindful of the doorway a step away. The man standing before me was not a fearsome reaper hell-bent on revenge. Nor was he the stoic guardian determined to protect me from my dark fate. Looking at him now, barefoot, hair mussed, and shirt unbuttoned to reveal the hard lines of his chest, I could see only the funny, caring man who made me feel things I refused to name.

"Evander," I breathed.

His eyes scanned the trees, taking in the subtle differences that marked the location. "Why?"

It wasn't an accusation, but I winced as the question struck me like a blow to the gut. "My mother. I cannot let her fall for me, not after—" I broke off, unwilling to poke the wound of my father's passing, still too fresh and raw.

He shook his head. "What's worth living for isn't always worth dying for. I would know."

A flash of utter devastation crossed his face, wiped away with the palm of his hand. After all this time, he was still hiding the broken pieces of himself, all the human parts he strived to be rid of. Would my leaving be his ultimate undoing?

"There's no guarantee Behryn is even waiting for me. I can find my mother, and you can retrieve us tonight. I'll only be gone a few hours." I smiled, but it was an approximation of the real thing. We both knew the probability of this being a trap, but Behryn had known exactly where to strike, and I wasn't willing to gamble away my mother to protect myself.

He stepped forward, and I slid my foot back until I felt the change in temperature. Evander's gaze tracked the movement, and he froze, despair pulling down the corners of his mouth and brows. His eyes lifted to mine, wide in panic. I watched as if in slow motion as his knees buckled, and he sank to the hard-packed road, palms open in surrender.

"I love you." Compared to his movements, his words came out in a rush. They hurtled for me across the short expanse, too quick to dodge.

"That is a cruel trick," I replied, the falsehood sticky on my tongue.

"I swear it's true. I can't go on pretending I don't love you, that I'm not *in love* with you. Tell me you feel it, too."

I shook my head, tears pooling at the edge of my vision. "I can't. I don't." Because if I admitted that I loved him, how could I ever walk away? But I knew the words for the lies they were, and I could not bear to voice them again. I turned my head so that only my darkened eye faced him. "If you love me," I whispered, voice breaking, "find me again."

I stepped backwards, the sound of Evander's scream following me into the living world. The forest came to life around me, and I knew there was no going back. Though the trees were still bare in the early winter chill, a muted rainbow of color littered the ground from the recent autumn shedding. The sunbeams shone brighter, birds called to one another, the wind smelled of crisp pine, and all of it paled in comparison to the beauty of being loved.

Tears ran freely down my cheeks as I reached for the world—the man—that was beyond my grasp. "I love you too," I said to the wind, if only to speak the truth once before the end.

Swiping my cheeks with the back of my hand, I dusted off my dress and pulled a single glove from my pocket. It was strange to cover my marks after weeks of not hiding, but my shadowed hand slid easily into the worn glove. I flexed my fingers, reacquainting myself with the feel. After pushing my hair forward over my mark, I set off for my home. If something happened to my mother while I delayed, then it was all for naught.

I exited the forest not far from Felwyck. While I'd expected there to be more traffic at this time of day, I stumbled at the first sign of the busy street. The road teemed with people heading into and away from town.

I checked the positioning of my hair over my face and kept my chin down. There wasn't time to hesitate, so I scurried as fast as I could manage without appearing suspicious. It was difficult to navigate through the overladen carts and carriages with only one eye. More than once, I collided with something and had to quickly change direction before anyone looked upon me too long. Someone called out in the crowd, but I couldn't know if it was to me they spoke without looking up. Ignoring them all, I gathered my skirts and broke into a run.

My family's estate lay on the close side of town, but my lungs heaved by the time the peaked roof came into view. I slowed as I turned a corner and was struck by the full majesty of the estate. If possible, the large white manor house looked more imposing in the light of day.

Once I veered from the main road, I saw no other servants or travelers on the way to the main house. It was possible the chill had driven them all inside. More likely, the upheaval of my father's passing had not yet settled among the household.

Ringing filled my ears as I stepped up to the main door. The sound pulled at a thread in my memory, but I shook my head and tapped three quick knocks on the door. The ringing persisted. A shiver snaked up my back, and I held my cloak together against the winter wind. Opening my fist, I pounded on the door. My ungloved hand stinging with the effort. The ringing took on a fever pitch.

Concern mounting, I tried the handle. It opened without constraint. I pushed through the door, alarmed when there was no footman to be found. I closed the door to the outside world, but the vexing sound persisted.

"Hello?" I yelled over the din.

A figure appeared from the hall, distinctly male, his features hidden in the bright backlight of a window. His steps were slow and measured as he approached. I danced from foot to foot, trying to get a better view.

The ringing silenced as he stepped into view.

"Hello, Katrin," Death purred.

Acknowledgements

This book was a struggle for me. Before this book, I'd only ever written standalones and I put a lot of pressure on myself to make my first series great. Luckily, I have a great group of friends who supported me every step of the way. Chani, Dee, Jess, Meg, and Rei, I treasure our friendship and the unwavering support you've shown me over the years. I will always look forward to our late-night (sometimes mid-morning) writing sessions. I still look forward to the day that we can all be published.

To those in the FaRoFeb discord server, your advice has been invaluable. Thank you for welcoming me among your ranks and being so forthcoming with information regarding all things Fantasy Romance. I am awed every day by the talent in that server and feel blessed to write alongside such amazing authors.

To my readers, thank you for wanting more from me. Your encouragement has kept me writing through the challenges of this past year. Please never temper your enthusiasm, it's like fuel to the writing fire.

Of course, I couldn't do this without my husband. Todd, thank you for all you do for me, for our family. We are so grateful to have you in our lives. I couldn't reach for my dreams without you to hold me up.

About the Author

Elle Backenstoe

Elle Backenstoe lives in Eastern Pennsylvania with her husband, son, and dog. She grew up with her nose buried in a book and sometimes emerges long enough to write some words of her own. She writes fantasy and romance, often together. Elle runs on pop punk music and Coke, and will always choose sweet over salty. When she's not reading or writing, you can find her at her home-away-from-home, the dance studio.

Find info about my other books at:
www.ellebackenstoe.com/books

Instagram and Threads: @ellebackenstoewrites
Tiktok and Facebook: @ellebackenstoe